DARKNESS FALLING

THE DARKWORLD SERIES: BOOK FIVE

EMMA L. ADAMS

Through many a dark and dreary vale
They passed, and many a region dolorous,
O'er many a frozen, many a fiery alp,
Rocks, caves, lakes, fens, bogs, dens, and shades of death—
A universe of death...
John Milton, *Paradise Lost*

"Deep into that darkness peering, long I stood there wondering fearing,
Doubting, dreaming dreams no mortals ever dared to dream before."

Edgar Allen Poe, 'The Raven'

1

MISSION

I leaned against the wall of my bedroom, eyes closed, like I could stop the world spinning just by ignoring it.

But the world wouldn't stop. Time ticked away by the minute, and every second that passed might bring the return of our enemy. Leo sat beside me on my bed, not speaking. Not asking what the human-demon girl had just said to me.

Lucifer wasn't dead.

I couldn't process it. In the past few days, I'd been attacked at my aunt's old house, spurned by the Inner Circle, witnessed a prison outbreak, been cornered by Leo's father, who was now possessed by a higher demon, arrested for outing myself as a human-demon, and escaped. Just tonight, I'd witnessed the sorcerer Lucifer break into the human world; watched my mother, the fortune teller, face Lucifer down and destroy him at the cost of her own life, and narrowly escaped a collapsing tunnel.

We had to leave campus as soon as possible, in case the

surviving members of the Venantium decided that I was dangerous and locked me up again—God knew where, seeing as their headquarters were now buried under the rubble. I couldn't deny it kind of served them right for building it underground in the first place. But nobody deserved to be buried alive in those tunnels.

Not even… her.

My eyes burned, and I became aware of Leo's hand in mine, gripping me tightly as though he was afraid I would disappear, just like the half-demon girl had. My other hand gripped the demon heart around my neck—the amethyst crystal that was the store of my demon side's magical energy. As if it heard my thoughts, felt my mental and physical exhaustion, the demon heart vibrated against my chest and new energy flooded me, making me feel less like collapsing from exhaustion. I opened my eyes, drawing in a breath, and met Leo's concerned gaze.

"What did she say?" His voice was hoarse, probably from tiredness and the desperation of our flight through a collapsing tunnel.

I shut out the memory—or tried to.

"Lucifer's not dead," I said tremulously. "You were right. Part of him's still in the Darkworld. He's tied to it. He can't die."

"Shit." Leo let out a breath. "Should have guessed the bastard had a backup plan."

"Yeah. And… and Mephistopheles's heart is missing, too."

There was more than that, more I didn't want to think about right now. But there could be no more secrets between us. I had to tell Leo everything.

"The others want me to help them," I said. "The other half-demons. I spoke to one of them. She… she was like me."

Leo didn't say anything, but let go of my hand, as though he'd forgotten he was still holding it. My heart spasmed painfully. *Please look at me.* Though he'd told me he regretted what had happened, I still could never forget what he'd said to me. *I don't want to look you in the eyes.*

"They say I can set them free," I said. "They're trapped in the Darkworld, in a kind of half-life, but they think I can help them."

"How?" he said, his voice hushed. "What you're saying is impossible—the Darkworld is just *there*. Without the Barrier, it'd be different. But the cost of that…"

Without the Barrier, *all* demons would be free. There didn't seem to be a way out of this that didn't involve sacrificing human lives to the demons.

We'd lost too many people already. And in the end, even the fortune-teller's sacrifice hadn't finished Lucifer off.

"I know," I said heavily. "Maybe it's something they want me to figure out. I'm too tired to think about it right now."

"Yeah," said Leo. "They're not going to give a straight answer, are they? That's not how demons operate."

No. They crept up on you and insidiously ruined your life from the inside.

"Maybe they can't say anything. I've been thinking… can Lucifer read minds? He's not a true demon, but he's in the Darkworld."

"You're asking me? I haven't a clue. If the Darkworld gives them that power, then maybe, yeah. There's no way for humans to know without going there themselves."

"Never mind, I was just thinking aloud." Even voicing my fears didn't make them go away. For all I knew, Lucifer was eavesdropping on us right now. The Darkworld was everywhere—everywhere in the world. No escaping it. And I'd not only escaped from right in front of him, I'd frozen the supposed king of all demons into an ice statue. I might as well have signed my own death warrant.

"Sorry," he said. "It's so... I just can't believe they're gone. I mean, we've been talking about how useless the Venantium are for years, but I think deep down I thought they had a handle on things. And now..."

"They're dead." I shook my head. I could hardly believe it either. "There are only two members of the Inner Circle left—well, that's if they survive going back underground." I didn't envy them that.

"I don't think Lucifer will come back underground," said Leo. "He'd need to find another demon heart, for one. Was the one he used hidden with the Venantium?"

"I have no idea," I said. "I never had a chance to ask."

Something else I couldn't ask the person who had all the answers. The fortune-teller was dead. Even though she'd revealed her true identity—Melivia Blackstone, my mother—over six months ago, I still had a hard time thinking of her as any relation of mine. She'd been the enigmatic fortune-teller for so long, and that was the way I would remember her—defiant even in death, singing an agonised song as she burned alive.

Melivia had escaped death by fire once before, as a young woman living in the mid-nineteenth century after she'd been seduced by Lucifer. He'd tricked her into summoning a demon, triggering the last demon wars. By that point, he and Melivia had disappeared into the Darkworld and hadn't returned until nearly a hundred and fifty years later—time had no meaning in the Darkworld, which was locked in a perpetual present. In order to return to life, they had to take possession of another body, one with a beating heart—in Melivia's case, a comatose young woman. Melivia was shocked to learn that the world had changed beyond recognition, and that Lucifer had lied to her. It was in that fragile state that the higher demon, Lucifer, had found her.

I had no idea how events had played out from there, only that she'd ended up pregnant by the higher demon, seen the human Lucifer's true colours and realised the danger he posed to her unborn child. She'd concocted an elaborate plan to hide the baby—me—by altering the memories of a family who'd recently lost their new born, and posing as my aunt. Influence and memory alteration were highly restricted branches of magic, but the fortune-teller had used them with impunity, taking on the identity of "Aunt Eve" for the first thirteen years of my life. By then, Lucifer had been defeated and a second demon war averted.

After "Aunt Eve" had moved away from her cottage in the Lake District, she'd slipped off the radar until I received a package from her for my eighteenth birthday, containing some money and an amethyst pendant, and a cryptic note telling me to "guard my heart well." I had thought this a little strange, but given that I'd started seeing invisible demons at the time, it hadn't exactly been the focus of my attention. But when my flatmate, Terrence, had taken the pendant and summoned a demon, I'd learned the truth about my identity as a human-demon, and that my power was contained in the crystal—which was actually my demon heart. He'd almost killed me, but I'd discovered that I was immune to demonic possession since I'm part demon myself, and I killed the demon inside him.

As for the demon inside me... she was a part of me. My real father was a higher demon, Lucifer. I'd met one of them—Belphegor—when the spirit of another half-demon had tried to get me framed for crimes I'd never committed. Five of the Inner Circle were now under the control of the higher demons Asmodeus, Beezlebub, Satan, Mammon, and Leviathan. I had no idea how long they'd been around for; the higher demons didn't seem to obey the usual rules of the Darkworld, and appeared whenever they liked. It was unusual for them to accept the authority of a human, but Lucifer could offer them what no one else could: access to our world.

That was, ultimately, what demons wanted. They might live in the Darkworld, but they wanted access to the human world. The false Lucifer had offered them the ultimate bargain. In exchange for their help, they'd have the world. Only Melivia's sacrifice had stopped him breaking the Barrier.

And now she was dead. My mother, the reluctant defender of humanity. Dead.

I'd hated her for most of the time I'd known her. I'd been enraged when the truth had come out about her identity, that she'd lied to me, manipulated me into living a life that wasn't mine. Until less than a year ago, I'd had a family. In one day, she'd destroyed the foundation of my life. When the Venantium had taken her prisoner and done something to her magic, it had broken the subliminal spell that made my "parents" believe I was their daughter. The awful part was how long it had taken me to realize something was wrong, but I'd been under a spell, too. It came out when Mephistopheles had tried to burn down my house to lure me into a multi-layered trap that nearly killed both Leo and me. Leo had been possessed by the demon, and the demon inside me had fought for control, nearly resulting in both our deaths.

Another debt I owed to the fortune-teller, for saving us.

That was the last time I'd seen Leo until now, and I still couldn't get used to his presence, let alone the fact that he was in my room. He'd taken off as soon as possible after the events of last March without even talking it through, with the argument that the demon inside me would never leave us in peace, and that we were a danger to each other. The memory still should have filled me with a searing rage, but I'd already lost my home and my family. I had no energy left to waste on petty arguments. Not when we had to run for our lives. Tonight.

I dug out my rucksack and started throwing clothes into it. What would I need? It was almost winter. Warm clothes were a must, but I could only fit so many in my rucksack. My television and laptop would have to stay behind. My iPod could come, but I wished I hadn't lost my phone. If the others and I were separated, I'd have no way of contacting them.

"I've a spare phone you can borrow," said Leo, as though he'd read my thoughts. "It's shit, but it works, and that's all that matters, right?"

I didn't say anything. Silence had grown between us, fuelled by absence. It felt stifling just being in the same room as him. I couldn't afford to think of what once we'd had, before we'd been set against each other. I wasn't the same person as before.

When I'd filled my bag to capacity, shoving in some photos of my friends and me at the last minute just in case I didn't have the chance to retrieve them later, I zipped the rucksack shut, and stood.

Tears pricked my eyes. I'd thought I had a future here. I'd thought this would be my new home, however temporary. I was still paying rent on that shitty old flat I'd rented in Manchester—I'd spent the summer there, since I'd been unable to go back to living with my once-parents. But Blackstone had always been different. It had been a haven, the only place I couldn't see demons, due to the strength of the Venantium's barriers. Now, however…

"Come on." I still couldn't quite look Leo in the eye. "Let's go."

The flat remained quiet; no one was in. My friends had probably gone to the student union bar, like any ordinary night. I'd lived two lives side by side for so long that the thought of leaving this one—my safe, normal life with friends who knew nothing about the Darkworld, nothing about demons or Lucifer or the Venantium—didn't bear thinking about. But now I had to leave, before Lucifer came back. He wanted me, the only human-demon, as his own, and as long as he existed, the only life I could have was that of a fugitive.

My normal human friends had no place in that life. I wouldn't do anything that might put them in danger, too.

Berenice's voice floated up from the ground floor as we walked downstairs. "They're obviously boning, we'll be waiting forever. I say we get the hell out of here."

"Berenice!" said Claudia.

"What? It's true. He wanted to rip her clothes off soon as he set eyes on her…"

She trailed off as she saw us approaching. "There they are," she said, unconvincingly.

Claudia had a rucksack, too; she'd obviously dashed back to her own flat to pack.

"Everyone got everything they need?" said Cyrus. "We can do a quick stop at your place on the way," he added, as Howard made to speak.

"We left our stuff there," Leo said to me. "There wasn't enough time to go home."

Cyrus and Leo had been travelling for the past few months, and had only flown back to England earlier that day. So much had changed in the last twenty-four hours. Yesterday and today were worlds apart.

"We're going back to Blackstone?" said Claudia.

"Quickest way to London is to get the train from Redthorne, through Manchester," said Cyrus bracingly. "We'll avoid the Venantium; just get the bus from near Howard's." His casual tone fooled none of us.

Manchester. I felt another pang. Cara, my best friend, wouldn't be at home, she'd be at university in Edinburgh. I supposed at least she was safe there. But it would have been nice to have time for one last Skype before we left. Just to warn her to stay as far away from me as humanly possible.

"Does your spare phone have credit?" I asked Leo.

"Yeah, I topped it up. Glad I hung onto it after I got my contract."

"I'm glad I made a note of people's numbers on paper," I said. I didn't know Cara's number by heart, but at some point I'd had the presence of mind to write it in a notebook, which I retrieved from my bag now.

The others looked at me.

"You're going to make a call now?" said Claudia.

I hesitated, then put the notebook away and slipped the phone back into my pocket. "Might wait till we're in London, actually. I just wanted to make sure she was safe. Cara," I added, in response to Leo's puzzled look.

"What about your other friends?" said Leo. "Your flat-mates? They weren't in the flat?"

"I think they'll be in the union bar." I glanced in that direction, from which a steadily growing volume of noise was issuing.

"Down it! Down it!" roared a chorus of voices.

"Time for one last drink?" said Leo.

"You're joking, right?" I looked at him incredulously.

"Maybe. Do you want to say goodbye?"

"Might be a better idea to just go. No awkward questions." I sighed. My chest tightened at the thought of leaving Alex and Sarah without as much as a note. Or a warning. "Are there any buses running?"

"Not on a Sunday. We'll have to walk…" Cyrus trailed off as a louder noise ripped through the night.

Screaming.

It wasn't a squeal of delight or drunken celebration, but a cry of pure terror. My heart plummeted.

For an instant, the six of us looked at each other. I could almost see the same thoughts cross the others' minds. *No. They've come here.*

Leo was the first to move. "Come on," he said, and ran toward the bar.

2

DEPARTURE

A harpy flew overhead, aiming for a group of people standing outside the bar. Claws outstretched, it dived. One girl screamed; her friends looked confused, at least until the bird landed on another girl's head, talons digging in.

"Stop that!" I yelled, and threw a handful of ice-fire at the harpy.

The girl screamed and ducked, but I hit the harpy, which exploded into black feathers.

The group scattered, falling over each other in an effort to get away. The first girl, the one who'd seen the harpy, shot a terrified glance at me as she stumbled across the lawn. Claudia gave me a wide-eyed look. I hadn't even thought to use Influence. *Shit.*

But there wasn't time to worry about that now. The harpies had revealed themselves, which meant this place was a target for Lucifer. My friends were in the bar, and I had to warn them. Without checking to see if the others followed, I ran ahead, pushing the glass door open.

Inside, the bar was cramped and noisy as ever. Apparently, no one had heard the disturbance outside. Club-house music pounded from the loudspeakers. Bar staff served endless shots, and a thousand people were packed into the tight space, talking, drinking and having a laugh. No one seemed aware that death waited on the other side of the door.

I stood on tiptoe, peering over the crowd to look for my friends. Alex and Sarah sat with several LitSoc members including Alex's boyfriend, Rex. I started making my way toward them, sidestepping Pete. Our old flatmate was, as usual, pissed off his face and pursuing Danielle, on whom he'd nursed a hopeless crush for the past year.

"Oi! Danielle!"

I halted as he staggered past, unease skittering down my spine. Last time I'd seen him, he'd talked of hearing voices in his flat, the same place a girl had hanged herself. Demons had some kind of influence there, but I couldn't say for certain whether Lucifer had really managed to connect with non-magic-users.

He turned to face me, and a gleam flickered in his eyes. A smirk twisted his lips, and he looked back at Danielle.

"Danielle!" he shouted across the bar. "I wanna talk to you!"

"I don't want to talk to you!" Danielle shouted back, from where she sat at a table with friends.

"But it's important!" Pete shouldered his way toward the bar, violently shoving a guy off his seat, into a nearby table.

Beer glasses went flying everywhere, and several people started yelling at him. Pete ignored them, climbing onto the seat to face the packed room.

"It's the end of the world!" he announced.

Shockingly, his proclamation met only with laughter from the crowd. But tension knotted inside me and I almost jumped out of my skin when someone came up next to me. Leo. I glanced back at the others. Claudia's eyebrows had disappeared into her hairline.

"Well, this is entertaining," said Berenice, dryly.

"Something's wrong," said Leo, who'd picked up the same bad vibes as me.

Pete spun on the chair, his gaze turning to meet mine, and at that moment, it became clear why. Goose bumps prickled at my skin, and the chill of the Darkworld pierced me from the inside out. Shadows moved along the ground —nebulous shadows that didn't belong to this world. They climbed the chair Pete stood on, wrapped around his body. His eyes changed to violet, and on his forehead a red gem shone: a demon heart.

Pete was possessed.

"It's the end of the fucking world," he said, still in Pete's voice. "It's judgment day for all of you. Starting with you, bitch."

His demon eyes locked on Danielle, who started to scream. Her chair slid out from under her and she crashed to the ground, glass flying. A horrible *crack* rang through the air, her neck snapped back, and she fell in a crumpled heap.

And then there was chaos. Screams rang out; the ground shook as everyone started running for the exit. Pete jumped off the chair, and I lost sight of him in the heaving crowd making for the doors. Caught in the rush, I struggled to keep my friends in sight whilst avoiding being trampled. *We have to kill the demon!* But I couldn't throw ice-fire indiscriminately, not with so many people around.

"We have to kill it!" I said, to the nearest person—Claudia. "We have to—"

"Ash, there might be more of them!" Claudia yelled in my ear. "The Barrier's broken—just *run*!"

I couldn't run, could only let the crowd carry me away. The mass of people pressed against the doors, but no one seemed to be able to get them open. Shadows filled the gaps between the doors and the frame, and the surface of the handles gleamed like ice.

"Bastard's sealed the exit!" yelled Leo, who'd appeared behind me. "Come on, people–fire!"

He moved away and was suddenly ablaze from head to toe, outlined in flames. The ice on the handles turned to water and dripped to the floor, but the shadows remained, sealing the door shut. I shouldered several people aside, calling on the Darkworld and pressing my hands to the shadows, but someone slammed into me, knocking me off my feet, and I threw my arms over my head to protect myself from a shower of glass. A window above the door had shattered, and people climbed on top of the heaving crowd, trying to reach it.

Someone cried, "That guy's on fire!" as Leo ran past.

"Shit," said Claudia's voice from somewhere nearby. "Way to expose ourselves."

"Little help?" said Leo, who was shooting fireballs at the door, trying to push it open without hitting anyone.

As I got to my feet, I saw the others. Howard held back the crowd with his large frame while Berenice cowered behind him, white-faced and trembling. Claudia and Cyrus stood side-by-side, throwing flames at the door from a distance.

I conjured ice-fire, which moved like liquid across my skin, rippling with power. The demon heart burned my chest from the pocket of my coat. People I'd known for over a year, students I'd shared classes with, stared at me in terror, dived out of the way as I held the swirling flames in my hands and threw myself at the glass door with every-thing I could.

The door groaned under the pressure, but still didn't give. I slammed my fists into it so hard the ice cracked and blood beaded my skin. A cracking sound above drew my eyes. The fluorescent ceiling lights shattered. Glass rained down on the shrieking, pushing crowd. Leo swore, flickering with fire again, and ran through the melee to join me by the door.

"Leo," I gasped, as the flames seared my skin even from a distance. "Put out the fire—people are going to get hurt!"

Laughter sounded, cold and inhuman. My blood froze. I knew the voice. Though I'd once thought all demons sounded exactly alike, I knew it.

Mephistopheles. No other demon took more delight from tormenting me.

"But Ashlyn, isn't it far more fun this way?" Pete pushed his way through the crowd. Mephistopheles's violet eyes gleamed in place of Pete's.

I hadn't particularly liked Pete, but no one deserved that fate. And any minute now, the demon might choose to switch hosts. He could kill anyone, any of my friends.

Darkness swept through the room, darkness that was more than the absence of light. It was like a living thing, spreading like an invasive weed. Shadows came alive, clinging to people's feet, climbing their bodies. Most didn't notice, in the general chaos, but some started screaming, trying to kick away the living shadows.

Then, they started dying.

A guy near me fell to the floor, emitting a choking sound. His hands pressed to his face, and blood started to seep through his fingers, as if from a nosebleed. But when he moved his hands I saw that blood was streaming from his eyes as well as his nose, and his mouth, too. He was choking on his own blood.

Stop! Please! I threw myself against the door again, ice-fire flaring around me. Leo hammered on the door, too, fire pushing the darkness away.

A girl grabbed at me from behind. At first I thought it was Claudia, but as I twisted to face her, violet eyes stared into mine. *Another demon?* Or had Mephistopheles switched hosts? Unconsciously, I moved to shield Leo from view.

"You can't save them, Ashlyn." Yes, it was Mephistopheles. Which meant Pete was…

"Stay away," I said, and directed the ice-fire at the demon's heart, in the centre of its forehead.

It would have been a clean shot, but the girl moved with an inhuman swiftness, leaping into the air. Instead, the ice-fire went towards a group of fleeing students, who shrieked and dived out of the way. Now the girl stood on a table covered in pieces of shattered glass.

"You can't escape me!" it said in a singsong voice. I called on the Darkworld, gathering shadows around me. People were running from *me*, now, thinking I was one of the monsters.

Then someone grabbed my arm. Rachel, my flatmate. Her nails dug in.

"Rachel, not now!" I said, keeping my eyes on Mephistopheles. I had to destroy his demon heart before he killed again.

"Ash," said Rachel, insistently, "He's coming…"

"Lucifer?" I said, cold horror rising. *Not again…*

"He's stirred them up… they're angry…" A gasp escaped her, and her head tipped back. Out of the corner of my eye, I saw the expression on her face change, her teeth baring, dilated eyes replaced by chips of violet. Struggling out of her grasp, I turned to face a forest of glittering eyes.

"Shit," I whispered.

"A mass demon summoning," Claudia croaked. I hadn't seen her come up beside me. Her face was drawn with the exhaustion of trying to break down the door. "We're really gonna die."

"No way," Leo said.

"Fight them, you morons!" shouted a voice. Howard.

He and Berenice had climbed onto on tables, picking off demons with an efficiency that surprised me. I knew neither of them had ever killed one before. Admittedly, Berenice's aim was often way off, but Howard's hobby of shooting down the Venantium's harpies from the sky was paying off now. Most of the fire he threw struck the demons right in the hearts. But there were too many of them. I spun on the spot, throwing ice-fire at the gleaming demon hearts, trying not to think about the humans whose lives had been taken. I'd lost sight of Mephistopheles, too. Cyrus and Leo had moved away, to shield survivors whilst striking out at the demons.

I have to kill them. But the ice-fire was too slow to take out more than one demon at a time. I couldn't keep track of everyone at once.

"Hi, Ashlyn."

A guy of around Howard's size jumped at me, knocking me off my feet. I gasped as the wind rushed out of me, my back striking the ground.

"Having fun? I'm trying to decide which of your friends to kill first."

"You stay away from them," I choked out, stabbing at him with ice-fire. He dodged easily, bulky arms still pinning me down.

Help! I tried to reach my demon side, but met only silence, like static at the other end of a phone line. *Help!* I reached out to the power within the crystal, felt my demon heart pulse like a real, human heart, and power rushed through me, throwing Mephistopheles aside. The demon roared in rage, but I'd already stabbed ice-fire right through the demon heart.

Anger rose inside me. The rage of the lost souls, the forgotten human-demons—it was still there, raw and blazing, ready to consume anything in its path. The anger rippled out through the Darkworld itself.

Shadows cracked like glass, and the cracks went even deeper, into the floor, like in an earthquake. The ground jarred beneath my feet as the cracks penetrated the earth and the stone walls of the building. Rachel tumbled away from me, the other demon hosts falling over each other as the ground trembled.

I was no longer in control. Cracks erupted in the walls, climbing towards the ceiling. The bar split in two with a crack, sending demons and humans alike sprawling.

"We have to get—out!" I screamed, and the demon screamed, too.

With a final, jarring screech, the room split. The ceiling fell in chunks of stone and a spray of dust, and I had a flash of deja vu from when the underground chamber had collapsed—the same sense of finality came with it, the same hopelessness. People were screaming, dying. I'd caused it, and I couldn't stop it.

But the demon—the demon was—

"Stop!"

The demon's emotions flashed through me; rage, desperation, and guilt. The Darkworld responded, shadowy tendrils reaching out from me to surround the struggling crowd, bolstering the collapsing floor. With a final burn of anger, I felt the half-demons, the furious half-shadows, withdraw, and with them, the other demons were sucked back into the darkness. Only humans remained.

And me.

The door had been ripped open during the chaos, leaving a way out.

"Come on!" Leo pushed himself up against the wreckage of a wall. White-faced and covered in dust, he directed people through the opening where the door had once been. Claudia joined him, Cyrus on her heels. None of them seemed to be harmed.

My body shook so hard my legs threatened to give out underneath me, but I still scanned the crowd, trying to work out if any of the survivors were possessed. I couldn't see my flatmates, either. Navigating the rubble, I joined my friends near the door.

"Ash!" said Leo, wrapping his arms around me. "Thank God—come on, nearly everyone's outside now."

I followed him through the wrecked doorway, staggering as the energy drained out of me. I let go of the power, and the shadows receded, leaving only rubble beneath my feet. The remains of the doorway promptly crumbled inwards, a mask of dust obscuring everything from sight.

I closed my eyes. I had no idea when or if my vision had become mine again, not the demon's. We were merging together, becoming one identity. What that meant, I didn't know.

That wasn't important now. I moved over to Leo, leaning on his shoulder as he pulled me close. I couldn't look at the wreckage behind us, the bodies of people I knew.

"I thought I'd lost you." His voice was rough from inhaling dust. "You're—she's getting stronger, isn't she?"

"Never mind that," I said. "What the hell are we going to do?"

Not that the Venantium's rules mattered now, but we'd all used magic pretty openly. I wasn't sure Influence could erase an experience like this. Any thought of subterfuge had gone out the window the moment the demon had appeared.

Huddles of students gathered on the lawns outside. Claudia, Cyrus, Berenice, and Howard stood apart. They'd all survived. Guilty relief flooded me, but I pushed it aside, my eyes roving over the… survivors. Looking for my flatmates.

I'll never forgive myself if they didn't make it.

"Ash!" yelled two voices. Alex and Sarah.

"Guys," I said, my voice cracking. My heart lifted. *They're alive.* I ran over to them, tears leaking from my eyes, adrenaline making my limbs shake.

"I don't suppose you feel like telling us when you turned into a freaking X-Man?" said Alex. "Or X-Woman? Whichever." She had her arms around Sarah, who was sobbing.

Rex sat beside her, his arm around her shoulder. He looked dazed, like he'd been hit with something heavy. Everyone dealt with shock differently.

No one should have to deal with this at all.

"Would you have believed me?" I said, wondering if it was best to try to give an abridged version of events, or just take the easy way out.

"Ash, this is *university.* Aka freak show central. I mean, we lived with an alien during our first term."

"Yeah," I said. "About that. He wasn't an alien, he was a sorcerer."

Three blank stares answered me. Rex looked even more dazed, like he'd taken another blow to the head.

"Like me," I went on. "Like all of us." I gestured to Leo and the others, who were deep in urgent conversation.

"Sorcerers," said Alex. "Right."

"Well, you wanted the truth, however absurd, right?" I said.

"Yeah," said Alex, "but what the hell does that have to do with the glowy eyes? Clementine—she killed someone." She swallowed. "I've known her forever. She wouldn't do that."

Sarah sobbed, burying her head in her hands.

"Those were demons," I said. "They're—well, they're magical parasites." I decided to fall back on the way Claudia had first described them to me. "They live in this place called the Darkworld, which is closed off, but a sorcerer just broke the Barrier. That's why they're here."

"I don't understand," Sarah sniffed. "Why'd they come here?"

"Um. Well. Blackstone is kind of right on top of the Barrier. It's complicated. There's an organisation that keeps the Barrier running and keep tabs on all sorcerers. But they're gone. They were mostly killed by this sorcerer called Lucifer."

"Lucifer?" Alex raised her eyebrows. "As in, Satan?"

"No, it's just the name he used. I told you it was complicated."

"I want to know," she said, firmly.

Crap. I didn't have time to argue. And she had the right to know the truth. So did Sarah.

"Okay. Crazy sorcerer Lucifer found a way to live in the Darkworld for hundreds of years and kept using demons to attack people. He's been dipping in and out of human history for ages, but the last time he appeared was twenty years ago. He was after my mother—wait, that part's *way* too complicated."

"Try me."

"I haven't…" I was aware that the others were shooting me urgent looks—Berenice in particular looked ready to walk off without me. "We have to leave, in case they come back. They're only after sorcerers. The demons, I mean. Lucifer's after me."

"You—why?"

"Because I'm half-demon," I said. "My parents weren't my parents. My mum was that crazy fortune-teller in Blackstone, only she wasn't really a fortune-teller. She was Lucifer's... lover, I guess, but she had an affair with a higher demon—they can take on human form. So she had to hide me with another family. I didn't find this out until recently."

Uh, what? said Alex's face. I could tell my friends hadn't expected anything as outlandish as that. Sarah looked at me like I'd said I'd been planted here by aliens. That would have been easier to explain.

"You could give celebrity scandals a run for their money," said Alex.

Well, that was one way of looking at it. "Um, right," I said. "Well, anyway, I've got to leave. Lucifer's after me so we need to get out of here."

"But where... where will you go?" Sarah blinked, another tear escaping.

"Shelter," I said. "I can't tell you where. Demons can read anyone's mind at any time, and I don't want them coming after you. I'll text you, I promise. We can't stay. I don't know how many of the Venantium survived, but, well, they don't like me much. They don't trust human-demons."

"So you're on your own?" said Alex.

"I have those guys," I said, gesturing toward Leo and the others.

"GameSoc, eh?" said Alex, referring to the alibi I used to use for meetings with the group.

"What, you think I should have told you I was going to practice magic and learn about demons?"

"I always thought this place looked like Hogwarts," said Alex. "Couldn't you at least give a demonstration?"

"Wasn't that enough?" I said, waving a hand in the direction of the ruined bar.

"That was you?"

"Partly. The demons blocked the door, but I have... demon magic. I can't really control it, though. I never meant to tear the place up."

"Holy shit," said Alex. "No wonder you have a crazy sorcerer on your tail."

"I never asked for this," I said. "I... I don't know if I'm coming back, if ever. But I thought you ought to know the truth. Even if you hate me for it."

"We don't hate you, Ash."

Their response echoed that of Claudia and the others when they'd found out I was a human-demon. Tears stung my eyes again.

"Thanks," I said, forcing a smile. "You know, that makes me feel slightly better. I hope... I hope I can come back."

"Same here," said Alex. "Hug?"

And the three of us embraced, there amongst the ruins, and tears ran down my cheeks as I thought of the life we'd once had, the life all of us had once had, before demons had torn it apart.

3

COMPLICATIONS

After one final goodbye, I went to join my other friends. None of them had stopped to say goodbye to anyone, but I supposed I'd been the only one to really get to know people outside of our group. I'd made friends before I'd known what I was, before I'd truly known the extent of the danger I posed to everyone. The others didn't have such attachments. Howard and Berenice's personalities put most people off. Cyrus and Leo had been away from here for months, and I supposed Claudia's party-girl façade didn't really leave room for serious friendships with non-magic-users.

Leo took my hand. "Ready?" he said.

I nodded.

Away from the bright lights of the student village, it was pitch-black in the forest. We conjured our own lights to create an avenue through the woods, but I hated that we couldn't see either side of us. Even the birdsong had faded to silence. Acorns and foliage crunched under our feet. Fallen leaves blew past, stirred in a mournful dance by the wind. At every turn, I expected something to leap out at us.

I just hoped the demons would leave the survivors alone.

Survivors. Like it had been a tragic accident—a train crash, or a natural disaster. Was that what the Venantium would disguise it as? If it even made the news. Blackstone was off the radar for most people. I remembered the blank looks I'd got when I'd told people at sixth form where I was going to university, how no one but me seemed to know there *was* a Blackstone University, even though it had showed up on the list when I was applying. When I'd tried to show Cara the university's website, it had crashed. Although most of the students there weren't sorcerers, it tended to draw people who had a minor connection to the Darkworld —or were what most people would call 'psychic.' The rest of the world more or less overlooked its existence. It had been Claudia who'd told me that this was due to the Venantium's barriers, which made it all but invisible to the outside world.

Alex and Sarah had known nothing about the world that existed beneath our feet. I'd not let anything slip, though there had been a few close calls, like that time I'd frozen a former flatmate—and *venator*—into a block of ice. Thinking about it, I hadn't seen David amongst the dead, so he must have got out of headquarters in one piece.

Claudia hissed a warning. A light flickered ahead. Several figures approached us.

It was a small group of *venators.* I recognised the leader as one of the men who'd taken me captive. He met my eyes with a hollow expression that hadn't been there when he and his friends had tackled me and taken me in; had that really just been a few hours ago?

"Ashlyn," he said, and managed to pack so much hate

into that word that I might otherwise have flinched. As it was, I hardly cared, not after what we'd been through at the union bar.

"You're too late," I said, coldly. "Campus has been attacked. People have died."

"Lucifer?" said another guy, his face pale under the conjured lights. He couldn't be older than me, nineteen or twenty. I remembered seeing him sobbing over a body earlier.

"Demons," I said.

"Impossible," said the first man, who still looked at me like I'd caused the whole thing. "The breach in the Barrier was repaired when Melivia Blackstone sacrificed herself."

"Maybe the Barrier's been broken for a while," said Leo. "Have you thought about that? The higher demons got through."

"The higher demons clearly don't go by the usual rules," said a blonde girl I recognised from meetings during the brief time I'd worked for the Venantium. "They come and go as they please. How many demons?"

I shook my head. "I don't know. I think we killed them all, but… there are survivors. You have to help them."

"We're evacuating the town," said the first man. "Blackstone's going to be put under quarantine until we can ascertain whether or not Lucifer's still here. The higher demons are unaccounted for; they disappeared when the tunnel collapsed, but I'm holding them responsible for any mass demon summonings."

"I didn't see any of them," I said. "But… Mephistopheles came back. It wouldn't surprise me if he summoned the others."

"A demon cannot cross the Barrier alone—those rules still apply."

I thought of Mephistopheles. He didn't live by any

rules, not like the other demons. If ever a demon bore a grudge, he did.

"Wait a moment," I said, my heart sinking as I remembered something else I'd overlooked. "Mephistopheles's demon heart was lost somewhere up at campus. If anyone touches it, he can possess them. Shit. I should have taken it…"

A choked noise came from Berenice. Mephistopheles was the one thing that truly scared her. The demon had some kind of hold over her, because he'd spared her life after killing her friends a few years ago. What that hold meant, I didn't know.

"He'll find us," she whispered, her face ghostly white beneath the rising moon.

"We don't know that," said Howard, putting an arm around her.

"Lucifer will find him a new body," she said. "He's his right-hand demon."

She had a point. In fact, any demon could resurrect infinite times. But Lucifer himself, as a human who'd cheated death, defied all the usual rules of the Darkworld. Not that I entirely knew what those rules were, but I knew that usually, to summon a demon required a contract of some kind. The sorcerer offered some of their own powers —magical energy, which no demon could resist—in exchange for the demon's service. Even possession required the victim to let the demon in, although since the alternative was death, most people said yes immediately, even non-sorcerers. Even Leo had, when it came down to it.

"We'll clear out of here before that happens," said Leo. "I didn't think of it, either. That thing's dangerous, anyway. Hope it was buried in the rubble. You lot," he added to the *venators,* "be careful with that thing.

Mephistopheles isn't like the other demons. He's an angry bastard."

"I think you need to have a little more faith in your superiors, Mr. Blake," said the man. "Do not presume that we are amateurs."

"Superiors?" Leo laughed humourlessly. "Your head-quarters are in ruins, five higher demons are on the loose, and a mass demon summoning just killed a bunch of inno-cent students under your watch. I think it's time to accept you're in over your heads."

"You—"

"Wait!" said the girl. "We've got to get a move on quickly. We'll need a ton of Influence."

"You're going to erase everyone's memories, right?" I said. "Do me a favour, okay? If you see two girls, Sarah Wren and Alex Park, leave their memories alone."

"Ash?" said Leo. "Are you sure?"

"Positive," I said. "They deserve the truth, and they deserve to be allowed to remember it. Alex will kick your ass if you try to mess with her memory, anyway."

"I don't completely agree with that," said the girl. "I still say we should test them for their magical potential."

One of the men argued, "We haven't time for that. We're at war. Hayley—"

"What happened to the others?" Cyrus broke in. "Hayley and Mr. Fraser?"

"They've been checking the tunnels for signs of Lucifer," said the younger guy. "We helped excavate what we could, but—but some demons must have got through the Barrier before it repaired itself. One of our own people got possessed, and the demon said Lucifer was coming back…"

"That I can believe," said Cyrus. "He has you in the palm of his hand, now, doesn't he?"

"We won't lose." But his dead-eyed look begged to differ.

None of the others looked particularly confident, either.

"Well, good luck with it," said Leo. "Try not to get anyone else killed."

"You, young man, ought to learn some respect."

"You ought to go fuck yourself," Leo retorted. "Innocent students are dead, and you're worrying about respect? And you wonder why I hate you people?"

"Leo. C'mon," said Cyrus. "It's not worth arguing. We have to leave."

"You're running away?" said the man, as though determined to get the last word in. "You call us cowards?"

"We're going to find a way to beat him," said Leo. "And then we're going to kill him."

"Damn straight," said Claudia.

For all their bravado, I knew they weren't as confident as they pretended to be. But what choice did we have but to fight on, no matter how hopeless and impossible it seemed?

We left the *venators* to carry on towards campus, and continued down the dark path. Winter had crowned the trees on either side with a coating of frost; brittle leaves crunched under my feet as I pushed on through the undergrowth. The others followed tensely, no one speaking.

The old Blackstone house greeted us as we emerged from the trees, as forlorn as ever, surrounded by an arc of scorched ground from the fire that had consumed the old manor, and the Blackstone family with it. Now that we were on the brink of another Demon War, I couldn't stop myself looking up at the house as though searching for a sign. But there was nothing but gaping rooms and mangled furniture, charred walls, and collapsed arches. There were no answers here.

Blackstone was eerily silent, too, with none of the usual sounds of students enjoying a night out. I wondered if the Venantium had evacuated them already, and if so, how on earth they'd managed it. The population couldn't be that large, but an entire town moving at once would be bound to attract some notice, surely.

We walked through the darkening streets to Howard's house, where everyone except Claudia and me disappeared inside.

"This is mental," she said, shaking her head. "What do we expect to find in London? Why would we be safer there than here? We'd be better off in the middle of a rainforest or something. Leo and Cy had the right idea."

"He'd find me," I said. "Wherever we go, the Dark-world's always there. Besides, that place in London—maybe someone there has answers about how to defeat him. That's what the half-demon implied, anyway."

She blinked. "The half-demon?"

Of course, I hadn't told her about my conversation with the half-demon. I relayed the mission I'd been given by the lost spirits eternally stuck in a half-life in the Darkworld.

Claudia sucked in a breath. "So, they're immortal? That's how Lucifer keeps living, right? He just goes back to the Darkworld when his human body dies."

"Well, yeah," I said. "But they aren't there by choice. They're like the half-demon—wait, it isn't the same one as last time," I clarified. "Not the one who tried to kill us. These are the other half-demons like her. They want me to set them free, and they said that was how we could kill Lucifer. In fact…" I frowned. "Now that I think about it, the half-demon—she said that breaking the Barrier would take away his immortality."

"Because he'd no longer be tied to the Darkworld?" said Claudia, working it out. "But... he *did* break the Barrier, didn't he?"

I shook my head. "I don't think that's what the half-demon meant. I think she wants me to get rid of the Barrier altogether."

"Wouldn't that unleash a load of demons?"

"Yeah, that's the tricky part. But if there was no Barrier, and we found Lucifer's demon heart and destroyed it, I guess... I guess that would actually kill him. For real."

"Seriously?"

I wasn't sure; that sounded too simple. Lucifer wouldn't have broken the Barrier if he'd thought there was a risk to his own life, would he?

"His demon heart was burned," I said. "In the—in the tunnels. But he's not dead. He can't be completely dependent on it." No. The Darkworld kept him living, just like the half-demons. That was what the half-demon had been trying to tell me. If we destroyed his heart—totally obliterated it, then he'd die as soon as the Barrier lifted. The Barrier wasn't the reason demons didn't invade our world. It was the source of their very essence, the reason that even after being killed in this world, they could never leave the Darkworld.

And... the same must be true of the fortune-teller, I realised with a sickening jolt. She'd had a demon heart, too, just like Lucifer. She'd dispersed the magic within it back into the Darkworld in order to defeat Lucifer, at the cost of her own life. But part of her must still be trapped there, along with the half-demons. *Oh God.*

"His heart will still be functional," said Claudia. "Or he'll find a new one. He's not a true demon, he won't be tied to one heart. Hell, more than one demon can use just one, if it has enough energy. That's why the Venantium keep defunct demon hearts in their headquarters, in case someone tries to use them again."

"And they used them to power the Barrier," I added.

"Well, those weren't technically demon hearts, just stores of energy. That's all a demon heart is, really."

Out of habit, I found myself reaching for mine. I squeezed it, feeling the coolness press into my palm. Demon hearts were both the source of their power and their weak point… Not only because destroying a demon's heart sent them back to the Darkworld, but because it was through a demon's heart that a sorcerer could control them. I had no idea how this worked for regular demons, but when Terrence and Jude got their hands on mine, they'd had control over my every move. I wished it wasn't such a vulnerable point, but it couldn't be avoided, at least that I knew of.

"Wait a minute," I said. "It *can't* be that simple. If Lucifer had already broken the Barrier, then those half-demons wouldn't have asked me to set them free."

"Shit." Claudia frowned. "You're right. There must be something else. Maybe ask the half-demon again? You really ought to get her name. This is just confusing."

At that moment, Howard emerged from the house. I raised my eyebrows at his huge backpacking rucksack.

"What? We don't know how long we'll be gone for."

Apparently, he'd packed both his and Berenice's possessions into one bag. All Berenice held was a flimsy handbag. *Figures.* Leo and Cyrus had opted for the more sensible option of ordinary-sized rucksacks.

"See, we've got all this camping stuff, but it's not exactly practical," said Cyrus.

"So we might end up sleeping on a picnic bench in Hyde Park," said Berenice. "Just what I've always wanted."

"You can sleep on the train," said Leo. "It's like… four hours, isn't it?"

I wasn't keen on the idea of spending that long in a confined space, but it was that or a seven-hour coach trip. Or walking.

We got lucky; a bus already was already waiting at the stop when we turned into the main street of Blackstone, and we managed to hop aboard. By mutual agreement, we used Influence to become invisible to others—not to avoid paying bus fare, but because we didn't want to risk anyone to see us leaving, or for the demons finding out where we were going. After all, demons could read anyone's mind at any time. There would be no hiding anything from Lucifer when he came back—all we could do was avoid making it easy for him and hope that his attention was elsewhere.

"Guess they haven't evacuated yet," Leo commented as we sat at the back on the top deck.

"There aren't many *venators* left, though," said Claudia. "I suppose it'll take a while."

In Redthorne, we made for the train station, a red brick building a couple of streets down from the bus stop. I couldn't stop looking around frantically as we waited on the platform, even though the still-active Influence cloaked us from view.

"I'm not paying eighty freaking pounds for a train ticket," Howard said, glaring at the ticket machine. "We'll stay undercover."

True enough, I didn't have that much cash on me—and whatever fortune my mother had left me, I didn't want to use my debit card if I could help it. I didn't quite trust Lucifer not to have figured out a way of tracking us through transactions or something. Maybe it was just paranoia, but he knew everything about Melivia, after all. Did he know about the money she'd given me? I doubted money mattered very much to the supposed leader of demons, but still.

Despite the constant worry, I was worn out from the turbulence of the day, and I managed to sleep for part of the journey. Leo shook me awake when we had to change trains in Manchester, and I groggily stood up, realising that the Influence hadn't disappeared when I'd dozed off, and the Darkworld still cloaked me in layers of shadow. It had to be the demon's doing, and for the first time, I was grateful for her presence.

We got on the second train, a direct route from Manchester to London, this time sneaking into the almost vacant first class carriage.

"Saving the world from demonic invasion ought to earn us a first class ticket, right?" said Leo.

But there was one small oversight.

"Did any of you get an address?" I asked. "For this night club?"

"Shit," said Claudia. "Didn't anyone think of that?"

"Apparently not," said Berenice, glaring at me as though it was my fault.

"I've never even been to London," I said defensively. *Come on. We'd nearly died, for crying out loud.*

"I have the address," said Cyrus, pulling a piece of paper from his pocket. "It was one of the places I researched when I was with the Venantium in America. Come to think of it, they'll be flying into one of the London airports soon…"

"Forget them," said Berenice. "Where is this place, anyway? Do you have a map?"

"Kind of." Cyrus passed her the paper, which showed

an unintelligible scribble that looked vaguely like a bird's eye view of central London.

"That's why we have Google Maps," said Leo, pulling out his phone. "If I could get a signal on this train, it'd help!"

"Brilliant," said Berenice. "So we get to wander around Trafalgar Square in the middle of the night when the country's under attack by demons."

None of us are thrilled about this, you know. Speaking of demons, it was unusual for me not to see any, but since we'd left Blackstone, no dark spaces had caught my attention. I'd been asleep, but I could usually feel when one was nearby—a cold prickling at my skin. Its absence made me suspicious. Had all the attention been drawn to Blackstone?

"We could just ask directions," said Claudia. "Use Influence."

"I don't like it," said Berenice. "We're going from the frying pan into the fire."

"It's that or die," said Leo. "Which would you prefer?"

Berenice didn't say anything, but snuggled closer to Howard. His fists were clenched. I could sense a temper tantrum brewing.

I found it harder to sleep this time around. It was eerily silent on the train at night, and the empty carriage seemed to be filled with small noises that made me jump. Every creak of the track set my nerves on edge. But it was my proximity to Leo that really bothered me. It was stupid, given everything that had happened, but for the past six months I'd told myself that even if he came back, all apologetic, I still wouldn't forgive him for leaving. But the world had tipped upside-down, and now was hardly the time for petty arguments.

And he'd told me he loved me.

I loved him, too. Stupid, blind as I was, I couldn't help it. Perhaps some people easily got over their first love, but I wasn't the type to give affection easily. I'd sooner be single for life than stuck with someone who didn't make me happy, and Leo did, effortlessly, just by being there. But right now, I wished he didn't, because it made me feel as though I wasn't in control of my own emotions—demon aside.

And if we survived this, I didn't think I could take it if he disappeared again.

4

HIDDEN

The train pulled into London around midnight. Still cloaked in Influence, Howard jumped over the ticket barrier and out into the main station, skidding across the polished marble floor. The rest of us followed more slowly, looking around for any signs of disquiet. Even at this hour, it was still packed with suitcase-toting tourists, some accompanied by small children. We dodged in and out of the crowd and ran down the escalator to the Underground.

I hated the idea of going underground again, given what had happened last time I'd been in a tunnel. Still, the Underground was as different as you could get from the stone walled, earthy tunnels of the Venantium. We rode three escalators down past tiled walls lined with advertisements. The incessant breeze—whether it came from the trains or extra-powerful air con, I had no idea—lifted the hair from my head. The low ceiling and narrow walls encased us, making me feel trapped despite the breeze. There were several unsavoury-looking figures hanging about at this time, but no one noticed us. I was grateful that the subway line we needed was still running, although we were cutting it close. I had no intention of joining the homeless people sleeping on the floor of the corridor under unfolded copies of the London Evening Standard.

Cyrus figured out which was the right train to get, luckily, because none of the rest of us knew where to start. We jumped aboard a train just before the sliding doors shut. The tube rushed through the tunnel, rattling along the track. Cyrus warned us to position ourselves by the doors so we'd be able to jump out at the right stop. We were the only people in the compartment, unusual for a busy line.

The train pulled into Charing Cross Station, and I was prepared to jump when a dark space opened on the platform. A tear in the universe like an open wound, exposing the darkness beneath. Coldness shot through me.

"Shit," I whispered, pointing. Leo's eyes widened.

"Come on!" Cyrus said, jumping off the train, seemingly oblivious to the dark space.

Behind me, Howard more or less shoved the rest of us out of the door, and I stumbled right into the darkness.

For an instant, the world appeared painted in two halves: one grey and dull, the other black as night. I staggered onto the platform, emerging on the other side of the dark space. Any ordinary person would see nothing amiss, but the dark space remained, cutting the platform in two. My eyes roved over it, searching for demon eyes, ghoul claws, shadow-beasts.

A hand grabbed mine. I jumped, my heart leaping to my throat.

"Don't freak me out like that!" said Leo, and the darkness disappeared as I turned around to face him.

"What do you think *you* just did to me?" I said. My heart raced at a million miles an hour and my breath came short. I could feel the presence of the dark space behind me.

"Sorry," said Leo. "I thought—I thought you just walked into the Darkworld. I couldn't see you at all."

"Because that's possible?" I stared at him. "Why would I do that, even if I could?"

"I don't know. I just panicked. Come on."

We went to join the others. A tramp lay propped up against the wall, so still he might have been dead. I didn't want to get too close.

"Mind telling me what that was about?" said Cyrus. "Provoking the demons is the last thing we want to do."

"I thought there was something there," I said, embarrassed by my overreaction. "A shadow-beast or something."

"There's nothing there," said Howard.

Leo took my hand again. "Never mind. How do we get out of this place?"

I couldn't imagine how commuters navigated these tunnels on a daily basis. Then again, given the number of traumatic experiences I'd had underground, it wasn't surprising that I wanted to avoid them for life now.

Thankfully, we reached the surface without incident. Unfamiliar streets surrounded us, lit by rows of streetlamps that spilled orange light onto the pavement. The roar of traffic persisted even at this hour.

"Right," said Cyrus, consulting the map again. "We're close, but this place is a bloody maze—we need to go this way."

After crossing a busy street, it became easy to tell where the action was. Girls in crippling heels wearing club-going gear staggered down the road whilst guys catcalled from nearby bars; a normal night on the high street in any city or town. I could hear the pounding music from nightclubs like a pulse beneath the cracked pavement, but it made me think of the fate of the union bar in Blackstone. Goose bumps broke out on my skin. I didn't want to walk into another club.

Satan's Pit was easy to spot. Unlike its sister branch in Redthorne, it actually looked like a nightclub rather than a shabby basement. It obviously cost a fortune to maintain, judging by all the flashing flame-like lights on its exterior. I wasn't sure where I'd put my ID, but using Influence again was probably our best bet to get us inside unnoticed. Just in case the demons had gotten here first.

If they have, God help us all.

"Wish I'd known about Influence when I was younger," said Berenice, as we ducked under the barrier outside, past the shivering people waiting in line. "I only used it to sneak into a nightclub once, and that was when I was on holiday in New York, 'cos I'm under twenty-one."

The entryway was carpeted in the same blood red as the other branch. A bored-looking guy who, for all I knew, could have been related to the door guy in Redthorne, stamped people's hands as they came in, whilst two burly security guards frisked anyone they thought looked suspicious. Nothing suggested this place hid any secret organisation.

Cyrus shrugged and made for the double doors at the back. "This is definitely the place," he said.

So we ventured inside, into a whirl of lights. The decorators had outdone themselves with this place; everything looked authentic, from the cobweb-strewn candelabra to the hellfire painted on the walls.

"Not really dressed for the occasion, are we?" said Claudia, visibly gaining a spring in her step from the deafening music. "I should've brought a dress."

She didn't look anywhere near as in her element as she

usually did, wearing shabby jeans with a hole in the knee, her hair tangled and matted. I became self-conscious that I didn't look any better. Despite my attempts to brush the dust out of my hair on the train, it still clung to me all over, debris from the tunnels and the collapsed student bar. The past twenty-four hours had done a number on all of us.

"Someone here must know something," said Cyrus, surveying the crowd. "Anyone spot any magic-users?"

Of course. I hadn't thought to check if anyone wore a shield. The Venantium had taught me how to see who was a magic-user, and I focused my vision, trying to see the shadows beneath the blinding lights. It wasn't easy, but gradually the Darkworld revealed itself in layers of shadow overlapping the visible world. The shadows were thickest around one individual, a guy in the corner who was dancing with a girl.

"What d'you think?" said Cyrus, nodding in his direction.

We edged toward him, pushing through the dancing, laughing crowd. People frowned as we brushed past, still cloaked in Influence. The guy was leaning right over the girl in a way that made me reluctant to interrupt. Between flashes of disco lights, I saw him move closer, a leer across his face—a familiar face…

"*Ryan?*" I said.

He turned, eyes widening in surprise. The girl he'd been ogling let out a shrill scream.

"Who *are* you!" she yelled in Ryan's face, leaping back. Several people nearby laughed, obviously thinking she was drunk. I knew better—Ryan was an incubus who made his target think he was the person they most desired. Generally, either a boyfriend or an ex. He'd tried that one on me when Cara and I had been in Australia over the summer. Though he'd told me he lived in London, I hadn't expected—or wanted—to run into him again. What the hell were the odds?

"Ash?" he said, gaping at me. "Timing?"

"You know this douche?" said Claudia.

"Unfortunately," I said. "We met in Australia. He's an incubus."

"Really?" Claudia, to my astonishment, hitched a flirtatious smile onto her face. "Hi, I'm Claudia."

He blinked. "Hey," he said, his mouth curving into a smile.

I flashed Claudia a glare, which she ignored entirely. "Can I talk to you for a moment?"

"Sure," he said, the other girl forgotten.

With a last terrified glance at Ryan, she tottered over to the group of people who'd been laughing at her, presumably her friends. She gave me a death-look worthy of Berenice as she wobbled past on her ridiculously spindly heels. *Really?* If anything, I'd done her a favour.

Ryan and Claudia were engaged in conversation. Claudia kept brushing against him in a way that made me gag. Presumably she was trying to sweet talk him into helping us, but I didn't like that it was the only way to get through to asshats like him. Surely just *asking* would do.

He waved the rest of us over, one hand on Claudia's arm. "There's a staircase in the corner of the other room, out through there." He pointed at a set of doors wide open into another room where a different kind of music was playing. "It's hidden, but you'll be able to see it. Follow the stairs. Someone down there'll be able to help."

His eyes were already on the crowd again, so I led the way through the doors without thanking him.

Techno-electric music blared in this room and the walls glittered blue. I made my way through the crowd, paying no heed to who I knocked aside.

Leo came up beside me. "*Where* did you meet that guy? You never mentioned knowing an incubus."

Oh, hell. "Do I have to tell you about everyone I meet?" I snapped. *For God's sake, I don't need this right now.* "A lot can happen in six months."

Leo flinched. "Sorry. I was just wondering, is all."

"We're definitely *not* friends. He gets his kicks out of seducing random girls by pretending to be their boyfriends."

"Mind tricks." Leo shook his head. "Sleazy bastard. He didn't hurt you, did he? Some of those incubi can be pretty vicious. Like vampires, but they do it on purpose."

"No, I scared him away. Nearly froze his face off."

"You did?"

"Yeah." My voice took on a defensive tone. Didn't he think I could take care of myself?

"Sorry. I was just shocked. Incubi are dangerous. I mean, they use their Darkworld connection to—"

"Mess with people's heads, I get it," I said. "You aren't exactly making this better, you know." Tiredness and worry made me sharper than I'd usually be. I didn't need him getting protective of me now.

"Sorry, Ash."

I didn't respond. Scanning the room, my eyes fell on a staircase in the corner. Like the fortune-teller's tent, it had been hidden in plain sight; the clubbers simply stayed a few feet back from that area as though the room ended there.

"That's our place," said Cyrus, nodding toward it.

Underground again.

But this time the stairs were metal, not stone, and led down a short way into a corridor. Here, several metal doors awaited us, with no clues as to what was behind each one.

Howard took the lead and hammered on the nearest.

"Hey! Is anyone here?" His voice rang through the corridor.

I counted six doors, all identical and without handles. It made me jump when the door on my right opened with a screech of metal.

"Who are you?" A dark-skinned young woman put her head out and frowned at us. She had a pink streak in her hair, and her fingernails were painted pink to match. She couldn't have been more than a few years older than us.

Behind her, I caught a glimpse of a room containing a long table strewn with books and papers.

"We came for shelter." Cyrus took control. "We're sorcerers, and we've travelled a long way. Can we stay here?"

"Well, I can't say that I'm keen to open our door to strangers during times like these, but we do have a policy that any sorcerer can stay with us. If you made it past our security, you must be safe. Where are you from?"

"We came from Blackstone," said Cyrus. "Do you know what's going on up there?"

The woman hesitated. Her eyes widened at the mention of Blackstone, and she ushered us inside, closing the door behind us.

Drawing in a breath, she faced us. "We aren't as up to date as we'd like to be, but I figure that the Venantium would have fallen by now. Has it?"

"Yes, it has," said Cyrus, his voice wavering slightly. It still didn't feel real, not even after we'd seen Lucifer with our own eyes. "Five of the Inner Circle are possessed by higher demons."

The girl's eyebrows shot up. "So it's true? Lucifer made contact with the Higher Ones?"

"Apparently," said Cyrus. "Lucifer's back. He killed half the Venantium, and attacked innocents at our university. We barely got away. We had a tip off that this was the only place to seek shelter with other sorcerers."

"You heard right. I'm Layla. This is Gareth." She pointed to a man at the table. I hadn't seen him as he was half-obscured by a stack of heavy-looking books.

"Hello," he said, peering around the books through thick-framed spectacles. "You came from Blackstone, you say?"

"Yeah," said Cyrus, warily.

"Have any of you visited the Venantium's library?"

"Sneaked in a few times, yeah," said Leo. "They don't like outsiders going in there."

"Still?" Layla shook her head.

"There's a book I think Lucifer may have used that might be in there," said Gareth, knocking a couple of books off the desk as he shifted his chair. "I've been researching. It's good that you showed up now; I've been looking for help."

"Slow down!" said Layla. "Sorry," she added, to us. "You must be tired. We have plenty of rooms available. This place was built to house over a hundred sorcerers. There's around twenty here now, but if what you say is true, then I'm expecting more people to show up soon. I'll show you where everything is."

She gestured us to follow her into the corridor again. Pushing open another door, she led us into another passageway lined with doors. It was wallpapered and carpeted in blue, as if it belonged to a hotel corridor not underneath a nightclub. The doors even had numbers.

"Any room that's unlocked is free," she said. "These two are the communal bathrooms, and there's another two down the far end. You have your own showers in your rooms, but the temperature can be a bit hit and miss. Just a warning. It might be noisy, too, with the club right over us.

Most of us tend to move around at night rather than during the day. Force of habit. The nightclub's open until six in the morning. Does anyone have any questions?"

"Yeah," said Howard. "My mum told me to come here. You seen her?"

"What's her name?"

"Becca Lloyd."

"I don't know anyone by that name. Sorry. Was she supposed to meet you somewhere?"

"She was imprisoned by the Venantium," said Howard, fists clenched at his sides. "She escaped and said she was coming here."

"Sorry, she isn't here."

"Then where the bloody hell is she, then?" Howard took a step forward, eyes narrowed.

"Don't you have her number?" said Layla, unfazed by his aggressiveness.

"Of course not. She's been in prison for five years, for fuck's sake."

"Howard!" said Cyrus, warningly.

"I'm going to look for her, then." He turned on his heel and made for the nearest door.

"Howard, she's not here!" said Berenice, rushing after him as he wrenched a door open on an empty room.

Howard let the door fall shut and turned to glare at her. "How do you know that?"

"I…" Berenice's lip trembled. She hated showing weakness, I knew, but like the rest of us, she'd been through hell in the past day.

"Fine," Howard snarled, and stalked off, out of the door and back toward the nightclub. Berenice hurried after him.

Claudia shook her head. "Well, I'm not following them."

"What's the betting he'll be gone by morning?" I said.

"Hope not," said Leo darkly. "We were damn lucky not to get attacked on the way here. Lucifer's people will be everywhere. We can't trust anyone."

"You can trust us," said Layla, who'd watched the whole scene with a calmness that surprised me. Her expression wasn't indifference, but suggested she'd seen far worse than Howard's hissy fits. "I'd even offer to go under the Venantium's scanners, if they existed any more—I'm assuming they haven't upgraded from the Angel Box?"

"They used it on me," I said. "I hope it got destroyed when the tunnel collapsed."

"Collapsed!" Layla's eyes widened. "Okay, I bet you guys have a lot to tell us. But sleep first. You look dead on your feet, and Gareth'll never let you go once he starts questioning. He's been down here for too long, looking for a way to beat Lucifer."

"Is that what you're doing?" I asked, my heart beating faster. "Do you think–do you think there's a way?"

"Who knows?" said Layla. "But I'm not giving in without a fight."

They must know something. We couldn't have come all this way for no reason.

"We're in," said Claudia. "We want to fight, too."

"You're more than welcome to give us as much or as little help as you like. We don't do contracts or anything like that, and we don't keep tabs on everyone like the Venantium do. Anytime you want to leave, feel free to."

"I think we'll be sticking around for a while," I said. "We're here to figure out how to fight Lucifer."

I only hoped that it wouldn't mean the death of all of us.

5

THEORY OF DARKNESS

I slept for a full twelve hours, despite the less-than-comfortable, lumpy mattress. The windowless, cell-like room bothered me less than I'd expected; it wasn't much worse than the dingy bedsit I'd rented in Manchester.

Unfortunately, my subconscious decided to treat me to a full replay of my flight through the collapsing tunnel, and I awoke gasping for breath, tears running down my face as I recalled the fortune-teller's last moments. Unexpectedly, the stark truth crashed over me; she was dead, never coming back. Would I ever get used to the idea that she was gone? She had never been actively involved in my life, not as herself, but I still felt her absence like a dark space had opened inside me. She'd been my hope that I could fight the demons. Without her, I had nowhere to turn to for help. She'd died to kill Lucifer: told me her death was the only way to finish him off... but he'd survived.

Untangling myself from the covers, I sat up, running a hand over my face. I caught sight of my reflection in the mirror. I'd become used to watching the half-demon of myself, a demon using my form, so seeing my actual reflection threw me a bit. The girl in the mirror didn't look like me. Matted dark brown hair, grown longer than I remembered for lack of a decent haircut in months. Shadowed dark eyes. Skinnier than before, smaller somehow. Fragile. The half-demon always looked assured. The real me just looked lost.

At least the shower was warm, though the en suite wasn't much bigger than a cupboard and the room felt a bit cell-like, with the absence of a window and the dim ceiling light. But I was so relieved to be alive and in a safe place that I didn't care. I showered quickly and pulled fresh clothes from my bag. The phone Leo had given me fell out of my coat pocket when I picked it up from where I'd left it draped on a chair. There was no signal underground. If I wanted to contact Cara, I'd have to go back onto the surface.

I didn't put on my coat, but fished the amethyst crystal from my pocket and hung it around my neck, tucked under my shirt.

Time to find the others. I pushed the door open and glanced either way down the corridor, unnerved by the silence. My watch informed me that it was one in the afternoon. I knocked on the room next to mine, Leo's, but no one answered.

Perhaps they're in the meeting room.

After knocking on Claudia's door, too, and getting no response, I decided to go and explore. There were four unknown doors in the main corridor, and I was curious as to what the group were keeping down here. Unfortunately, only one of them was unlocked, and behind it was a room filled with so many boxes that I couldn't take a step inside for fear of knocking something over. I knocked on the meeting room door instead.

"Thought you'd show up at some point!" said Claudia, waving at me from the other side of the table. "I knocked on your room about an hour ago, but you were dead to the world."

"I must have slept through it," I said. All the others were there—even Howard and Berenice. So she'd stopped him from running off. *Good.* I'd half-expected to run into a group of strangers, but the only newcomers were Gareth and Layla. The latter smiled at me from behind a laptop.

"Your university's in the papers," Gareth informed me. He sat in the same seat he'd occupied last night, and by the look of things he hadn't moved since then, if his tousled hair and red-rimmed eyes were anything to go by. He sipped from a mug of black coffee.

"What cover story did the Venantium use?" I said, pulling out a chair.

"Some kind of explosion," said Leo, yawning.

"Hell, I need to ring my parents," said Claudia. "They'll be going apeshit."

"Will they know what really happened?" I asked, wondering whether the Venantium had got Blackstone under quarantine yet, and how on earth they were even going about doing that.

"By now, yeah." She got to her feet. "Nothing's going to attack me outside, is it?"

"No, but use the back door of the club." Layla came over, carrying a plate of toast. "If you want anything to eat or drink, Ash, help yourself over there. We don't really have cooks here, so everyone has to chip in."

"Sounds fair," I said. I was starving, actually. Adrenaline had made me forget I hadn't eaten in over twenty-four hours.

There was a small kitchen in an alcove at the back of the room, complete with microwave and kettle, but no proper oven. I slotted some bread into the toaster whilst surveying the room. The table was still covered in papers, and Gareth had divided his stack of books in two. They looked as ancient as some of those in the Venantium's library, spines wrinkled with age.

"What about the rest of you?" Layla asked. Unlike Gareth, she looked as though she'd actually snatched a few hours of sleep. She wore purple today and had painted her nails to match. "Do you need to phone anyone?"

"Nope," said Leo, as Cyrus said "No," almost at the same time. "Our parents are dead. So's our guardian."

"I'm sorry." Sympathy shone in her eyes. I wondered if she'd lost anyone.

"Well, I don't know where *my* parents are," said Howard, through gritted teeth.

"What about you, Berenice?" said Cyrus. "Isn't your dad a lecturer at the university?"

"Yeah," she said, sullenly. "We argued."

"I'm guessing he wasn't in the union bar, then?" said Leo. "Because even *you* aren't that heartless."

"Look, he hates Howard, okay?" snapped Berenice. "I don't want to speak to him. And God knows whether my mum's alive or dead."

Layla gaped at her. Even Gareth looked up from his books, his jaw hanging open.

"She joined the Venantium," Cyrus explained. "Like our father. Never came back for family or anything."

There was an awkward pause, where the only sound was the faint hum of the kettle boiling.

"Shit," said Layla. "But—you said the Venantium was attacked, right?"

"Yeah, but she's not there, she's in France," said Berenice. "She moved to the EU's branch years ago."

"You never told us that," said Cyrus, eyebrows raised in surprise.

Berenice gave one of her ever-unconvincing shrugs. "Does it matter?"

Cyrus turned to Layla. "What about you?" he asked. "I hope it isn't a rude question. How long have you lived here?"

"A while. My parents started this place up originally. They made an enemy of a necromancer after they turned him in to the Venantium. But he had friends. They hid here for years, but just when they finally thought it was safe to go to the surface again, they were attacked." She blinked, and I saw a flash of tears in her eyes. "But it wasn't enough to pay the debt, he said. He wants me dead, too, and his cult could be anywhere." She looked down at the stack of books on the table.

"I'm sorry," said Cyrus. "Our guardian, William Melmoth, was murdered, too."

"Melmoth?" said Gareth, moving the books in front of him aside. "He's dead?"

"You knew him?" said Leo. "We found out that there was a hell of a lot of things he kept from us. The fact that he was looking for a cure for vampirism, for one."

"Last I heard, he was researching the possibilities," said Gareth, taking one of the books and flipping it open to the contents page. I caught sight of the image of a demon and turned my back. "He came to borrow some of our books a couple of years ago."

"Which ones?" said Leo, an edge to his voice.

"I can't remember... he was looking into the history of the Darkworld connection, if I remember right. After all, the Vampire's Curse is the result of a faulty connection, as is the condition that incubi and succubi suffer from."

I thought of what Lucifer had said, about vampires

being able to take in infinite energy. It was well known that vampires had to take energy from others, usually through biting them and tapping into their magical energy as a demon would. Conrad had suffered from it, too. According to Lucifer, the reason Mr. Melmoth had abandoned his pursuit of a cure was because he'd realised that vampires could be a valuable weapon, and he'd intended to take advantage of this. Lucifer had implied Mr. Melmoth had intended to use vampires to combat him, but had been unable to share this before his death. I wasn't sure whether Leo and Cyrus believed him, or that I believed it myself. I'd never really known Mr. Melmoth, having only met him once, and not under the best circumstances: when he'd attacked me, thinking I was the half-demon. But Leo had trusted him.

"You have a lot of books here?" said Leo. So he wasn't going to ask about his late guardian, after all.

"Yes." Gareth put down the book he'd been skimming and looked up at him. "That was what I was going to ask you last night. You said you'd been to the library in Blackstone–"

"Yeah, we regularly snuck in," Howard said. "Harpy-dodging was our thing."

Gareth blinked. "Did you read any of the books?"

"Yeah," said Leo. "Mainly guides to magic and fighting demons."

Yeah, and... I shut out the thought of the other book I'd found there. Melivia's diary. I turned my back, busying myself making coffee and buttering toast. It was only a matter of time before I'd have to say my bit.

"Ah," said Gareth, leaning forward and resting his elbows on the table. "Did you find anything on the history of the Venantium, or have they hidden all those books?"

"We weren't really looking," said Leo. "I mean, the

Venantium's history's alluded to in pretty much every book anyway."

"I think there might be something in the Venantium's past that will help us defeat Lucifer," said Gareth solemnly.

I turned around again, to see Cyrus exchange raised eyebrows with Leo. Claudia leaned forward, her mouth pulled into a frown.

"Really?" Berenice looked even more unimpressed than the others. "Well, we're *not* going back to Blackstone now. The tunnels collapsed, the library's probably a heap of rubble."

Gareth looked wounded. I wasn't sure whether it was her tone or the idea of the books being buried. I grabbed my toast and coffee and went to join them at the table.

"You met Lucifer, right?" he said.

I said nothing, shifting a stack of books aside to make room for my plate.

"Met him?" Berenice gave a hollow laugh. "Yeah, he nearly killed us."

"He's been the subject of my research for some time."

"I'm sure he'd be happy to know," said Berenice, narrowing her eyes at him. "Do you have a death wish?"

Gareth shuffled papers, his face flushed. "No—of course not. Just an academic interest... the idea that anyone can survive in the Darkworld is fascinating to me. Do you know when he first appeared?"

First appeared? I'd never really thought about it. Certainly not in an academic sense. I'd been more interested in how to defeat him.

"Appeared?" I said. "He was human once, we know that much."

"Human?" said Gareth, frowning like he didn't believe me. "He's appeared at certain points in human history, leaving his mark, even though most people wouldn't know it was him. For instance, the Demon Wars. The name Lucifer is thrown around, but few connect the same sorcerer with the terror campaign twenty years ago—the last time he appeared. Only those who believe it's possible to travel to the Darkworld. If that's true… my entire theory hinges on the possibility."

"It's definitely the same guy?" said Layla. "My parents believed it, but I never really put much stock in the idea of immortality. I mean, the Darkworld isn't a place for humans. It's physically impossible to go there."

"He's not immortal," I said. When Layla's eyebrows shot up, I went on, "Well, we think there's a way to beat him. We're just trying to figure out how."

"But he's been to the Darkworld?" said Gareth. He hadn't reacted to my claim that Lucifer wasn't immortal.

I wished I could analyse this as objectively as he did, but my head was fogged with worry. For my friends, in Blackstone and here, and for myself.

"Yes," I said. "The fortune-teller…" Grief closed my throat as the dark space inside me reminded me of its presence. I blinked rapidly, determined not to dissolve into tears.

"Who is this… fortune-teller?" said Layla, curiously.

The words were there, but I couldn't say them. Leo gave my arm a squeeze.

"She was important to Ash," he said. "Is it okay if I tell them?"

I nodded, my eyes fixed on the toast I suddenly didn't feel like eating anymore. I picked up one of the newspapers on the table, just for something to do with my hands.

"The fortune-teller was this cryptic woman who lived in Blackstone. She was a sorcerer who operated on her own, separate from the Venantium, and she wanted to help people. But it turned out she…" Again, he looked to me for permission, and this time, I spoke.

"She wasn't who she seemed. She wasn't even from our time. She went to the Darkworld, like Lucifer. *With* Lucifer. She was Melivia Blackstone." I heard Gareth start to ask something, but blocked it out, pretending to be speaking into an empty room. It was easier than acknowledging that I was speaking the truth, as though my telling someone made it truer, irreversible.

"She was lured into the Darkworld by Lucifer after he tricked her into summoning a demon. That was what started the Demon Wars, but she didn't know about that. Time doesn't pass in the same way there, so she didn't know that when she came back to the human world, everyone she knew would be dead, and the world would have totally changed. She stayed with him, but…"

There's nothing to lose now, I told myself. They could kick me out and it wouldn't make a blind bit of difference. We were only delaying the inevitable. At the very least, they'd be more understanding than the Venantium had been.

"There was a higher demon. This was twenty years ago. She got pregnant, sneaked away from Lucifer after she realised, too late, that he'd duped her from the start. She fought against him, and he hasn't come back since. She knew he'd only gone to the Darkworld, and it was only a matter of time before he came back. She knew that his first target would be her child. Me."

There. I'd said it.

"I'm half demon," I said. "That's why he's after me. I'm the last one. And Melivia—she's dead. She sacrificed herself to kill him, but he didn't die." Damn, I couldn't cry now. But there was nothing I could do to stop the tears dripping down my face.

"And now he's—he's coming for me. Feel free to kick

me out." I swallowed, eyes on the ground, then lifted my head as Leo squeezed my hand.

"No one's kicking you out," said Leo, with a warning glance at Layla, who, like Gareth, was gaping at me. I didn't blame them; I had just dropped a bombshell on them.

"We're going to have to talk about this with the others," said Layla. "They're nocturnal, most of them, but they'll be around."

"Ashlyn," said Gareth, his expression brightening as though a thought had just occurred to him. "That's your name, isn't it?"

"Yes," I said, warily, wiping my eyes.

"Ashlyn, I think you may have the answers I'm looking for. If I can prove my theory right, there may be a way… your story proves beyond doubt that it's possible for a human to survive in the Darkworld for any period of time. I've been on the right track, but if I just had access to a history book… I've only had speculation, thus far."

"And what's this theory?" said Leo, possibly in an effort to draw the attention away from me. At any other time, I might have been interested in what Gareth had to say, but right now, I just wanted to disappear.

"That Lucifer's identity has been in front of us all the time," said Gareth, solemnly. "There are only a handful of sorcerers in history who have been notorious enough to make it into the records—the last two were Mathers and Crowley, demonologists who lived in the 1920s. The Hermetic Order of the Golden Dawn was around at the time—most people think their claims of having summoned demons were just trickery. Clever, clever sorcerers, clever enough to play games with the higher demons… too bad it killed them in the end. But this Lucifer would have gone by another name, once. We just need to find what that name was."

"And how'll that help kill him?" said Berenice, her usual snide tone back in place. "Knowing someone's name doesn't make a damned bit of difference. Besides, he's more powerful now than he would have been then, he'd have learned all this crazy shit from the Darkworld. Demons don't teach embroidery and dance."

Even I couldn't help snorting at *that* image. Like it or not, I couldn't deny that she had a good point.

"Actually," said Leo, "there *is* something we can learn about him. We can learn if he has powerful enemies. Any allies would be welcome at this point."

"If he does, they'd be dead," I said. "Besides, the entire Venantium couldn't stand against him."

"But those human-demons," said Leo. "They stood up to him. There has to be something…"

"Do you… do you mean you want me to try to talk to her again?" I said, dropping my voice. The idea of trying to communicate with the demon in my mind didn't appeal, but maybe if I could talk to her, it would avoid her anger exploding and blowing things up next time.

Leo blinked at me. "Is that okay?"

"Well, yeah, I guess. Except it wasn't her who answered last time, it was the half-demon."

"Huh?" said Cyrus, staring at the two of us—along with everyone else in the room.

"What haven't you told us this time?" Berenice demanded. "You need to stop being so bloody cryptic. You're as bad as…"

Thankfully, she cut herself off before she finished her sentence, but anger blazed within me all the same.

"You don't tell people every detail of your life," I said icily. "Some things are no one's business." But now wasn't the time for secrets. "For your information, the half-demon's one of the half-demons who helped us. They were human-demons once, back during one of Lucifer's campaigns, but he slaughtered them himself. They've been there all this time, angry and vengeful, and they saved us from him. The half-demon spoke to me—I think it's because *I'm* half-demon that they asked for my help." I stared defiantly across the table. "If you're going to kick me out, I'd prefer you get it over with now."

"Hold on there," said Layla. "You've given us a bunch to take in. I can't say for sure that the others will be accepting, but I'm not going to kick you out. Hell, we have that sleazeball Ryan in here, he's a danger to every female who crosses the threshold unless someone's there to keep an eye on him."

"Half-demons?" said Gareth. "You know, in all my years of research, that isn't an area I've really touched upon. How does that work?"

Great. Like I signed up to teach a lesson in human-demons. "Well. I have… I used to think I had a demon living in my head, and it's kind of true, but we're also the same person. It's complicated."

"Symbiotic?"

"I guess. She's less… feeling than a human would be. Fearless. She puts her own safety first, and…" I trailed off. I hadn't meant to reveal so much of myself. But wasn't that what all humans were like at the core? Strip everything away and the survival instinct prevailed. Did demons have that, or did they think themselves invincible? Was I talking about the demon–or myself, the human, Ashlyn?

"Well," I said, "she's useful to have around in a fight, anyway." But when I'd fought Lucifer, I'd thought *I* was more in control than the demon.

"I can see why," said Layla. She returned her attention

to her laptop, frowning at the screen. "Well, there's no news on the Venantium."

"What, they have their own website?" I said sceptically.

"No, but our network here's hooked up to all the news feeds worldwide, and I've set it up so it hones in on any article that hints at anything related to demons, the Darkworld, magic—anything like that. It was my parents' idea."

"That's amazing," said Cyrus, leaning forward.

"It is," I agreed. "How's that possible? Just with technology, or is magic involved as well?" Hell, I was hardly a computer expert. Technology defeated me more often than not.

"A bit of both," said Layla. "I'd say it's the future, but you know the Venantium like to uphold their traditions."

"Melmoth was into that sort of thing," said Gareth. "Did you know the Venantium's underground computers run on magic energy? It's stored in them, like demon hearts."

"What?" said Leo, his head jerking toward Gareth. "That's... why the hell didn't he tell us?"

He looked at Cyrus, who shrugged.

"Maybe he didn't want us building one?" he suggested.

"Bull crap," said Leo, shaking his head.

The idea of magic-based computers made my mind spin. "I didn't know that was even possible," I said.

"That's what this laptop runs on," Layla said, lifting it. "See? No plug."

I stared. "There's a demon heart inside it?"

"A stone of power, yes."

No way. "Isn't that dangerous?" I said. "That energy—someone could take it and summon a demon, right?"

The others all looked at Layla, too. This went against everything we'd been told about the Darkworld—and demon hearts. But then, was it really a surprise the Venantium had lied to us again?

"That's not how it works," said Layla. "The Venantium don't like the right information to get out there in case people get ideas, but you need to do something very specific to contact a demon, and you don't necessarily need a stone of power to do it. This is just the anchor. You're basically telling it to draw magic from the stone and not from you."

"The Barrier's like a demon heart, too," said Leo. "That's what Lucifer tried to destroy. The Venantium hid it with the other demon hearts they have in their stores."

"But he didn't destroy the Barrier, did he?" I said. "It's still there. So he must have failed."

"Even if he did, the crux is still buried in Blackstone," said Leo darkly. "No—it can't be that easy." He gave me a significant look.

Of course, he was thinking of the half-demons who'd asked me to help them. They wouldn't ask for my help if they thought Lucifer would destroy the Barrier anyway. *Damn, I need to talk to the half-demon again.*

There was too much I didn't know, too much I hadn't taken the trouble to find out. Now our main source of information had gone, and we were more clueless than ever.

As the thought crossed my mind, an icy chill swept through me, and I felt a presence touch my mind. The half-demon.

"I'm here, Ashlyn. We need to talk."

6

HEART OF ICE

I felt the half-demon's presence touch the edge of my mind again, urgent and insistent. My own demon rose, too, and the two presences combined made my vision waver.

"Hold on," I said, standing. "I just—I just need to go and check on something. I'll be back."

Everyone stared as I ran from the room, before ice started growing on my palms and shadows climbed up my legs. I half-ran back to my temporary room. The door shut with a snap, and not a moment too soon. Power flooded from my demon heart to my fingertips and ice began to spread out, fanning across the floor and climbing the walls like a fast-growing plant.

Hold on!

The half-demon materialised in front of me. My exact double.

"You didn't need to do that," I said, looking at the ice-coated bed I'd been going to lie on.

"You have better things to do than sit around chatting," the half-

demon retorted. *"You can't get complacent, Ashlyn. Lucifer is still hunting you."*

"Complacent!" I raised my eyebrows. "I've been here a few hours. I'm not relaxing. We need to find a way to beat him. What's so urgent, anyway?"

"You need to know more about what you are, Ashlyn. Do you remember our last 'lesson'?"

"You mean the time when you told me I... I suck the life out of people? Hard to forget." Not that I hadn't tried, though. And I still hadn't told Leo about it. Intentionally or not, I automatically took energy from others when I was close to them.

"Love is the most complex of human emotions. I know that even more, now..." She blinked, and my heart dropped at the sight of her eyes glistening with tears. *"You began to take energy, vitality from him. Just like a demon would."*

I unconsciously grabbed for the demon heart, feeling its power still thrumming as it kept the ice imprisoning the room.

"Can it go on forever?" I asked, aloud. "There's a limit to the power in this—right?"

"I assume so. I don't know. When I was... living, I never thought to investigate my own demon heart. A minimal amount of magical energy is required in order to create an anchor, but yours contains a depth of power rarely seen. It was your heart that attracted demons' attention to you from the beginning."

"It's not an anchor for me," I said. "Is it? Why do human-demons need a demon heart like this? It's just an extra weakness, isn't it?" Because I'd lose myself, and everything else, the instant someone took that power from me. My strength was my biggest weakness, and would put me at the mercy of any sorcerer who got hold of it. If not for those half-demons down in the underground chambers,

Lucifer would have taken me under his control, using Melivia to do so.

"That's certainly what Lucifer thought. And yet, human-demons are unique, and I don't think it's a bad thing, even if... even if it leads to terrible errors of judgment on the part of others. You can access a power nobody else can, given the opportunity. Even Lucifer is limited by his demon servants, and he has a heart of his own. He created it himself. That's how he manifested."

True—and he'd killed Conrad to do so. "I guess, since he isn't human anymore... but he can possess a human body, right? He doesn't *need* the heart. Melivia Blackstone didn't, when she came back from the Darkworld. She had one, but she couldn't use its power."

"Melivia had not given herself to the Darkworld's influence as much as Lucifer did. Despite being unable to access the true extent of the power in her demon heart, she could still use magic far beyond an ordinary sorcerer—even though the person she possessed wasn't a magic user. Lucifer, however, must possess a powerful magic user if he even wants to access his magic. A limit he imposed on himself."

"What do you mean by that?" I asked. "Don't vampires have the same ability as I do—to take power from others?" They had—and Lucifer basically said they could gain as much power of their own as a regular demon. But Lucifer was a liar. Could I take what he said as truth?

"They do. But they have no demon heart to store the energy, and they can't retain it for long, thanks to their curse."

"So it's not true, that Mr. Melmoth was thinking of using them as an army?"

The half-demon hesitated.

"Tell me. I won't tell Leo, if you think he'd be better off not knowing." I wasn't sure I meant that. I'd had enough of lying for a lifetime. And Leo would want to know the truth. It wasn't my right to keep it from him.

"You will tell him, Ashlyn. I can sense you're tired of lying. But

never mind. William Melmoth might have briefly entertained the idea, but he never acted upon it, and it was Lucifer who destroyed his research."

I breathed out. "He didn't destroy it himself?"

"No. He would never have denied his fellows a chance at a normal life."

"Leo will be glad to hear that," I said. Some of the tension in the room eased, and the ice began to recede from the walls. I felt the hum of power as the pendant took the magical energy back into itself. It made my skin tingle.

"I didn't used to be able to feel that," I said, watching the now glowing pendant. "Why can I feel the power moving now?"

"You're more attuned to it. Interesting how fast your heart absorbs magical energy. No wonder it has such an effect on you."

I frowned at her. "What does that mean?"

"I can't say for certain—only that your heart is an important piece of the puzzle of how to defeat Lucifer. Demons throughout the Darkworld talk about it."

They do? I turned the amethyst in my hands. Outwardly, it still looked unremarkable, like a piece of crystal anyone could buy on the market. It sure didn't feel like the centre of Darkworld.

Something occurred to me. "If you burned my demon heart, why would it kill my human side as well as the demon? If you survived the death of your mortal body, why can't it work the other way around?"

"That… that is a complex question. How I died… they burned my heart and body at the same time. But perhaps, if your heart was destroyed separately… but you've felt the pain before, haven't you?"

I could sense a different kind of pain coming from the voice, like she was remembering something terrible. Her own death.

"The pain would surely kill you."

I shivered at the memory of that time Jude had almost killed me by setting my demon heart aflame. I'd been reduced to nothing but pain, and was sure if it had continued, I'd have faded out of existence. "Okay. Just wondering."

"Ask me whatever you like, Ashyln. I would do anything to see Lucifer dealt the fate he deserves."

"Um. Okay." I tried to remember what else I'd wondered about. "How is it that I have human blood and a half-demon heart? I know demons are spirits, but how can they be bonded to humans? And where does the power in the demon heart come from in the first place?" All things I'd pondered more than once, and even the *Seven Princes of the Darkworld* book hadn't given me answers. But then, maybe there were some things you could only know if you were part of the Darkworld itself. I doubted any of the authors of the books in the Venantium's library had been.

"You ask questions human-demons have wanted to know the answers to for centuries. Trust me, I've heard them all already, and I don't know why a spiritual being and a biological creature of flesh and blood can be bonded. Perhaps the higher demons know, since they can be both at the same time. Perhaps, at some point during conception, the higher demon gives a part of him or herself to the human, and that it somehow becomes lodged in the child's mind. I know there's a transfer of power—that's why your demon heart comes with the power of a higher demon already in it. The higher demon Lucifer's power is in yours. No one knows if any higher demon has more power than another, but Lucifer has the reputation as the most cunning and powerful of demons—that's most likely why the human sorcerer chose to take his name."

"That, or he fancied styling himself after a rebel angel." I turned over the crystal again, sure there was something I was overlooking. Whilst we'd been talking, the ice covering the walls and floor had almost gone—thankfully, this particular ice didn't melt, so my room was relatively dry. I checked my rucksack just in case—and stiffened when old book pages brushed against my fingertips.

I hadn't packed any old books. In my rush, I'd barely remembered my e-reader.

Heart beating fast, I pulled out Melivia Blackstone's diary.

When did I pack this? It had been a long time since I'd seen it—in fact, I thought the fortune-teller had taken it back. Had this been her last act? Was there a clue in here, after all, or was I over-thinking things again?

I looked up at the half-demon, whose guilty expression confirmed my suspicions.

"You knew about this?"

"Your mother cared for you a lot, Ashlyn. She did it for your safety. If you were captured on your way here, you wouldn't be able to recall packing the book and there would be nothing in your memory to suggest that you knew anything about it."

She messed with my mind? Again? A lance of pain cut through the old anger. Even at the end, she'd used Influence on me rather than giving me a choice.

I flipped open the diary with shaking hands. A page marker fell out, marking a passage early on in the diary, in the midst of Melivia's tedious description of dressing for her eighteenth birthday. To be precise, the part where she mentioned stealing a priceless family jewel from her parents' room.

A glittering amethyst, she called it. *When I touch it, it gives me the most peculiar feeling. I do not know why, but I feel like it belongs to me.*

The page marker had landed upright, and written on it, in the fortune-teller's hand, were the words, *Turn to the ending. It will make sense, Ashlyn.*

I turned to the final page, where Melivia had written a letter, twenty years ago. Again, a passage was highlighted.

"I will conceal this diary in a place where the right person may find it someday, along with the crystal I fear was the catalyst for it all. That, too, survives, and is now a monument to my shame."

"The crystal," I said, looking from the amethyst to the pages and back again. "This one. Why is it important?"

But the half-demon had vanished. A crashing sound outside made me jump. I put down the diary and ran to the door. Expecting to see Leo or one of the others, it disarmed me to find Ryan in the act of opening another door.

"Oh," he said, flushing. "Um… hi, Ash."

"Hi," I muttered, turning back to my room. I really wasn't in the mood to talk to him right now.

"Uh, Ash?" he said. "I never had the chance to apologise for what happened."

"For being an asshole? Forget it," I said.

"It's not…" He hadn't been this uncertain the last time I'd seen him. "It's not entirely under my control. I mean… I thought you might know what it feels like."

Being an incubus meant he fed on human lust through the Darkworld connection—that much I knew. But, truth to be told, it wasn't exactly something I'd looked into, even less considered might be similar in any way to having a demon living in the back of my mind.

"I don't get the urge to masquerade as people's exes," I said tightly.

He stepped closer to me. "I'm sorry, Ash," he said, again. "Look—it's the end of the world. Well, that's what people are saying, anyway. Do we really want to be fighting each other?"

"I'm not fighting anyone except Lucifer and his

demons," I said. "I just think it'd be better if we stayed away from each other."

"Afraid your boyfriend might get jealous?"

There was a hint of a smile on his face, and he'd moved closer to me than I'd thought. His crazily long eyelashes framed the brightest blue eyes I'd ever seen. He looked like the kind of guy who modelled on magazine covers... and I was absolutely uninterested. I turned away, deciding to head back to the meeting room to see if any more news had come in from Blackstone.

Ryan moved in front of me. Somehow, one of his hands was suddenly cupping my chin whilst the other wrapped around my neck. Before I could even think to struggle, he'd tilted my head up—and pressed ice-cold lips to mine.

The demon rose inside me, roaring anger and icy fire. My whole body shuddered, and shadows rose around the two of us, jagged and so sharp I almost felt them cut into my skin as they climbed my legs. Ryan's mouth smiled against mine, and my vision flashed purple. I pulled back, the demon taking over entirely. Dark ice spread beneath my feet, like solid shadows. Letting go of Ryan was like trying to pry apart two magnets. The effort made my muscles scream—it was like the shadows *wanted* us to move closer together.

"Come to me, demon," he crooned. "We belong together, you and I."

"Like hell you do," said a voice.

My heart stopped. *Leo.*

I twisted to look at him, the demon still looking through my eyes, and one glance at the hardened expression on his face told me he'd seen everything.

That was enough for me to regain control of my own body. I wrenched away from Ryan, skidding on the icy floor. Black ice crawled up the walls and across the ceiling. I'd never seen anything like it before.

"What the hell is wrong with you?" I demanded.

Ryan's face spasmed, turning from seductive to horrified in a second. "Shit. Shit… it's the demon." He shook his head violently. "It's never been this—never."

"Stop trying to cover yourself," said Leo, coldly. "What the hell were you doing to Ash?"

He doesn't blame me, I couldn't help thinking, before giving myself a mental kick.

"I… I…" That was more like the Ryan I'd met in Australia.

"Get out," said Leo. "If you go near Ash again, you'll regret it."

Ryan was noticeably shaking now, the whites of his eyes visible as he looked from the ice to me and back again.

"Come on," he said. "Give me a second chance? I don't want to go out there—not while Lucifer might be outside…"

"Should have thought of that earlier," I said.

"Get the hell out," Leo told him.

With the two of us glaring at him, Ryan didn't dare argue. As he fled, I breathed out, the demon's presence retreating as the ice slipped from the walls.

Leo came up behind me. "You okay?"

I turned around, feeling my hands tingling like I'd touched a live wire. *Why does he still do that to me?* I willed the cool, logical demon to return, but she stayed dormant.

"Layla said that's been happening a lot."

I blinked, confused. This wasn't how I'd imagined this conversation would play out. "Huh?"

"In the past couple of days, it's like all the vampires, succubi, and incubi in London have gone berserk. Attacking people left right and centre."

"Do you think it might be because of Lucifer?" My voice was even, disguising my ridiculous fluttering heart. *He doesn't blame me.*

"Wouldn't surprise me," said Leo. "They're tuned into the Darkworld more, I guess. Conrad…"

My heart twisted. Conrad's death had been mercifully quick, but Lucifer using his body and warping it into a monster filled me with numbing horror. We *had* to get on with finding a way to beat him.

"What were you doing, anyway?" Leo asked me.

Oh, right. I forgot. "I found something," I said. "I think it's important."

7

DEMON'S LEGACY

L eo read the passages in Melivia's diary as I pointed them out, but he was none the wiser for what it might mean.

"Family heirloom," he said. "That's what the fortune-teller called the crystal at first, right?"

"Yeah," I said.

"So it was important even before it became a demon heart. And it has… the higher demon Lucifer's magical energy stored in it?"

"Yeah. Apparently that's what happens when a human-demon is, uh, conceived." I felt a flush rise to my cheeks. For God's sake, why was it embarrassing to talk to Leo about this? He was the only guy I'd slept with anyway, even if things had gone so horribly wrong with us. Maybe it was because I knew the connection was still there. I knew I still wanted him, and I hated myself for it. Only the attack from Lucifer had thrown us back together, and he could easily abandon me again. The unspoken words were so present, I could almost hear them as whispers in my ears. I could tell him to leave me alone, and save myself more future heartache, but what was the point? We might all die within the week anyway.

I stood, abruptly. "Should we check on the others? What's happening out there, anyway?"

"Not a lot. Layla's looking for news, Gareth's looking for theories. Oh, and Howard's threatening to run off again."

"What if he does?"

"Then he's an idiot." Leo shrugged.

"But he could get killed."

Leo sighed. "We can't take responsibility for everyone. We're the only people who care about finding a way to kill Lucifer."

"Yeah, but…" I threw down the diary, my anger at the fortune-teller sparking again. "She couldn't give me any decent hint, could she? Even now…"

Another piece of paper fluttered to the ground. I picked it up, recognising the familiar handwriting.

"Two demons named Lucifer made me what I am. One has my love, the other, my heart, and we are forever bonded. Ashlyn. I am truly sorry. Of all the wrongs I have done, you are my greatest regret."

My insides turned to ice. *Her greatest regret? Is that all I am?* Before she'd died, she'd told me I was her legacy, that she wouldn't let me die. Instead, she'd abandoned me, and to add insult to injury, refused to see me as an independent person even in the end.

The world wavered before my eyes. Tears choked me again, and Leo's arms around me were all it took to undo me completely.

She regretted me. I was nothing to her. She hadn't given me the chance to fight Lucifer and had sacrificed herself and left me in an even worse mess than before.

"I—I just can't believe she's really gone," I sobbed. "And she—she regrets that I was ever born."

"You can't know that, Ash," Leo murmured, rocking me like I was a child. "She loved you. You know she did. If she regrets anything, it's the pain she's caused you."

I didn't argue. I didn't have the strength for it. I just let Leo rock me and cried until my tears were spent.

~

I BLINKED AWAKE. I'd fallen asleep in Leo's arms, lying back on the bed. I twisted over and saw that his eyes were closed, too. My heart twisted with painful longing. *Damn it.*

There was a sharp knock on the door. Leo jolted awake, springing into a sitting position.

"Who's there?" I said.

"Claudia," she called. "I just wondered if you two were hungry. Gareth's ordering pizza. I don't think he can cope with the idea of so many people trying to use the kitchen at once."

"Sounds good," I said, jumping up and running over to the door.

Claudia stepped back as I opened it. I could almost see the questions in her eyes, and I knew exactly what she thought Leo and I had been up to.

"Why's it so cold in there?"

I shrugged. I hadn't noticed. *Side effect of the ice magic, maybe?* Or the demon, as usual.

Leo had sat up on the bed in as dignified a way as possible. "Ash found Melivia's diary again," he said, getting up, diary in hand.

"She tricked me into packing it and forgetting about it," I said. "More Influence. But there's nothing useful in there, anyway. Has Gareth figured anything out?"

"He's been impossible," said Claudia, rolling her eyes. "He keeps shouting out the names of random famous sorcerers. He's convinced Lucifer was a Renaissance-era heretic or some nonsense like that. I mean, why does it matter?"

I shrugged. "I'm up for pizza, anyway."

Leo and I followed Claudia back to the meeting room. It looked more or less exactly as I'd left it, except Berenice and Howard were conspicuously absent. Layla and Cyrus were engaged in conversation, but both looked up when we came in.

"Hi," said Layla, stifling a yawn. "I might actually go to bed at a civilised time tonight. The club's pretty quiet."

"Oh yeah, we kicked Ryan out," said Leo, sitting down.

Layla blinked. "Oh God, what did he do?"

"He attacked me. I'm okay," I added, hastily.

"Shit." Layla shook her head. "Sorry. We claim to offer shelter to all sorcerers, and he's never *attacked* anyone before—pissed a bunch of people off, of course, but never anything serious."

"What about that time with Fiona?" said Gareth, stacking more books on the desk.

"I think she did more harm to him, to be honest," said Layla. "I'd feel sorry for him if he wasn't such a douchebag. He makes enemies wherever he goes."

"I have no sympathy," I said. "Where are Howard and Berenice?"

"Around." Claudia shrugged. "They disappeared not long after you two did."

Her knowing look made me prickle with irritation. Why had I been stupid enough to fall asleep?

"Do you own this place, then?" Leo asked Layla, in an attempt to change the subject.

"I have a share in it. The building belonged to my parents and a few other sorcerers, but the old crew aren't really around anymore."

"You're always here?" said Claudia. "Is this like your job, then?"

"Officially, yeah, but I'm also halfway through my doctorate at King's College. Gareth's studying, too—well, he's always studying something or other. He has a PhD in the history of ancient civilisations."

"I half expected you to say he had a doctorate in demonic studies," I said. "I bet that's an actual thing now."

"Probably, but it'd be a bit conspicuous," said Layla. "The Venantium wouldn't like it."

I glanced at Gareth, who was up to his ears in a book so large it resembled a small boulder.

"Hey. Gareth." Layla prodded him with a pen. "Ash wants to know about your thesis."

"She does?" he blinked. "You probably wouldn't find it interesting."

"Ash is going to be a lecturer," said Leo, to my immense surprise.

"I am?" I said, rather stupidly, as Gareth looked up at me.

"Come on, Ash, it's inevitable." He smiled at me, which was distracting if nothing else. Come on. Did he really think we'd get out of this mess in one piece?

"That's assuming I ever get to live a normal life," I said.

Leo snorted. "What, and he's normal?"

"Hey!" said Gareth. "If you'd met as many people as I have, you'd see I fall low on the crazy scale."

"Can't argue with that," I said, thinking of Terrence. Pete came to mind, too, and I felt an unexpected surge of sadness—most of it for poor Danielle. "Tell me, anyway," I said, pushing the dark memories away. "What does history have to do with demons?"

"Everything!" His eyes gleamed with the manic look of

one truly engrossed in his subject. "I see myself as more of a detective than a historian, dedicated to uncovering the truth behind the lies the Venantium feed their recruits. Did you know that many ancient civilisations worshipped demons? The great philosopher Socrates saw them as a sign of divine inspiration, and the word 'demon' itself actually comes from the ancient Greek *daimon*, a word that denotes a spirit or divine being—or a guardian angel. Our modern mythology polarises good and evil, angels and demons, but spirits in the ancient world were seen as they are, morally ambivalent beings. Of course, there were conflicts—ancient Mesopotamia was plagued by demon-summoning sorcerers vying for supremacy. When religions began to preach that all demons were evil, under the dominion of Satan, that gave rise to the belief that..."

"Enough!" said Layla. "You'll scare them off."

"We don't scare easy," said Leo—like me, he watched Gareth with rapt attention. "So, what are your views on demons, then? I know the Venantium are liars, and I'd like a second opinion."

So did I. They'd doctored history, but to what extent? Was anything they preached true?

Gareth paused thoughtfully before replying. "I approach demons with a scientist's eye. To understand something, you need to know its rules and principles. The Darkworld isn't what you'd call an exact science, but it still runs by rules in the same way our universe has natural laws. The Venantium guards that knowledge jealously, out of the fear that adventurous sorcerers with an interest in science might use that knowledge for evil purposes. My goal is to uncover those rules."

"Any particular reason?" said Claudia.

"It's a puzzle that demands to be solved," said Gareth, simply.

"Apparently it's worth spending your life in hiding for," said Layla, shaking her head.

"The great thinkers have always been persecuted," said Gareth, then suddenly seized another book from the pile. "Surely not," he muttered. "Could Lucifer truly be one of the great early scientists?"

"If he is, he's gone way off the rails," said Claudia. "Why does it *matter?*"

Gareth, absorbed in his book, ignored her. "There was John Dee," he said. "Thought by many to have been a wizard. He was a celebrated alchemist in his day. Naturally, he *was* a magic-user—I believe one of the early supporters of the creation of the Venantium... but was Lucifer *before* or *after* the Venantium's inception?"

Claudia rolled her eyes. Layla had switched on her laptop again. I fidgeted, wishing I'd brought something to do. Leo sat beside me, and I was always conscious of his presence.

"What did people do about demons before the Venantium?" I asked Gareth.

"That would depend on the culture and beliefs of each nation during each time period," he said. "Certainly people were more open-minded about sorcery in the ancient world, but records are scarce until the 1500s and the creation of the Venantium. Then, sorcerers went into hiding for the most part—certainly when people were being persecuted for witchcraft. People knew magic existed, and it terrified them. And yet, there are records of reported demon attacks, possession... exorcisms could be performed only by a priest, and their methods would have had no effect upon a true demon. Of course, the most contested event amongst the Venantium, the one they have tried to cover up... is the creation of human-demons."

He gave me a quick glance, hesitating to continue.

I felt the demon stir in the back of my mind, and sadness choked me again, an emotion that wasn't mine. *Those lost souls,* I thought. *Have they really been there for five hundred years?*

"Tell me more," I said. "I want to know."

"The idea always fascinated me," he said. "The impossible fusion of human and demon. My interest–and the project that cost me my safety from demons—was an investigation into the movements of the seven higher demons over the past few years. Most accounts skim over the idea of humans and demons interbreeding, but the one case of a sorcerer subduing a higher demon is from the sixteenth century, and it is surrounded by anecdotes about half-demons walking amongst regular humans."

"That was Lucifer," I whispered. "He killed them all."

Gareth's eyes widened. "Are you sure?" he said. "How do you know?"

"One of the half-demons told me."

"Then it is without doubt that Lucifer was most active in this era, more than five hundred years ago," he said. "The question, of course, is *why.*"

"Five hundred years is nothing in the Darkworld," said Claudia.

"He's clearly been planning this for a while," said Leo. "He already had the higher demons under his control— God knows how long they've actually been possessing the Inner Circle. Maybe even since the last elections. This is years in the making—who knows, maybe centuries."

A horrible possibility occurred to me. "Gareth," I said. "Was it only one higher demon who fathered the half-demons? Or were they all here?"

"Accounts refer to the father-creature as being named Lucifer."

I closed my eyes. "Well," I said. "That explains why my

father's never been keen to meet me." The half-demons were my *siblings,* in some sense.

"So the human Lucifer has control over *six* of the higher demons?" Claudia's eyes widened. "Wait a minute —who's missing, then? Asmodeus, Mammon, Beezlebub, Satan, Leviathan…"

"Belphegor," said Leo. "The one who killed the half-demon."

"Brilliant," said Claudia. "Well, that's us screwed, then."

"Your father?" said Gareth, blinking at me in bewilderment.

"Yeah, Lucifer the higher demon," I said. "Well, he's a better role model than the human Lucifer, anyway."

Gareth looked nonplussed at the sarcasm. I'd spoken more or less on autopilot; at least half my mind was still occupied with the horrible idea of the half-demons, my siblings, being stuck in the Darkworld for five centuries. Could this situation get any more messed up?

"If there's one thing we know for sure about Lucifer the sorcerer," said Gareth, "it's that he wants to be known. Almost every mention of his name in the history books looks like an attempt to stroke his own ego. I think he *wanted* to leave a legacy behind. If only he had kept a journal."

"Not likely we'd be able to get hold of it if he did," said Cyrus.

"I'm *not* looking up the lost diary of Lucifer," said Claudia, slamming a hand on the desk. "In all honesty, I don't give a rat's ass. No offence, I'm sure your work's very interesting, but I can't deal with being shut away. I need something useful to do while we're stuck here otherwise I'll go insane." She stood, as if to prove her point.

"You could do worse than help with his research," said

Layla. "He'll find ways to rope you into helping, anyway. I never intended to go to university, but living underground with this guy changed my mind."

Gareth adjusted his glasses, clearly embarrassed. But the others were nodding. As for me, I knew confronting Lucifer now would be suicide. The answers about what happened to Melivia had been in the past. Could there be a clue buried in hundreds of years of history that would help us beat Lucifer?

"We could do worse," I echoed. "It's all a part of finding a way to beat him, right?"

Claudia sighed. "Fine. But I'm going to Satan's Pit tonight. Might as well make the most of living under a night club, right?"

8

IMPATIENCE

No news had come from the Venantium by the next day. I opted out of going clubbing with Claudia, pleading a headache. In reality, I couldn't face being around people when I felt so messed up inside. I knew that was Claudia's way of letting off steam and forgetting the outside world, but it didn't work the same way for me. I kept thinking about Blackstone and the world I'd left behind, and my friends, Sarah and Alex. Had the Venantium wiped their memories? Would they even remember me? I berated myself for worrying about something so self-centred when it was a better alternative to being dead.

Like Pete, Danielle, a hundred other students. The whole scene replayed in my nightmares, except this time, I was the demon killing people, laughing as the union bar crumbled around us. I awoke in a cold sweat, gasping for breath, ice crystals on the palms of my hands. It took a minute for me to realise the screaming in my head wasn't residue from the nightmare. And it wasn't screaming—at least, not *human* screaming.

It came from the Darkworld.

What's happening?

The half-demon appeared at the foot of my bed, semi-transparent with a terrified expression on her face.

"The sorcerer Lucifer's woken up," she whispered.

Beads of icy water slid down my spine. "*What—*"

"He's angry," said the half-demon. "His fury holds no bounds. Even Mephistopheles—" She broke off as the shadows around her rippled. "Stay hidden, Ash."

She faded away. Heart thumping, I jumped out of bed. Lucifer had awoken. What did that mean for us? He had the run of the Darkworld—if he wanted to, he could appear anywhere in the world. He could find us here. Nowhere, was safe. Then again, we'd not come here looking for safety. We'd come to find a way to beat him.

Still, I dressed as quickly as possible and all but ran to the meeting room. Out of the Blackstone group, only Cyrus and Leo were up, but Gareth occupied his usual position behind a stack of books, and Layla was surfing the net on her laptop.

"What's up?" said Leo, taking in my dishevelled appearance.

"I just spoke to the half-demon," I said. "She said Lucifer's awakened—whatever that means. It's stirred up the whole Darkworld."

"Seriously?"

All eyes were on me. Even Gareth looked up from his books.

"Yeah, of course. I don't know what that means for us, but—"

"He won't be able to find this place," said Layla. "For one thing, it's under too many protective barriers. Even the Venantium can't find it. For another, he's going to go for the Barrier first. Didn't you say he's been lurking in the

Darkworld for centuries, waiting to break it? I can't see him abandoning that plan now. He sounds like the type to bide his time until the right moment."

"I don't know," I said. "He's really angry—it wouldn't surprise me if he blames us for what happened to him. The fortune-teller's already—" I swallowed.

It was easier to refer to her as that, as though even in death she didn't have a name. Easier than acknowledging her as a person… as my mother.

"We'll just have to stay indoors and sit tight," said Layla.

I felt too restless to stay underground, but I nodded. Walking outside would only draw attention to the others. What could we do, then? The sound of the demons screaming lurked at the back of my head. What was Lucifer doing, taking out his anger on his fellow demons?

"I thought Lucifer was all about world domination, anyway," I said. "What better way to make the world fear him than a massive exposure of his powers? Most people can't even use magic. The world would be completely at his mercy."

"Trust me, when Lucifer wants to reveal his power to the world, we'll know about it," Cyrus said, grimly. "He'll shout it from the rooftops. Or his version of that, which is probably a mass slaughter."

Yeah. He's probably right. What happened at the student union bar was just the beginning.

"You know," said Gareth, thoughtfully, "in all of history, Lucifer has never done anything that might expose all sorcerers to the non-magic users. I wonder why?"

"Fair point," said Leo. "That's odd. He wasn't scared of what the Venantium would do to him, even back when they used torture."

Good point. "Yeah, he's an ego-maniac," I said. "You'd think publicly terrorising non-magic-users might help his cause. The ratio of sorcerers isn't exactly high, is it?"

"Less than one percent of the population," said Gareth. "Zero point zero four percent, to be precise."

Everyone stared at him. How many people in the world was that?

"Who the hell figured that one out?" said Leo. "Did someone do a head count of all the magic-users?"

'The Venantium have records," said Gareth, with a hint of embarrassment; I wondered if he'd stolen the information somehow. "But unregistered sorcerers wouldn't show up, of course, so the statistics are a bit skewed."

"He was after the Barrier, not magic-users, anyway," said Leo. "We know that much. He wants to set the demons free... and I guess he'll kill anyone who stands against him, but that doesn't say much about his actual plan."

No. We were still in the dark on that one. Except now he was awake, and if the half-demon was right, time was running out.

"He was in Blackstone for a reason," I said. "That means the Barrier's definitely there—right? But he didn't manage to break it."

"The fortune-teller stopped him," said Cyrus. "But you're right—those demon hearts were the Barrier. Or at least, *he* thought so, and he's had centuries in the Darkworld to figure it out. It can't be common knowledge though, otherwise loads of demons would have gone after it."

"Maybe the higher demons told him," I said. "Think about it. They can walk into our world whenever they want."

"They can?" Gareth's face fell, almost comically.

I guessed *that* hadn't shown up in his research.

"They walked right past the barriers," I said. "Five of them have been in the Venantium's Inner Circle for years. And Belphegor appeared when Jude ripped open the Darkworld. The Barrier didn't hold him back."

An uncomfortable silence descended. I could see the truth sinking in for the others. "We've been at their mercy for years," said Layla. "It's the only explanation… but they spared humans. They don't have the limits Lucifer does. They can take on human form, tear the world to pieces if they wanted to. But they haven't… why?"

"Another mystery," said Gareth, who seemed to have recovered from the shock. "I'll have to look into that one! Demon psychology… think of the possibilities."

Seriously? How could he react to Armageddon like it was an intellectual puzzle?

"Demon psychology? Seriously?" Leo shook his head. "If you ask me, it's Lucifer's psychology that really matters. I mean, we *assume* he'd make a spectacle of his power. But think about it, he's hidden in the Darkworld for years. He's good at concealing stuff. Maybe not exposing himself is his way of showing how powerful he really is, that he can send the Venantium all over the world into chaos without even acting."

Humans and demons. In the end, that was what it came down to. Lucifer, a human, had engineered destruction by using demons. Possessing humans allowed demons to reach their full potential. If they possessed a sorcerer, they were granted instant access to their own powers by using the sorcerer's magical energy. Meanwhile, the terrifying powers of the demon were just the thing to give the sorcerer an edge over their enemies—even if it was like standing near a naked flame, and only a matter of time before the demon turned on them. Most sorcerers paid the price eventually, simply because demons were strong and cunning by nature, and humans tended to underestimate them. Was it in human nature to see everything different as beneath them?

"But he did make a show of it," I pointed out. "He killed a lot of people. And in the union bar…" I shook away the image before it could creep up on me again. And what I'd felt before—the Darkworld breaking. I couldn't sense it now, but that didn't mean Lucifer was sitting around waiting for us to make a move.

Leo looked down. "True, but that was only one incident. It's worrying about what he might do next that's got everyone in a panic. The demons' greatest weapon is our fear. Melmoth told me that so many sorcerers learn the theory of how to kill a demon, then freeze up when faced with that situation in real life. Ultimately, knowing that you're facing an enemy that can break into your mind at any point… well, no matter how good a magic-user you are, it's not enough."

Yeah. Just look how many of them had died in the end and watched Lucifer rise without even fighting. And yet my friends and I—who had the bare minimum of formal training—had gotten out alive.

"Very wise!" said Gareth. "The same may be said of the creation of the Barrier itself. One demon killing could generate enough fear that the sorcerers actually put up a barrier around the whole world to keep them out."

"You know, I'm starting to see why the Venantium think you're a danger to them," said Cyrus. "Your views contradict pretty much everything they stand for. Not that it's a bad thing."

Gareth went slightly red, like Cyrus had given him a high compliment.

"Anyway," said Leo, "I think it's Mephistopheles we really need to worry about. He's the one who attacked the union bar."

"I was wondering about that," said Cyrus. "Why'd he target there?"

Uneasiness rose within me. I'd forgotten about that. Mephistopheles's heart had disappeared. He could possess anyone at any time if they so much as touched his dormant heart. If someone had picked it up…

"So we have two enemies to worry about?" said Layla. "Mephistopheles… that name sounds familiar."

"A demon," said Leo, his eyes narrowing, fists clenching on the table. "The worst."

"He's Lucifer's right hand demon," I explained. "He came back before Lucifer did, but the fortune-teller took away his demon heart. Afterwards… it was him who attacked the university. He's powerful–really powerful."

Gareth made a choked noise. "You made an enemy of the most notorious demon in history? *And* Lucifer?"

"Notorious?" I echoed.

"Oh yes," said Gareth, whose hands were shaking. At least he was finally having a normal reaction to the depth of the trouble we were in. "The two are mentioned in conjunction with one another, many times. Lucifer and Mephistopheles." He fell silent.

"I'm going to check who else is around," said Layla. "I'll make sure Ryan hasn't sneaked back in. Two of the others attacked people too. Vampires, I mean."

"If Lucifer's awakening, maybe that's why they're going stir-crazy," said Cyrus.

That sounded about right to me. But how many inno-cent people would get caught in the crossfire? *I wish we could do something. Anything other than sit here discussing wild theories.*

"Yeah, that's what I thought," said Leo. "I don't like it. He said something about using vampires as energy sources…"

I knew he was thinking about what Lucifer had said, when he'd insinuated that Mr. Melmoth had kept quiet about his attempts to find a cure for vampirism for his own gain. I wanted to tell him what the half-demon said, but the words stuck in my throat.

"Where are the others?" I said, instead.

"Probably asleep," said Leo. "Claudia must have got back—well, after I fell asleep. And Berenice and Howard went out, too."

"You mean, outside?" I said, worry starting to flicker, even though I didn't particularly *like* either of them. I didn't think I could handle losing anyone else.

"No clue."

"Berenice stopped Howard running off," said Cyrus. "But he's still adamant that his mother's somewhere here. I just hope he doesn't do anything stupid."

So did I, if just because it would put the rest of us in danger, too. Now wasn't the time for rash decisions.

"Shit," said Layla, glancing up from her laptop. "Okay. That was fast. The Venantium's just issued a warning. One of the sorcerer forums just posted it."

"What does it say?" asked Leo, leaning over the table.

"Says that due to an external threat, the Venantium are declaring war on the Darkworld. Anything goes. I think that means we're allowed to use magic publicly, if we're attacked."

"Well, that's good news," said Leo. "I mean, we'd rather avoid being arrested than save our own lives, right?"

"It's the best we're going to get out of them," said

Layla. "Right. I'm going to see who else is in and pass on the message."

As she stood up, the door slammed open and Claudia rushed in.

"What's up?" said Cyrus.

"There's a problem," said Claudia, to Layla. "Half the Venantium's on your doorstep."

Layla hesitated for a minute, mouth slightly open. Then she kicked her chair aside and ran out of the room. Gareth looked like he was debating whether to follow, but sank back into his seat when raised voices sounded outside, and buried himself in his book again.

"Did they say what happened?" I asked Claudia. She hovered near the door, her hair looking like a bird's nest. Had she even gone to sleep?

"I couldn't get a word in edgeways," said Claudia. "Hayley was trying to keep them in order."

"What happened to you?" I said.

"I may have got a bit drunk last night and forgot the way to my room."

"What, you slept out there in the night club?" said Cyrus, with a snort.

There was a slightly embarrassed silence.

"You didn't hook up with someone, did you?" said Cyrus.

"Maybe." Claudia looked at him defiantly. "So what? It's not like I planned on sleeping. Not after…"

The atmosphere switched to serious as though someone had flicked a switch. I wasn't the only person having trouble processing the last few days.

"But is it safe out there?" said Cyrus. "I mean—it's your business, I know, but did you go back to this guy's house?"

"He's staying in a hotel, and to be honest, I was too

drunk to care," said Claudia. "What can I say? He had a fancy car and offered me a lift back to his hotel. And he had room service. I came back here like an hour ago—got a bit lost trying to find my way around the streets."

"You lunatic," said Cyrus, shaking his head. "Look, I know it's not my place to interfere. I mean, I know we're not really a group anymore. I was happy to let you guys shoot harpies and get up to crazy high jinks when there wasn't any real risk, but this... this isn't a game."

"I know that," said Claudia, biting her lip. "I won't do it again. Happy?"

"I—look," said Cyrus, holding his hands up in a placating gesture. "I just don't want you guys getting hurt out there. I know no one listened to me anyway—"

"Sure we did," said Leo. "We just chose to ignore your advice. But it's Howard you should be talking to. I hope he and Berenice haven't wandered off somewhere outside."

"Me too," said Cyrus, with a nervous glance over his shoulder. I felt the same—especially after what I'd heard from the half-demon that morning. If Lucifer was awake, he could reach anyone outside.

"Yeah," said Claudia. "I know it was stupid. I mean it, I won't do it again. I just needed... last night, I just needed to be with someone who didn't ask questions. Someone I didn't know."

"I get it," said Cyrus. "But now... things are pretty bad out there."

"I know," said Claudia. "My parents are freaking so much. They actually told me I'd be safer here than at home."

Cyrus blinked. "Really?"

"Yeah. No one knows what's going to happen out there, but this is one of the few places left that actually has a decent amount of security. For all the good that'd do if Lucifer came." She gave a short laugh.

"Don't tell me you're giving up?" said Cyrus.

"No," said Claudia, unconvincingly. "But, well… we're up against an insane enemy, and I'm not sure all these wild theories will do any good."

Nor was I. But we'd learned *some* things. Any piece of information might lead to the answers. I'd rather chase wild theories than accept that Lucifer would tear the Dark-world itself to pieces to find me.

"Hey!" said Gareth, who'd kept his head buried inside his book for most of the conversation. "Wild theories have solved more problems than people think. Never underestimate the power of the human imagination. The demons don't have that. They have no concept of original thinking."

"I thought the whole reason for the problem was because Lucifer *is* human," said Claudia. "A human with the powers of a demon."

"Everyone's worst nightmare," said Leo darkly.

The voices outside grew louder. I heard Layla saying, "We have plenty of rooms, don't worry–help him through. Gareth!"

Gareth jumped. "Yes?" he called.

Layla's face appeared in the doorway. "Have you checked the medical stores lately? A few people are hurt."

"Yes! Of course. We're well stocked." He remained seated, however.

"Why'd they come here?" said Leo. "That makes no sense—they're not even supposed to know about this place, right?"

Layla opened the door. "I don't suppose any of you know first aid?"

"Me," said Claudia to my surprise, and stood up.

"Same," said Cyrus, joining her. "What do we need to do?"

"Harpies attacked them on the way down. Help me get them into the medical room."

Cyrus and Claudia followed her outside. Gareth sank back into his seat, muttering something about not liking the sight of blood.

"We're in the middle of a war, mate," said Leo. "Get used to it." And he hurried after his brother.

I followed. It was that or stay behind with Gareth. I'd been attacked by harpies before, but I had no idea what it was the fortune-teller had put on the wounds. Still, there might be some way I could help. I needed to *do* something before I went crazy.

Outside the door was total chaos. People ran up and down, shouting instructions, most wearing the blue uniform of the Venantium. I recognised a few of them, confirming my guess that they'd come straight from Black-stone. I hovered awkwardly on the outskirts, not wanting to get in the way.

Then someone smacked into me. "Hey—Ash! You made it here?"

It was Freya. To my astonishment, she hugged me. I remembered seeing her crying over her fallen comrades— including her twin brother–the day before. My heart clenched and tears stung the back of my eyes.

"What happened?" I asked. "Did Hayley bring you here?"

"Yes, we—oh God, Ash, it was awful. Blackstone's a ruin. Lucifer's taken it."

"Taken it?" I echoed. My heart beat fast, and a chill trickled down my spine. When the Darkworld had opened… what had he done?

"Mephistopheles possessed Mr Fraser," said Freya. "I

didn't see it happen, but he—he attacked us. We thought we were safe. We'd got most people under Influence and the last buses left Blackstone—we had to drain the energy out of most of our demon hearts to get enough power to Influence everyone into leaving. We were supposed to regroup afterwards, but, but…" She trembled all over. "Everything shook, like an earthquake, and then the sky went dark; all the lights went out. There were shadow-beasts, ghouls, harpies everywhere. Mr Fraser was leading them, and he… he was possessed. He spoke to us. He said it was fitting that Blackstone would be the stage for mankind's final stand."

Horror coursed through me. Mephistopheles had done it again, ripped lives apart, waged war on the human race. Right now, I hated him even more than Lucifer. Anger pulsed like white-hot fire beneath my skin.

"I'll kill the bastard," I whispered, feeling the demon's emotions stir, becoming one with my own. Freya backed away slightly, fear glistening in her red-rimmed eyes.

"He—he had a message for you," she said. "I don't know if he thought you were still in Blackstone, but he said he's coming for you."

My throat closed up. So he did want me dead.

"He won't kill us," I heard myself say. "I won't let him hurt anyone else."

Freya was quietly sobbing now. I held her, anger having pushed my own tears away. I looked around. Leo was helping people climb down the stairs to the shelter. Strange, how one person could be such a mass of contradictions. Not that I was one to talk. Since when was I so conflicted about which of my emotions were the human's and which were the demon's? Humanity was more than survival instinct. Emotions were one of the things that made us so complex. Love and hate. I'd seen demons express hate, even pleasure, but love? It seemed incongruous.

What scared me most was Mephistopheles's ability to hate. He could literally tear the world apart with it. What if he was on the *venators'* trail? Then we'd have to leave. Run.

I paced the corridors while *venators* and other people I didn't know moved about, getting everyone settled into rooms. Apparently, their other headquarters wasn't equipped for visitors, though it made me uneasy that so many of them had come here in such a conspicuous way. If any other sorcerers had been watching, and if Mephistopheles had followed them…

I finally found Hayley, guiding the last of the group downstairs.

"Can I talk to you for a moment?" I asked.

"Ash?" she said. "You made it here."

"Yeah, we did," I said. "I was just wondering about Mephistopheles and Lucifer. Did they know you were coming here?"

"You're asking me what Lucifer knows? I've no idea." She shook her head, wearily. "Mephistopheles, on the other hand, well, someone killed the demon in Mr Fraser. It was too late to save him, of course." She closed her eyes, her forehead screwed up.

Another person dead. Another life we couldn't save. Mr Fraser had been one of the few reasonable leading members of the Venantium, and I could tell that Hayley was having a hard time keeping everyone together now she was the only survivor from the Inner Circle.

She drew in a deep breath. "Anyway, I need to call a meeting."

"Wait just a second," said a voice, as two more people came downstairs.

Berenice and Howard. The latter narrowed his eyes at Hayley.

"What are you people doing here?" he demanded.

"Same as you," said Hayley.

"You're the ones responsible for this mess," said Howard.

"Howard!" said Cyrus, coming out of the meeting room. "That's enough!"

"Shut up," Howard told Cyrus. To Hayley, he said, "I have a question. You can answer, or any of you *venators* can, but either way, someone's going to tell me. Where are my parents?"

"I told you," said Hayley, "I don't know—"

"You'll find out," he said, advancing toward her. "I'm not taking any more shit from you people. The world's ending as it is."

Hayley stood her ground. "I can check with the representatives here in London, but that's the best I can do. I'm sorry for your loss, but there's simply too many people missing for me to know specifics."

"Whatever," said Howard, making for the stairs. "I'll just go find your representatives, then. You people have fucked me around for too long."

"Howard!" Berenice ran after him as he disappeared upstairs.

Hayley sighed. "He won't find them," she said. "They have almost as many barriers around them as this place does. I'm impressed," she added to Layla, who'd just come out of one of the other rooms.

"Just doing my bit to keep people safe," said Layla. "I'm afraid I'll have to be harsh, though. Two of your people were threatening one of my guests earlier. I'm not standing for that."

"I'll speak to them," said Hayley. "Alone. Thank you for telling me."

She headed toward the open door at the corridor's end. I turned back to Layla.

"Are you sure no one followed them here?"

"No one can be sure of anything these days," she said.

9

SPEAK OF THE DEVIL

Understandably, our group wasn't invited into the *venators'* private meeting. Instead, once Leo, Claudia and Cyrus had come back from helping people, we ended up going back into the meeting room. Berenice and Howard joined us, once she managed to drag Howard back from trying to pester the *venators*. I guessed he'd concluded that it really was impossible to go after the London group alone and expect to find their hidden headquarters.

Cyrus and Layla seemed to be getting along, but the rest of us sat in tense silence. I read one of Gareth's books, for lack of anything else useful to do. I wished I had my laptop, but that was back in Blackstone along with most of my other possessions. The book wasn't particularly relevant to the situation, though the title, *Lost Souls of the Darkworld*, sounded suitably morbid.

Finally, Howard stormed out of the room with a ferocity that startled even Berenice. She hesitated to follow him. I wondered if they'd argued earlier.

"I know!" Gareth said, looking up from his books with

eyes shining like a scientist on the brink of a new discovery. "I know who Lucifer is!" he said.

"Try us," said Claudia, apparently unimpressed.

My heart jumped in my chest. *He knows?*

"You gave me the idea yourself, Ashlyn," he said, nodding at me. "If this Mephistopheles is indeed Lucifer's right hand demon, so to speak, then it seems we find ourselves facing the solution to a conundrum that has mystified scholars for centuries!"

"And what's that?" I asked.

Claudia drummed her fingers on the desk in a *just say it already* gesture.

"You mentioned the famous literary work the other day, Ashlyn. *Doctor Faustus.*"

"Yeah," I said slowly. "So?"

Gareth held up the yellow-paged book he'd been perusing. "The Faust tale was based on a real individual, a sorcerer who possessed extraordinary magic. He was a legend in his time, and people said he'd made a deal with the Devil. Then he disappeared. But his death was never recorded."

"You can say that about a million historical figures," said Leo. "Like Nicholas Flamel. He was meant to be immortal, right?"

"Yes, but the stories seem unusually apt in this case. If Marlowe's take on the legend is to be believed, Faust's pact was with the devil's second-in-command, Mephistopheles."

"Yes, and he was also pulled to pieces by devils," I said.

"You can't take every word literally," said Gareth.

"Sounds like that's exactly what you're doing," said Leo, almost as unimpressed-sounding as Claudia. "But selectively. I'm not buying this. In any case, it won't help us here."

"That's where you're wrong," said Gareth. "In fact,

this is exactly what we needed to know! If the original contract Faust made was with Mephistopheles, then he is the demon that holds Lucifer's life in his hands. In other words, he is the only demon capable of killing Lucifer."

That got everyone's attention. Even Claudia and Berenice gaped at him. As for me, my heart started racing. Could he mean what I thought he was implying? I caught Leo's eye, but he looked just as confused.

"I thought you said you hadn't experimented with demonic magic!" said Layla. "How in hell would you know that if you hadn't dealt directly with demons?"

"I have resources. Well, I did." He sighed. "I'm not proud of it, but I was once part of a cult. Don't look at me like that, Layla, some of the others here were the same."

"Figures," said Leo, giving him in disgusted glance.

"It was purely for research purposes!" Gareth said defensively. "I was intrigued to learn about modern views on the occult from independent sorcerers, and I went to a few meetings. That's all."

"And then got arrested," added Layla, rolling her eyes at him.

"Well, yes. How was I to know the Venantium had staked out the meeting place?"

"Honestly. You're a danger to yourself, Gareth."

Gareth blinked his owl-like eyes. "Well, it was worth it for the information I discovered. The cult's, um, leader, so to speak, planned to make a contract with a demon. He told us in detail how he planned to go about doing this. You see, when a demon is summoned, the first few seconds are crucial. If it dominates the sorcerer's mind, that's it. Your control is gone, and so, in most cases, is your life."

My eyes flickered toward Leo; I couldn't help it. He'd let a demon into his mind, himself. One second he'd been Leo, the next, not. But Mephistopheles had spared his life, intending to torment me. If the fortune-teller hadn't intervened…

Leo's fists were clenched on the table, like the same thing was on his mind. Berenice had gone deadly still, her eyes bright and her face pale as milk.

"But in order to ensure their own control, the sorcerer must make a bargain with the demon. This is usually done by summoning the demon to the brink of the Barrier, but not actually into our world. Through the veil of the Darkworld, the two communicate, and the sorcerer gets the demon to state his desired terms. Why, I cannot say. They are amoral and the idea of deceit means very little to them. They are not above using any means possible to trick the sorcerer into making a bargain that doesn't work out in their favour. But once stated the bargain cannot be revoked. It's a spoken agreement, a binding contract, and a peculiar one—I never did find out why a demon cannot go back on their word. But if Mephistopheles and Faust made a contract, some record of it might exist somewhere. So, in order to defeat Lucifer, that is what we need to find."

"We need to find the contract… if it exists?" I said. "Where the hell would we even start?"

"Fair point," said Gareth. "I imagine that Lucifer would have hidden it cleverly. Perhaps even on his person?"

"That makes no sense, he doesn't even have the same body," said Claudia. "God knows which poor sod got it this time."

The last body he'd used had been Conrad's. I shuddered at the memory of Lucifer snapping Conrad's neck and warping his body into a monstrous form.

"Well, it's a start."

"Yeah, well, it's not enough," said Berenice, her voice shaky. "That doesn't tell us how he got five higher demons under his control."

"The higher demons, again," said Gareth, more to himself than anything. "They are a constant factor in the Lucifer tales. The last known time a higher demon visited our world was during Lucifer's last attack, twenty years ago. I was comparing the leaflets." He held up a pamphlet that looked not unlike the one Claudia had once stolen from the Venantium, albeit faded with age and exposure to sunlight.

Surrender your life before you surrender your soul, this one proclaimed.

"That's like the one I found in Melmoth's office," said Leo.

"Your guardian was instrumental in that case, wasn't he?" said Gareth. "By all accounts, he was the one who killed the sorcerer!"

"Yeah, he did. But I guess Lucifer just slunk back to the Darkworld." Leo's eyes narrowed.

"Twenty years ago," Gareth muttered. "So many coincidences. The elusive higher demons made an appearance, and Lucifer declared war on the Venantium. They were baffled that he couldn't be possessed, he seemed to be immune... is he?" He turned his bespectacled gaze on me.

"Is he what?" I said, wondering why he was addressing me. How would I know about Lucifer?

"Is he immune? Can he be possessed?"

"I don't know," I said. "If he's in a human body, then maybe, but he's more or less totally separated himself now. He's more demon than human. He's the one who does the possessing."

"He is not a human-demon," said Gareth, and I didn't care for the undertones in his voice.

So he thought *I'd* possess someone, given the chance? Or maybe I was being jumpy for no reason.

"Yeah, Ash is the lucky one who can't be possessed," said Berenice. "She doesn't know the meaning of fear."

"That's a lie," I said, bristling. "I didn't know anything about my powers when I faced Terrence. When I saw he was possessed, I thought I was going to die. I almost did. Don't talk about what you don't understand."

"What I don't understand?" Berenice leapt to her feet, her eyes dark with anger. "You don't know anything about me. I stared death in the face when I was sixteen and a demon tore my two best friends to pieces before my eyes. So you lot can shut up about Lucifer not making big gestures. He showed his power to me, all right? And he's coming back for me, like he's coming for all of us."

A shiver raced through me. This wasn't like typical pessimistic Berenice–it was more than that. She really believed it. I'd thought the same myself, more than once.

"We'll kill him first," said Cyrus, but he didn't sound convincing.

"Stop deluding yourself," she spat. "I'm going to find Howard."

And she flounced out of the room. Everyone stared after her.

"Is that true?" said Layla. "About Lucifer killing her friends?"

'Yeah, it's true," I said. Thanks to a demon-induced nightmare, I'd been forced to witness that very scene myself.

"Lucifer's really marked her as his?" said Gareth.

"I don't know," I said. "We're all on his hit list, but I'm not sure he's bothered to figure out who to kill first."

Claudia stood. "I'm going to my room," she said.

Silence filled the room in her wake. The *venators'* arrival had set everyone on edge. What we knew couldn't beat

Lucifer. Where else could we get information, short of speaking to the demons themselves?

Did I really just think that? But my only source of information in the Darkworld was the half-demon, and now she was gone, too. I couldn't risk trying to speak to her again, in case Lucifer was listening in.

I reached to the demon in my own mind. If she could take over so easily when I was angry or in danger, then why wouldn't she talk to me? She knew as well as I did that we needed to stop Lucifer. I mean, she *was* me.

I stood up. "I'm going, too," I said.

"You okay, Ash?" said Leo.

I nodded. "Fine. I'm fine. I'll be back in a bit."

I walked out of the room, and tried to contact the demon the instant the door closed behind me. I felt the Darkworld at the periphery of my awareness, but couldn't get any closer. Had whatever happened to the Darkworld earlier permanently cut off my access? *No. It can't be too late.*

Answer me! I yelled at the demon. *You know how urgent this is. Please, just talk to me.*

Nothing.

Futile tears sprang to my eyes. Every hope had failed. Even the Venantium had gone. Mr. Fraser was just another of the dead. Our hope had died with the fortune-teller.

"Ash?"

A rush of warmth told me Leo was behind me even before he spoke.

"You okay?" said Leo.

I nodded. Then I shook my head. No more words were needed. He hugged me again, arms enfolding me like a soft blanket. He steered me along the corridor, away from the sound of voices, and I walked mechanically, trying to concentrate on him and only him, not on the darkness growing inside me, the gaping hole of self-blame and despair.

"They didn't deserve it," I whispered. "So many people died…"

"I know," he said. "I know."

"How can we—how can any of us fight that?"

He didn't answer. I didn't even realise we'd reached my room until the door closed behind us.

"I hate this," he said, quietly. "I hate hiding away. Running away feels so wrong."

"You did it to me," I whispered, before I could stop myself.

"I told you I was wrong about that," said Leo. "You have no idea how much I regret…"

"Don't," I said, putting my finger to his lips.

"Huh?"

"Regret can destroy a person. Look at the fortune-teller. Regret defined her whole life. Even in the end, she…"

But it was selfish, I knew, to dwell on the words of a dead woman when the living needed my help. Selfish to resent my mother regretting my very existence when so many were dead.

"It's only human, Ash. Regret can be a good thing. How else can you learn from your mistakes?"

"Well, there's that," I conceded. "But it can drive you mad, wondering what might have been. And—"

I was just like her, I thought. *I regretted everything. I wished I could have done something to stop everything going wrong last year, like I could have stopped Mephistopheles from getting at Leo…*

And even now, regret for all the lives lost weighed on me. I felt I could never be free of it. Not as long as Lucifer and Mephistopheles still existed.

"Don't I know it," said Leo. "Hell, my dad's a prime

example. I don't know if it was that he blamed himself for Mum's death or just that he wanted to do something, anything to distract himself from the pain of it, but he never let up. I remember coming home from school to find Cy's stuff and mine all packed up in the hall. My dad was there, and he looked like he hadn't slept in a week. I don't think he did, after Mum died. He never comforted Cy and me, either. I was six, Cy was eight. He packed everything into the car, and dropped us off at a children's home. I think Cy got what was happening quicker than I did. Took me a while to realise we'd been abandoned."

"I'm so sorry," I whispered.

"That place wasn't so bad," said Leo, shrugging. "It worked out pretty well. He'd had the sense to pick a place with a high proportion of magic-users, so the *venators* used to call round frequently. People our father knew. A few years later, Melmoth showed up one day and said he wanted to adopt us. Took a while, of course, but they came around. I think he might have used Influence on them, but yeah. That was that. I did see my dad again, of course. Melmoth wanted Cy and me educated in the workings of the Venantium so he sometimes took us along—not to important meetings or anything, obviously, but just to look around. Once I tried to talk to Dad, but he brushed me off. That was when I realised he'd gone. The person who'd once loved me and Cy and Mum, I mean. His eyes were just like a demon's. And right now, to be honest, I can't tell the difference."

He spoke in a hollow tone, but I didn't miss the pain underlying it. My heart ached for him.

"I've been thinking about it. I know, it's stupid, what with everything going on, but I can't help wondering whether there was any of him left, before the higher demon took control. t drives me crazy that I'll never know."

"You can never know everything about a person," I said. "It's demons who have the mind-reading ability, and they don't have empathy to back it up."

"I know," he said heavily. "Well, how have I lived with myself for the past few months, knowing I treated you like shit? I've gone over it in my mind a thousand times. It's maddening."

"Me, too," I said. "But there's a time and a place for self-blame, and this isn't it."

I meant this about us as much as about the recent events. Even with Mephistopheles and Lucifer out there, even with our hours potentially numbered, I couldn't let the moment slip away. Not again.

He nodded. "Who needs demons when we did such a good job driving each other crazy?"

That coaxed a smile out of me, despite it all. "You know, I've asked myself a hundred times why I never gave up on you."

"Not me. I always knew why I regretted letting you go."

He moved closer, and my breath hitched.

His voice dropped an octave. "Do you know what scared me most of all? The idea that if I came back, you wouldn't be here anymore."

I studied the floor. "I thought you'd never come back." I felt him move next to me until his hand brushed against mine. Warmth radiated from him. I gave in and looked into his eyes, saw the remorse plainly reflected back at me.

His voice was a whisper. "You should have told me."

"You should have told me you gave a crap about my existence."

He winced. "I can apologise up until the end of the world, but I have a feeling that isn't far away anyway."

"We don't have to talk," I whispered, and kissed him.

All doubt fled my mind, and I held onto him against the end of it all.

10

SHADOW FALLING

Morning arrived too soon for my liking. My eyes flickered open, my head rested on Leo's chest, and I felt a sense of peace reverberating through my body. I smiled, content to shut the cold and darkness out and concentrate on the warm feeling of closeness…

An unwelcome thought chased away all my contentment, and I sat up, trying not to jostle Leo awake. Was I draining energy from him? Was that why I felt so warm?

I tried to ask the demon, but still didn't feel her presence. Maybe she'd stayed away because there was no place for a demon in the intimacy of being with the person I loved. Of course, sex demons existed—Ryan, for one—but that wasn't the same thing. Or perhaps the demon just wanted to give me some privacy.

I looked at Leo, tuned into his quiet breathing. I ran my hand through his hair, feeling tingles shoot up my arm. *Demons could never understand this.*

Leo's eyes opened a crack. "Hey, beautiful."

My heart flipped over. "Hey, sexy."

"Cliché much?" said Leo, kissing me.

When we stopped to breathe, I said, "You're allowed to use clichés when you're in love. And it's the apocalypse."

"Well, now," said Leo, cupping my face in his hands. "Let's not spoil things."

He kissed me again, long and slow, and I felt every nerve stand on end.

"How's this for a cliché? Make love to me like it's the end of the world." And he pulled the duvet over us again.

"I THINK the others know what we've been up to," I said, sometime later, as I lay with my head in his arms once again.

"Who cares?"

"Well," I said. "We should probably join them at some point."

"Nah. Let's just wait until they start looking for us."

"We can't stay here forever," I pointed out, shifting my legs over the edge of the bed.

"I know," he said. "But it's nice to forget."

That word alone triggered unwelcome memories. I sat up properly, rubbing my arms, where goose bumps formed again.

Tell him, I thought, trying to will the words to come.

"Leo," I said. "Do you feel cold at all?"

"Me?" he said. "No. Are you cold?"

"I… well, it's just something the… the half-demon told me. She said I'm always cold because I'm tuned into the Darkworld."

"I figured that," said Leo. "But you said it doesn't bother you."

"Not really," I said. *Just say it. Go on. Get it over with.*

"There's something else, though. Apparently I can take warmth from other people. She said... I've been doing it for ages. I think I did it to you."

A pause. Leo didn't move or speak. My breath stuck in my lungs. *Please. Don't push me away again.*

Bracing myself, I turned to look at him. One eyebrow was raised, but he didn't look like he was about to run for his life.

"Really?" he said. "I don't feel like I've had the life sucked out of me, so you have one advantage over Melmoth."

I blinked, confused at how calmly he was taking it. "Huh? Doesn't it bother you?"

"Melmoth bit me once. Accidentally. I think after a vampire bites you, you tend to look at things differently. It's not like you set out to suck all life and warmth out of me."

"No," I said. "She said that—well, love had something to do with it. Like an emotional thing. I don't know. I mean, demons don't *have* emotions. The human-demon only understood because she used to be human, once."

And I have to help them. I got to my feet, stretching.

"Honestly, Ash, it's nothing. Even if you did it of your own free will. Kind of flattering, really." He laughed.

I'd shared part of myself with him, again, and it made me breathe a little easier, but it also brought a sense of emotional exposure. Like with each part of myself I gave away, the more I opened myself up to potential heartbreak. Even now, I felt the instinct to run away before I got hurt again.

Mind reading was impossible. All I could do was trust. And yet that was the fundamentally human thing, the idea of putting my happiness in someone else's hands whilst simultaneously holding his close to my heart. Demons could never understand this. Even if the world ended today, I'd have one less regret, and a memory even the darkness couldn't push away.

"Come on," he said, kissing me again. "Let's go join the party."

⁓

WHEN WE WALKED into the meeting room, Gareth was still postulating on the subject of Lucifer as Johann Faust, the scholar. Claudia doodled on a piece of paper, looking bored out of her mind, whilst Layla and Cyrus had started talking about something else without Gareth even noticing. Worry spiked inexplicably, even though I knew there was nothing Leo or I could have done in the past twelve hours to help the situation. We were still in the dark about how to beat Lucifer.

"Legends tell," he said, "of a book buried beneath a castle in Germany, which enables one to control all spirits. This must be the devil's handbook!"

"If non-sorcerers came up with that one, it'll be long out of date," said Claudia. "Seriously, what use is this crap?" She tapped her pen on the desk.

"Perhaps," said Gareth. "But it's worth considering what books he used to concoct his evil deeds! We already have the Lesser Key of Solomon—naturally, the version available for public reading is highly edited."

"I give up," said Claudia. "Nice of you two to join us, anyway," she added to Leo and me.

"Anything new?" said Leo, sitting down.

I did likewise. He wound his hand into mine, our fingers clasped under the table.

"No," she said.

"Actually, I did reach one important conclusion!" said

Gareth. "The legends all agree on one thing: that Faust tricked the devil unfairly. That's important."

"What, we should feel sorry for Mephistopheles?" said Leo, one eyebrow raised. "No way in hell is that happening."

"No, of course not! But think about it–demons never forget a grudge, and being tricked by a human is something demons will never forgive. Mark my words, he hasn't forgotten, even after all these years. Mephistopheles is still waiting for his chance for revenge on Lucifer."

"Interesting," said Leo. "But it doesn't help us. They're equally dangerous whether they're on the same side or not, and it's not like we can ask Mephistopheles what makes Lucifer tick."

Even if it was true, none of this would help me break the Barrier. But I wasn't ready to share that particular goal with the others yet. Gareth would doubtless bombard me with useless books, the others would see it as a suicidal goal that would end with us all dead, and I didn't quite trust word not to get out to the Venantium.

"Um, not to burst your bubble or anything," said Claudia, "but Mephistopheles wants *us* dead, not Lucifer. Besides we've bigger problems." She turned to Leo and me. "Howard won't leave the *venators* alone. Even Berenice can't talk any sense into him."

"Seriously?" I said, though it didn't surprise me.

"Yeah. I have a bad feeling he's going to do something stupid. Keeping him cooped up is a bad idea."

"That one's trouble," said Layla.

No one argued, but an uneasy silence filled the room. We really were just living on borrowed time, holding our breath until Lucifer made a move.

Everyone jumped when the door opened, and Hayley came in.

"Hi," Hayley said, wearily. She looked drawn, haggard even, far from the capable woman who'd rallied everyone in Blackstone. *What must it be like trying to hold together an organisation that's falling apart?*

"Hello," said Gareth. "I've found some information that might be of great interest to you and your colleagues."

"Not now, Gareth," she said. "We were contacted by Mephistopheles earlier."

Everyone looked up sharply. My heart started beating fast. *Not again... not so soon.*

"He's given us an ultimatum," she said, grimly. "Apparently almost wiping us out wasn't enough. Lucifer has his sights on world domination, and he says that unless we give him access to our overseas contact information—how to find the other branches of the Venantium—then he'll kill us one by one. And... and they found a body on the street earlier. One of yours."

"One of..." Gareth's face paled. "Who?"

"A young man. Blond. Two of my colleagues brought him in."

"Ryan Goddard," said Layla. I felt a rush of relief, and was then sickened with myself.

My attention snapped back to the present when the door flew open again, hitting the wall with a crash. Berenice appeared, her face stark white.

"Howard," she said, out of breath and wild-eyed. "He's gone."

"Gone?" Leo echoed. "What, he's taken off?"

"No. They have him." She held up her phone.

There was a faint buzz of static. Then a voice, cold as icy knives.

"If you want to save him, come to the Embankment. Now."

11

DEVIL'S BRIDGE

W e all looked at each other, shock leaving a ringing silence in the room. Even though the voice was unfamiliar, the chill that slid down my spine, the prickling of the Darkworld, told me there was only one person it could belong to. Only one demon. Mephistopheles.

Berenice trembled all over, but she held herself upright. "I'm going," she said. "I don't care what any of you say, I'm going to save him."

"What do you take us for?" said Cyrus, getting to his feet with a determined glint in his eye.

"Yeah, we're not going to let him hurt either of you," said Leo, his hand sliding out of mine as he got up.

"Agreed," said Claudia.

Berenice glared at me when I stood. "Mephistopheles wants me dead, too," I said. "I'm coming."

"Suit yourself," she said coldly.

"Mephistopheles?" said Gareth, looking wide-eyed between us. "The devil's second-in-command?"

Berenice ignored him, slamming out of the room.

Cyrus and Leo ran after her with Claudia and me on their heels. Fear pulsed through me. I couldn't let that demon kill anyone else. The image of Leo being possessed rose in my mind and I bit down on the fear, let the iciness of the Darkworld flood me and take control. This time, the demon answered immediately, rejoicing at being let free.

"Ash?" said Leo, taking a step away as he saw that my eyes had begun to glow violet.

"It's okay," I said, in my own voice. "I know what I'm doing."

Truthfully, I didn't. But now the demon and I had an understanding. I would never, ever let Mephistopheles near him again.

Even though the day was overcast, the sky looked bright compared to the artificial lights of the underground headquarters. But there was something unnatural about it all the same.

The journey across the city was little more than a blur of dodging tourists and running through traffic. Everything looked strange to me through a demon's eyes, oddly bleached of colour. Demons didn't have the same appreciation for beauty that humans did, and yet Mephistopheles himself had complained of being *trapped* in the Darkworld…

We reached the end of Northumberland Avenue, narrowly avoiding being knocked over by a tour bus, and found ourselves facing the Thames. The Embankment Bridge waited before us, and I could sense him even though I couldn't see the demon. Yet.

Then my gaze fixated on a point in the centre of the bridge, a shadowy figure standing still amongst the crowd.

We climbed the stairs, knocking into yet more tourists, who moved either side of the silent figure, heedless of the darkness that rippled across the bridge and into the Thames River. The London Eye stood out on the right, strange through the curtain of darkness. Boats still crossed the river; traffic still ran on the road beneath us.

Howard stood alone, a manic grin stretching his face, violet eyes gleaming. The crowd parted and closed around him in waves, faces turned forward.

Berenice let out a choked scream. "Howard!"

"You're late," crooned the demon.

"Let him go!" Berenice shouted.

"What would be the fun in that?" Mephistopheles spread Howard's arms wide. *"Do you like the world Lucifer's creating?"*

At once, every person crossing the bridge stopped, and turned to face us as one. Although their eyes weren't glowing, it was plain that they weren't in control of their own actions.

I felt the demon in me recoil, her shock resonating with my own. *How did he do that?*

"Not such great odds now, are they?"

"Let them go!" Leo shouted.

"Oh, spare me the heroism, Master Blake. You and I have unfinished business."

"Don't you dare," I said, taking a step forward, ice coating my hands.

"And you, Miss Temple, should not presume yourself invincible."

Pain shot through my arm, and blood poured as though from a knife wound. But nothing had touched me. The blood trickled down my arm to the ground, forming letters. I watched in horror as it spelled out words on the tarmac. *You are mine, Ashlyn.*

Then the pain faded as the demon rose to the surface again, her anger cancelling out my fear and pushing the pain back to the human part of me.

"You still don't know the extent of your abilities. Space has no

meaning for us. I could break his neck." One of the frozen tourists crumpled. *"Or hers."* Another fell.

"Stop!" Ice-fire rose to my fingertips and I prepared to launch myself at the demon.

"Don't!" Berenice cried, grabbing at my arm. "He'll hurt Howard!"

"Your boyfriend is already mine," said Mephistopheles, grinning at us. *"I have come here to offer you all an ultimatum. You see, when young Ashlyn here provoked me and took away my prize, she had no idea what horror she unleashed."*

Berenice turned accusing eyes on me. "What have you done?"

"She and that meddling woman thwarted my desires and caused me a great deal of pain. No demon forgets a grudge—and you have had the misfortune to provoke the next great higher demon. Lucifer has promised me enough power to join the Seven, if I help. That was our agreement."

"So what?" I countered.

"We already know you're both egotistical bastards," Leo yelled in agreement.

"You will regret ever insulting me. Ashlyn, merely killing you is no longer of interest to me, or even killing your friends. I will no longer be merciful. I will destroy everyone you hold dear, one at a time, in a way that will leave you broken. Only when you are utterly alone and bereft will I put my ultimate purpose to you. You will not die. You will linger forever, eaten away by your regrets and haunted by the deaths of your friends. And you brought this on yourself."

A man standing blankly nearby fell to the ground.

"Dropping like flies, aren't they? Admit it to me, Ashlyn. I want you to acknowledge my power."

"No chance." I felt numb inside, but the demon spoke through me all the same. Blood dripped down my arm, and I knew that when I returned to awareness, it would hurt a lot.

"As for you, Miss Payne. If you want him to live… you will have to come with me."

"Don't!" Cyrus shouted, as Berenice stepped forward, the tourists parting around her.

"I have to!" she said. "I have to—I can't let him die."

There was nothing any of us could do to stop her. Of course, this was Mephistopheles's plan. He held Howard's life in his hands, just like he had with Leo, and I didn't dare move for fear of provoking him.

"I'm glad we reached an understanding."

Berenice walked slowly toward Howard. Helplessness weighed me down. Neither of them deserved to be tormented by Mephistopheles. *Is it my fault?*

"Oh yes, Ashlyn," Mephistopheles said. *"All the blame lies with you. May your friends' fates torment you forever."*

And with a laugh, he embraced Berenice. Even from here, I could see she was shaking all over.

"Stop," I whispered. "Stop that."

Mephistopheles turned Howard's head to look directly at Leo. *"You're next, bro."*

Then he raised Howard's hands. Shadows rose from the Thames either side of the bridge, livid and writhing like dark flames. They obscured everything in front of us. I heard Mephistopheles's laughter echo from behind the wall of shadow flames, and images flickered before me.

Fire was everywhere—true flames climbing up to the sky that was suddenly a mass of roiling grey clouds. Bolts of lightning lit everything up in flashes, like club lights, pulsing red and blue and green, and still the flames climbed higher. I could see buildings outlined against the scorching hue, familiar ones. Blackstone burned in the fire.

The fire roared, devouring Blackstone, devouring everyone I knew. Each single image etched itself onto my mind. Claudia falling into the fire, Cyrus dropping to the ground, Leo's eyes meeting mine before the light within them was extinguished...

I could no longer see my friends beside me—all that existed was a nightmare video clip playing over and over again. I shook all over, the fight going out of me as I opened myself to the darkness.

"I might not be able to possess you, but I can break you, Ashlyn."

"No." My voice was barely a whimper, but it was there. "No."

I willed the demon to come to the surface, and she did, her vision replacing mine. The flow of images stuttered and stopped, and all I could see was darkness.

Then the world came back into focus and Mephistopheles was gone.

Pain stabbed my arm where blood still dripped from the wound. People on the bridge had returned to awareness, judging by the screaming. Bodies lay everywhere. I whirled around, heart beating like a jackhammer. Relief swept through me when I saw Leo beside me. Claudia and Cyrus stood there, too, none of them moving. By the expressions on their faces, I realised with a jolt that they were trapped in visions, too.

"Leo!" I said, shaking his arm. "Leo! Wake up! It's just a vision."

His mouth was half-open, eyes glazed in an expression of pure terror.

"Leo! Please. Please come back!"

The panic rose again. *No. Don't let me lose him again.* Blood ran down my arm, but I didn't care about that, not even the dull, throbbing pain. Nothing was worse than the expression on Leo's face.

"I can help." The demon's voice cut through the horror numbing my mind.

How?

"Let me show you."

The Darkworld covered my vision again, but familiar this time, with no images of horror and flames. Instead, I saw different images. Leo and me. Our conversation earlier that day. The past few weeks. Him in my underground room, holding Melivia's diary. The two of us in my room, him holding my hand as I faded away into the Darkworld.

Then a gap. I reached deeper into Leo's mind, for the long-ago memories I knew were still there. Leo and I at the cinema, at the burger bar, walking hand in hand through campus, talking, laughing. Lying on his bed on campus, locked together as though Hell itself couldn't tear us apart.

"Ash?"

Slowly, reality came back into focus. My nails dug into his hand.

"Leo," I said, half-dazed. "Thank God."

"What—what happened? I saw…"

"A vision," I said. "Help me help the others."

Claudia and Cyrus still stood rigid, each locked in a private nightmare world.

"We'd better get a move on," said Leo, glancing around.

Police in bright yellow jackets had begun to congregate around the bridge. *Like they can do a thing. Where the hell are the venators?* But my demon had surrounded us in Influence, and we couldn't move Cyrus and Claudia in this state. Blood trickled down my wrist and my vision had started to go fuzzy, but we had to act now.

I quickly called on the Darkworld. I felt Leo beside me as I entered the visions again, and using that sixth sense, I directed him to help his brother whilst I helped Claudia.

Again, a rush of memories. I focused on bringing the positive ones to the surface, and was surprised to see how many of them involved us. Our group. Discussions in the

Games Room, joking and bantering, pool nights in the campus bar. As I reminded her of who she really was, I felt her awareness return and blinked the darkness away. Leo and Cyrus looked at me, and Claudia blinked, half-choking on a sob.

"Thanks, Ash," she said.

"Yeah," said Leo, hugging me. "You're amazing."

I felt tears sting my eyes, and closed them, feeling so, so tired. "I couldn't save them."

"None of us could, Ash."

Leo's hands dug into my shoulders, grounding me in the present. "We'll find a way to stop him hurting anyone else. I promise."

"He… he almost broke us."

"But he didn't. We're alive."

"Just about." The cut on my arm demanded my attention, and Leo gasped as he noticed it.

"That bastard—"

"Could be worse," I said, grimacing in pain.

"We have to get that checked out," said Leo. "Come on. Let's get off the bridge."

We moved away, dodging tourists who paid us no attention; again, the demon kept Influence on autopilot. I felt overwhelmingly grateful for her presence now.

Folly as it might be, for every breath in my lungs, for every heartbeat, I'd remind myself of that. *I am alive.* Not merely existing, as demons did. Living.

But for how much longer?

Now the demon had gone, all the fear I'd suppressed racked me with shudders and it was all I could do not to break down. Berenice and Howard, both gone. It felt unreal that the world around us could just go on, regardless. Crowds milled around, cars clogged the roads, and boats crossed the river, ferrying tourists.

Leo held onto my hand, and I gripped it tight, as though I could somehow hang onto sanity that way. The cold, empty place inside me threatened to pull me in again.

He's alive. You're alive. But that gave me little comfort, knowing that Mephistopheles had killed Howard because of me. That Berenice was now at his mercy because of his grudge. And that I was utterly powerless. He could be anywhere, and looking for him alone would be futile. When he wanted to be found, I had a horrible feeling it would be very, very clear.

We made our way through the crowded streets to Satan's Pit. This time, the journey seemed to take no time at all. I felt detached from reality, and the others' silence cemented that. The drab grey sky and the tourist landmarks seemed part of a different world.

Claudia knew the way back, and the rest of us unconsciously followed her lead. Nevertheless, it surprised me to see the nightclub still there, standing exactly as we'd left it. A few hours felt like an eternity. Claudia led the way downstairs and into the meeting room.

"What happened?" said Layla, jumping to her feet the instant we came in. "You're—are you all okay?"

"Ash is hurt," said Leo immediately. "Not serious. Come on, we have to clean that cut." He steered me over to the sink.

My limbs were like dead weights, and blood soaked my sleeve. However, once I removed my jacket, I saw the cut was shallow, despite all the blood. Judging by the icy numbness, maybe the demon had sealed it.

"I'm okay," I insisted.

"Two of our friends are dead," said Claudia, sounding like she hardly believed it. "So we need a plan to take down the bastard before he kills anyone else."

Layla's hands clapped to her mouth. "Oh, God. I'm

sorry."

Gareth said nothing, unusually subdued. I could swear he hadn't changed position since we'd last been here.

"I have a first-aid kit," he mumbled, stumbling to his feet and out of the room.

Layla sank into her seat again, trembling all over. "I should have told you... I'm sorry, it's my fault. I just never thought he..."

Tears streamed down her face. Mine were locked away somewhere, screaming to get out, but I gripped Leo's hand and determined to stay focused before I broke down completely.

"What?" said Claudia. "Why's it your fault?"

"Hayley—she came to talk to me." Layla swallowed. "She said that she'd been talking to your friend about his parents—that he wouldn't quit until he'd found answers. That's why he went out alone."

"It's not your fault." Cyrus sat down beside her and put his arm around her. "Howard never listens to anyone. Hell, I'm... I was the closest to a friend he ever had, and he treated me like shit."

He stared ahead with the same deadened expression Leo wore when he spoke of their father.

"Really," said Claudia. "If anything, it's our fault for not being able to control him."

"It's my fault," I said.

"Ash, don't be ridiculous," said Leo.

"Why deny it?" I felt my throat close up. "I'm the real target. I've got to leave. He'll come after you guys next."

"Ash," said Leo. "I know how you feel. Don't go after Mephistopheles. Or Berenice. It'll get you killed."

I blinked at him through tears. "I could say the same to you."

"I don't have a death wish, as much as I want to kill the

bastard."

"Likewise," I said. "But I'm not having anyone else's death on my conscience. I'll go… I don't know. Back to Manchester? Cara won't be there."

"Ash, don't be stupid. I know it's hard, but Howard only got caught because he went outside."

"Look," said Layla, who'd managed to get her tears under control. "I know this is a bad time, but Hayley… she asked to speak to you later. She didn't say why."

"Fine," I said, tonelessly. "It's better than doing nothing. Where have the *venators* been, anyway? Did they not notice a bunch of demons out there?"

"I have no idea," said Layla. "It's possible the shields around here stop them from sensing demons outside."

"Great," said Claudia. "I'm not talking to any of them. It's their damn fault Howard's dead."

Dead. I couldn't listen to that word. I turned toward the door, letting go of Leo's hand.

"Ash?"

"Hold on," I said. "I just need a moment."

My chest felt tight, like I couldn't get enough air into my lungs. I felt myself unravelling and the room seemed too small, too stifling. I didn't want to sit inside. I wanted to run, and keep running, until the grief and guilt inside me spent itself, but it wouldn't be enough. I couldn't rest until Mephistopheles was dead.

Berenice and I had never been friends. Hell, we'd *loathed* each other, really. And Howard had always struck me as unbelievably self-absorbed and unfeeling, except where Berenice was concerned. The two were the match made in hell and strangely suited to each other, and no demon had the right to tear them apart. No one had the right to do that to anyone.

Human law might not be perfect, but demons literally

got away with murder because no one ever stood up to them. True enough, no one *could*. Despair rose in my chest, choking me. I stumbled from the room.

Pull yourself together.

I clenched my fists, squeezing my eyes shut, and rested my forehead on the wall. *I have to find a way.* Killing Mephistopheles would only send him back to the Dark-world. That monster had no concept of guilt; immortality was no punishment to him. No punishment was bad enough, anyway. Only true death, destruction of his demon heart, would truly end him and keep him from harming anyone else.

Breaking the Barrier. Setting the souls free. And killing Mephistopheles, and Lucifer, for good.

I repeated the three goals in my head. *My* goals. Mine, and the demon's. Together we'd figure it out. *We will.*

"Please," I whispered, to the demon. "I know you hate me. But I need your help. Please talk to me."

Only silence answered.

"Ash?" Leo said from behind me. "You okay?"

"Sure," I said hoarsely, turning to let him hug me.

"Stupid question, I know," he said. "Uh… Gareth?"

Gareth shuffled out of a nearby room, clutching a bag. "First-aid kit," he said. "I'm sorry."

I let Leo fuss over the cut, even though it was barely a superficial wound, and right now, anger pushed away the pain.

"I'm fine," I insisted, finally. "We should… we should go back in there."

"Yeah. But I think we should talk to Hayley. Maybe she knows something we don't about how to find him. And kill him before he can harm anyone else."

"Damn straight," I said, wiping the last of the tears from my eyes. I was done crying.

12

ULTIMATUM

Hayley, it turned out, was just as surprised as Layla to find that any of us had survived. She came into the meeting room alone, which struck me as suspicious. I hadn't seen any of the other *venators* around, either.

"They're at the London HQ," she said. "We're working together to take down Mephistopheles. The damage he did on the bridge… the team are working to cover it up."

"Great," said Claudia, sarcasm dripping form her voice. "So they'll intervene when the fighting's over, but not when our friends are getting killed?"

"None of us knew anything was wrong," said Hayley defensively. "He communicated with you?"

"He used Howard's phone," I explained.

We should have told them. But we'd had no time, and the Venantium couldn't have made the slightest difference. Once Mephistopheles set his sights on someone, they were dead.

"He told us to come to the bridge if we wanted to save

Howard. But… he's possessing him, and now he's taken our other friend with him."

"Your people are the ones who stirred him up," Claudia growled. "That's what Layla said, anyway."

Layla stiffened, looking at Hayley.

"Hey, don't drag Layla into this again," said Cyrus. "She couldn't have known he'd do something that stupid. That's on us. We all know what Howard's like."

"That doesn't change the fact that you told him something about his parents." Claudia still glared at Hayley. "Right?"

"It wasn't my decision," said Hayley, running a hand through her hair. "God knows I've got enough to deal with already. The fact of the matter is that Mr. Lloyd—Howard's father—passed away from a sickness in prison two years ago. His wife suffers from an undiagnosed mental illness. My colleagues refused them the help they needed."

A horrified silence filled the room.

"I claim responsibility for it," said Hayley, "but I wasn't in charge of the cells, and no one can deny that the two of them used illegal magic."

"What did they even do?" said Claudia, in horror struck tones.

Hayley drew in a deep breath. "They conspired to murder a senior member of the Venantium. They were caught in the middle of a demon-summoning spell. They fought back with demonic magic, and were restrained. The Inner Circle themselves had to get involved in order to restrain them, and it was decided that Howard shouldn't be told the truth."

More silence. Ripples of shock coursed through the room. I couldn't even wrap my head around the idea. Maybe it was for the best that Howard had never found out…

Stop that. You don't know he's really dead.

The gaping hole inside me threatened to drag me in again.

"That's..." Cyrus's voice sounded distant, as though coming from the other side of a glass wall. "That's still not your decision."

"You asked for the truth. I gave it to you." She sighed, running a hand through her dishevelled hair. She looked like she hadn't slept in days. "I'm sorry. Believe me. But you should know that stopping Mephistopheles and Lucifer is imperative right now. Mephistopheles sent a warning to us, too."

"He did?" I said, staring at her. *You might have mentioned before.*

"He used mind-communication. Told us he could read our every thought and could kill us at any time. I don't think he can get past the wards though, at least not alone, which means Lucifer hasn't broken them yet."

I shivered. Even if I did figure out how to break the Barrier myself, I'd have to be close enough to Lucifer and Mephistopheles to kill them, otherwise I'd only be doing them a favour by removing their only obstacle to dominating the world.

I had the sensation of teetering on a tightrope, always one step away from falling into oblivion. Except that if I fell, so would the world. It was too much. Once again, hopelessness constricted my chest.

"Ash, we need your help."

I turned to Hayley. "You? Or the Venantium?"

"Both. What's left of us have assimilated into the London branch, and we want to fight against him. You—all of you—are admirable fighters, and you, Ash? Well, I'm glad you're on the side of good."

I didn't acknowledge the compliment. "The Venantium

hate human-demons," I said. "How do I know you won't turn on me? You might be reasonable, but your colleagues have different opinions. I have enough enemies already, to be honest. Besides, we're fighting Lucifer ourselves."

"I'm just asking you to meet with the leaders of the London branch. Things are run differently here, not so old-fashioned. They're all keen to meet you."

"Why should we risk our lives in going outside?" Leo countered. "Mephistopheles will still be in London."

"Ready to attack again. We can't afford to delay," said Hayley. "Believe me, we're no threat to any of you. We don't need any more enemies."

"I guess," said Claudia, looking at me. "I suppose we could do worse. They might know something we don't."

I had a feeling it was more the feeling that we had to do *something* that motivated her. But I felt the same. Maybe it was a good idea to talk to the supposed experts, even if they did think me an abomination. We were outnumbered by far, and Mephistopheles had managed to get at us once already. Maybe he was *letting* us stay alive.

"All right," I said. "We'll come to hear you out."

Hayley nodded, looking immensely relieved. "Thanks, Ashlyn. You're a source of hope to all of us. Whatever the Venantium might think of your kind, all the witnesses who escaped from Lucifer in the catacombs saw that it was the spirits of half-demons who defended us."

"How…?"

"It couldn't have been anything else. Most of us heard the voices. It's a remarkable thing."

Tragic, more like, I thought. The spirits had been people once, before their lives were brutally cut short, condemning them to an eternity in the shadows. But it was more unnerving than reassuring that the *venators* knew about it. I couldn't let them find out what the half-demon had asked me to do. Even now, they'd surely stick to their old principles, no matter what Hayley seemed to think.

Hayley's gaze swept over the others. "Ashlyn, our time's limited. I hope you'll understand."

"Oh, believe me, I do."

"Are you ready to come with us now?"

I nodded, getting to my feet. Leo stood, too, still holding my hand.

Cyrus sighed. "I suppose it's pointless to say I think this is a bad idea?"

"Ash goes, I go," said Leo simply, and squeezed my hand.

Hayley's eyes flickered in that direction, and her mouth tightened.

"Right. Are you…?" She gave Gareth a questioning look.

He shuddered. "I'm afraid not. I'm no fighter, but I have some interesting research which I'm sure will be of value to your investigation. I am sure that the others will pass on my conclusions."

"Yeah, sure, whatever," said Claudia. "Come on."

Once again, we were putting our fates in the hands of the Venantium. I didn't like it, but right now, survival was the priority. If I had to disappear when this was all over—well, I didn't want to think about that, but it was better than the alternative, a world ruled by Lucifer.

We followed Hayley back upstairs to the nightclub. Several other *venators* waited there, looking around uneasily. They still wore their uniforms, unwilling to break tradition even with the world collapsing around them. I looked at Leo, who nodded, his face set.

Time to face the *venators*. Again.

Outside, the world looked the same. It bothered me how *ordinary* the city seemed, not at all as though it housed a sadistic killer. Grey clouds clustered around the buildings and apartments, interspersed with green stretches of park. Flocks of pigeons dive-bombed picnickers on the grass and on the steps outside the National Gallery. I could hear the sounds of life going on as usual, crowds and chatter and the hum of city life. The smell of petrol mingled with cigarette smoke. It wasn't pleasant.

"I'm afraid it's a bit of a walk," said Hayley. "We don't like to use public transportation if we can help it. Especially now."

I still couldn't help glancing in the direction of the bridge where Mephistopheles had met us. Where those people had died. Now, tourists were crossing again. It seemed unreal, like it belonged to another world.

I still felt more like an intruder than a tourist in the capital, but I couldn't help admiring the landmarks we passed, including Big Ben and the Houses of Parliament. I wondered if the government had a clue what was going on. Unlikely.

"There are *venator* representatives within Parliament," Hayley told us, as if she'd read my mind. "They're responsible for seeing that no one is targeted by a demon attack, but to be honest, demons tend to leave politicians alone. They're the reason we have another branch here, anyway."

I nodded. That made sense.

I still found it strange that a whole world existed beneath our feet, even though in London, travelling underground was second nature. We crossed Westminster Bridge, dodging around yet more tourists and flag-draped stands selling souvenirs—who in their right mind wanted a T-shirt that said 'Mind the Gap', really?—and followed the main road until we came to a park.

There, I saw something odd. A pair of wooden doors set into a statue of a gargoyle that stood alone on the grass, like it had belonged to a grand church or cathedral which had since been torn down.

"Nice Influence," Claudia remarked. "Looks like it's missing a cemetery, though."

"They took the old church down," said Hayley, confirming my guess. She pulled a key from her pocket, and I noticed to my puzzlement that there wasn't a lock in the door. But she held the key out anyway, pressed it to the wood, and it sank inward, into a lock that wasn't visible to my eyes.

The key turned, and with a grating sound, the doors opened onto a passageway. I felt a familiar shiver of dread.

Hayley walked through the doors, followed by the other two *venators*. Claudia went next. Leo squeezed my hand, and I nodded. *We can do this.*

We went after the others, Cyrus bringing up the rear.

It was just like being in the tunnels under Blackstone again—stone-walled tunnels smoothly dug out of the earth by long ago magical means. An underground labyrinth that only *venators* could navigate. Hayley walked ahead, glancing down each passageway as we neared it, presumably to ensure no trap awaited us. But there was the same silence that always pervaded the headquarters in Blackstone here, the kind I associated with a prison. Or a morgue.

Eventually we came to a wider tunnel, lit with electric lighting just like the hideout. This tunnel's walls were decorated with the same kind of paintings that adorned the Blackstone Headquarters' entrance hall, scenes from Milton's *Paradise Lost* of the damned descending into Hell.

If the Venantium saw the apocalypse coming, then why weren't they prepared?

We crossed the tunnel, footsteps echoing on the stone floor. Leo still held my hand as we went deeper into the

Venantium's lair. A pair of tall oak doors waited at the end, and another person strode out to meet us.

He was in his mid-forties, I'd guess, grey-haired and wiry-looking. His gaze passed from each of us to the next, assessing.

"Ashlyn?" He looked directly at me.

I nodded, my throat dry.

"Excellent. Most excellent. Come with me, all of you. I am Jonathan Stirling, the acting leader of this division of the Venantium."

His insincere smile instantly put me on edge.

"Won't you and your friends come with me?"

Through the oak doors, we found a room that could have been the exact double of the Venantium's meeting hall, like the interior of an old church crossed with a court-room. I'd only been in that particular room once, when Leo's father had warned of the threat of Lucifer, and announced the fortune-teller's detainment. Had Mr Blake been under Lucifer's influence even then? We'd probably never know. I turned my attention back to the present, and the crowd waiting for us inside the hall.

I couldn't believe the size of the audience. Almost all of the seats in the hall were filled, and every single indi-vidual wore the Venantium's uniform. Because of the small number who'd made it out of Blackstone, most were new faces. It almost drew my attention away from the carvings on the walls and ceiling, which were stone renderings of the grim paintings on the walls in the corridors. Twisted manifestations of the human form intermixed with depic-tions of demonic beasts, some of which resembled shadow-beasts, others which looked nothing like anything I'd seen before: fanged, clawed, hideous monsters that stretched the limits of the human imagination.

In other words, not what I particularly wanted to see

underground, knowing there was a madman with all of those creatures at his disposal on the loose who wanted us dead.

I made for the aisle leading to an empty row of seats, but Jonathan Stirling waved us to follow him. With a lurch of the heart, I realised he was leading us to the stage at the front of the hall, right in front of a thousand eyes that were suddenly looking directly at me.

Hell. Public speaking was definitely not my thing.

Leo and Cyrus didn't look too pleased, either. Claudia scanned the audience, probably searching for people she knew. There were a few familiar faces but I had that odd feeling of disconnection that always came with nerves, like giving a presentation to my seminar group at university. Or an interview. Funny how my Oxford interview came to mind now. Looking back, that was child's play. *Try keeping your head together when the whole world might depend on you.*

Jonathan Stirling stepped to the raised platform at the front of the stage, where a microphone stood on a stand. He took it, and addressed the crowd.

"*Venators,*" he intoned, and I could imagine him to be the kind of legendary public speaker who could capture the hearts of an entire room in seconds. "I have called you here this time to give you some excellent news. An extraordinary group of sorcerers have offered themselves to help our cause."

"Offered ourselves? Makes us sound like a sacrifice," Claudia muttered.

I tensed, but Jonathan didn't seem to hear her.

"As you are all aware, Mephistopheles has given us twenty-four hours in which to give him our location. This, as you know, is out of the question. He's attacked several other branches worldwide. Ireland, Egypt, Australia."

My insides lurched.

"Twenty-four hours," he repeated, and I glanced at Leo, out of the corner of my eye. Although his expression was unreadable, the grip of his hand on mine indicated he was as uneasy as I was. This wasn't what Hayley had told us.

"And so, I came to a decision. Miss Hayley Fairfax informed me that a certain individual was currently in London, a person of particular value in this war. Both Lucifer and his chief demon Mephistopheles want this individual on their side. She is unique not only amongst humans, but amongst sorcerers. Ashlyn Temple is a human-demon, the last of her kind, and has all the advantages we do not in the fight against Lucifer."

He'd just *said* it—he'd told every single person in the room my secret. I couldn't look anyone in the eyes now. My tongue felt glued to the roof of my mouth, and I couldn't utter a word, not even to contradict him. I was just as vulnerable as any sorcerer faced with Lucifer.

"Ashlyn would be a valuable weapon for our cause. However, she is unstable, and the Venantium do not ally themselves with demons. So, I have made my decision. Please know that this was not an easy choice to make, but our own survival is of paramount importance. I have agreed to deliver Ashlyn to the demon Mephistopheles tomorrow, rather than disclose our whereabouts to the enemy. The demons have been searching her out, at the cost of many lives. It is the only way to end the slaughter of our people."

A ringing silence followed his words. Possibly, the ringing was in my own ears, and had caused me to mishear. Who in their right mind would believe handing me over to the enemy would solve anything?

Beneath the ringing, I heard someone speak. Leo's hand slipped out of mine, and he stepped forward.

"Don't listen to another word," he told the mute audience. "Don't let him lie to you. Handing Ash over won't stop Mephistopheles or Lucifer from threatening you. The demon likes killing too much to give it up, even if he gets hold of Ash. And he kills because he enjoys it. It's *not* her fault."

"Be quiet," Jonathan Stirling said, but the restless audience ignored his words. "Mr. Blake, you ought to mind your tongue."

Leo stood his ground. "Only when you tell people the truth. And I'm not going to let you kill Ash."

Yeah. I'm not going to let that happen, either. How had we managed to land in this mess? We were in the spotlight, with hundreds of powerful sorcerers surrounding us. There was no obvious escape, and I wouldn't let any of the others get killed.

"Wouldn't you prefer to know your girlfriend died in the name of a great cause, for the good of us all?"

"Like hell," said Leo. "My dad told me you were a crook, but I didn't believe a word he said. He was right this time, though. You're not getting Ash, or any of us, come to that. Better focus on actually fighting Lucifer before he wipes you all out."

"It's true," I said. "We're not your enemy here."

"How dare you," said Jonathan Stirling, looking at Leo, not me. "You dare speak so disparagingly of us, when we do so much to defend you? Your father gave himself up to a higher demon. Now his son, an unregistered sorcerer, comes here and insults us. You're treading a thin line, Mr Blake."

"Don't associate me with that bastard."

"I refuse to let you damage morale even further. Eileen, take them to the cells."

A woman in the front row stood. She was tall, made

taller by heels that looked extreme, even by Claudia's standards, and had a short bob of black hair. With her impeccable suit, she could have been any businesswoman, were it not for the badge of the Venantium on her jacket.

She looked directly at me, and the world froze.

Ice flooded me, so deep it came to the surface, and I felt it crystallise right there on my skin. The woman's stare cut through me, but I couldn't pinpoint the exact expression. It could have been anger, hate, righteousness, malevolence, even piety. But something in it brought the demon in me to the brink, a whisper in my ears that she was a very dangerous woman.

Like I hadn't figured that one out already.

The ice ran through me to my feet and into the ground, manifesting in jagged spikes and spreading over the platform. *Impossible.* I'd thought only demons could use ice-magic. This woman was strong, crazy strong. I couldn't move at all. An image rose to the front of my mind of a long-forgotten dream, where I was encased in ice, imprisoned before a crowd that gawked at me like an animal in the zoo. The ice didn't cover me all over like the dream, but I felt it all the same, entrapping me. I couldn't even turn my head to look at Leo. *What the hell is she doing to me?*

"Ashlyn Temple, you are ours," she said.

I tried to tell her *no way*, but even the demon in me couldn't break through the ice. I heard her screaming in my head, and I knew the sound would be coming out of my own mouth, could I open it.

Then the woman spoke to me directly in my mind, as a demon would, *"Ashlyn Temple, you are ours. Do not resist me."*

I tried to mentally push her away, but hit a block. She was too strong. It was like running into a brick wall, and my mental defences crumpled before her. Shadows invaded my mind, and I faded away into emptiness.

13

RAISING HELL

"*Ashlyn Temple!*"

The demon's voice echoed in my ears, jolting me back to awareness. My neck ached and cold stone pressed against my back from where I lay, at an awkward angle, on the floor. I sat up, wincing. I was in a cell, which didn't surprise me in the slightest. Barely three metres square in size, it had no furniture, and the door was barred.

Darkness made it hard to see in here, with not so much as a candle to penetrate the gloom. I conjured a light, relief seeping into me when it worked fine. My connection wasn't damaged.

Hells. What did she do to me? So much for having allies. A host of new enemies, though? *Not fair, universe.*

"*She's a dark magic-user, Ashlyn. She uses demonic magic.*"

I looked up at the half-demon, who hovered faintly in front of the door. "I got that much," I muttered. "You didn't see where the others are, did you?"

"*In another part of the headquarters. I will lead you there.*"

"Perks of a demon's all-seeing vision," I said, rubbing the back of my neck.

"She'll be coming back for you, Ashlyn."

"Brilliant," I said. "As long as she doesn't hurt the others, though…"

"She has Leo in the Angel Box."

"Shit." I jumped to my feet, ignoring the pain that throbbed through my head. "Might you have mentioned that first?"

I ran to the door and pressed my hands to the bars, remembering an old trick I'd used to escape the Venantium's cells last time.

"You were insensible, Ashlyn. She used magic on you that would have killed a regular human."

"Are the others okay?"

The half-demons hesitated. I turned to face her.

"Tell me!"

"Leo's brother is injured."

I swore again. "I have to get Leo out of the Angel Box."

I called on the demon and gripped the bars, tightly. The pendant burned, and ice spread over my fingers, burning cold. I directed the magic toward the bolts holding the door shut. The door rippled all over as the ice spread over the surface. *At least they didn't block my connection.*

"She wouldn't have been able to torture you otherwise. She needed it to break into your mind."

"She's crazy," I said. "Just when I thought the Venantium couldn't get any more twisted."

The bolts dissolved at my touch, and the door hissed open. I stepped out, the half-demon at my side. *I have to find Leo…* I moved the conjured light to hover over my head and followed the half-demon down the corridor. The neighbouring cells were empty, and fear for Leo gripped my chest. My hands shook harder as I walked, but the demon's presence bolstered me. I didn't know what I'd do if that woman hurt him—

No, I *did* know. I'd kill her.

The pendant burned again, sharply. Urgency swept me into a run and shadows gathered around me, Influence prepared to shield me should I run into anyone.

But there was no need. Soon enough, another light spilled onto the stone floor—the eerie, alien light of an Angel Box. *Leo.*

The door to the room was wide open. My eyes instantly focused on the prone form on the floor of the glass box. The world lurched beneath me, and shadows crept in at the corners of my vision. *No. God, no!*

"Leo!" I ran over, heart hammering in my ears.

He looked up, and relief flooded me.

"Thank God," I breathed, pressing my palms to the glass, tears pricking my eyes. He looked unhurt, only a bit dazed.

"Ash? How did you—?"

"Come on," I said, running my hands over the glass walls, searching for the opening.

Leo sat up, wincing. "Where'd that bitch go? I think I blacked out." The thick glass distorted his voice, but he sounded okay.

"That woman?" How had she overcome my demon so easily? I hadn't seen, nor had I known anyone had power like that.

Leo stood. "You've got it. Mr Stirling's delightful wife, as it turns out."

"His wife?"

"They're made for each other." He pressed his hands against the glass. "Crap. No exit."

"Don't worry about it," I said. The half-demon had already stepped up to open the glass door.

Leo stared.

"You can see her?" I said, following his gaze. The half-demon made quick work of the invisible bolts holding the door shut, and it sprang open.

"Yeah. Who is it? Your… demon?"

"Nah, she's in here." I tapped my head. "This is, um, another of the half-demons. I never asked your name," I said, slightly apologetic.

The half-demon blinked at me, surprise crossing her face. *"Anthea. Once. Most demons do not take on a name unless they intend to manifest, and us half-shadows least of all."*

"Anthea," I said. "Thank you."

It was unnerving to see tears in my eyes when my own were now dry. The half-demon and I stared at each other, and I had the strange feeling that I'd crossed some sort of boundary.

"Come on," I said to Leo.

"I don't like this," he said, ducking out of the box. "I don't remember her leaving. This feels… off."

"I'm suspicious that no one was guarding me," I said.

At that moment, the demon heart flared again, burning cold against my chest. Leo and I both flinched as the Darkworld struck, cold and merciless.

Demons.

"Shit," he said, looking around.

"We have to find the others!" I said.

"Cy's down that way, I think." Leo pointed vaguely down the corridor.

The half-demon—Anthea—led the way. She appeared as a blurred shadow, distorted by the blue lights that sprang up in the candles along the walls. As we followed her, more of the candles flared to life, and a thrill of horror went through me when I saw that, like the candles in Blackstone, the holders were alive. Harpies. The birds blinked bulging yellow eyes, spread black-feathered wings. Their talons and curved beaks gleamed in the candlelight.

"No freaking way," said Leo, skidding to a halt.

"Shield!" I said, and called on the Darkworld. Shadows moved around me, and Leo, catching on, helped me to pull the shield around us. Not a moment too soon. The harpies launched themselves into the air as one, and flew around in circles, letting out chilling cries. But they couldn't get past our shield.

We ran around a corner, still beneath the shield, and into another corridor of cells.

"Cy?" yelled Leo, and the walls caught his voice and threw it back at us.

A hoarse cry answered his call.

We found Cyrus in the last cell from the end, and Claudia, too. They'd been thrown in there together, and lay in a heap on the floor, Cyrus's head at Claudia's feet. Neither moved when we came to the door.

"Shit," said Leo.

I was already frantically directing magic at the door, melting the lock with ice-fire.

"Cy!" Leo shouted, as I forced the door open.

Claudia stirred feebly. "Took your time," she slurred.

"What did they do to you?" I said, squeezing through the gap in the door. Leo followed, and ran over to his brother.

"Cy!"

He grasped Cyrus by the shoulders and shook him, violently.

"Don't die on me. Don't you fucking dare."

Cyrus groaned. "What... the..."

I recoiled as I saw that his clothes were stained with

blood. He groaned again. Leo helped him into a sitting position, swearing softly.

The side of Cyrus's head was a mess of dried and fresh blood, as though he'd been struck with a heavy object, or perhaps when he'd landed on the stone floor. His arm hung at an angle, either fractured or broken. There was so much blood...

His eyes flickered open. "Goddammit, I feel rough."

"Thank hell," said Leo. "Come on—we have to go."

The harpies' screeches rang through the corridor, and although I knew they couldn't see us, the pendant's constant burning against my chest told me that the danger was still there.

Something dark had entered the tunnels. Whether the Venantium had invited it in or not hardly mattered. We needed to get out.

"Can you walk?" Leo helped his brother stand, whilst I awkwardly tried to help Claudia. She looked shaken up, but not seriously hurt. "They... threw us in here," she said, her voice slightly slurred. "Wanted you and Leo. Hurt him —to get to you."

"Bastards," said Leo through clenched teeth. "Well, they didn't get much chance to hurt me. I was only in that box for about five minutes. One mind-attack and I passed out."

I winced, wanting to hug him, but he was encumbered with Cyrus, and Claudia wasn't looking too clever either. She never sounded that incoherent even when she'd been drinking. I wondered if she was concussed. *This is bad. If there really are demons...*

"I can walk," Claudia insisted, slipping out from under my arm and stumbling ahead. I stayed directly behind her to make sure she didn't fall.

Leo, supporting Cyrus, followed us. I pulled the shield

like it was a cloak, ensuring it covered all of us. Harpies still swooped overhead, screeching and wheeling about. *Are they looking for us?* Or were they reacting to the Darkworld? With every pulse of the pendant against my chest, I felt the Darkworld stir like a tremor in the earth, a tidal wave, a force of nature, a living entity. Something big was moving around us. I felt it in my very bones. The demon inside me *trembled*, and it gave me a thrill of horror when I realised. She was scared.

I'd thought demons couldn't feel fear. Then again, I'd seen plenty lately to contradict that. Like Mephistopheles.

Our progress was painfully slow. Blood continued to drip down Cyrus's face, and Leo could barely keep him upright. Claudia was steadier, but I feared all of us were walking right into a trap.

At last, we came to a place I recognised: the corridor where we'd entered the meeting hall.

Where the hell is everyone? Silence. I looked at Leo, who leaned against a wall to take some of Cyrus's weight off him. Claudia sagged against the wall, too. I made a tentative step in the direction of the meeting room door, which was slightly open.

The half-demon appeared in front of us so suddenly, my heart tried to leap out of my throat.

"Don't do that!" I said to her, as she turned to face me.

"You can't stay here," she said. "You have to hide. All of you."

"Hide?" I echoed.

"He's looking for you, Ashlyn."

"Who?" My voice cracked. "Mephistopheles? Or Lucifer?"

Before Anthea could answer, someone came around the corner. Human.

Eileen Stirling now looked more like a car-crash

survivor than a high-class businesswoman. Her suit was in disarray, blood dripped from one arm, and her eyes caught me like twin daggers as she took in the sight of the four of us, two half-conscious, the other two stock still.

"You," she said quietly. "This is all your doing, Miss Temple. You've brought the devil to our doorstep."

"You brought it on yourself," I said. I was still petrified of her, but I couldn't show it. Not now.

"Defiant even in the face of death? I could kill any one of you with ease."

"You're a demonic magic-user," Leo said. "Tell me who's the bad guy here?"

"That would defeat the purpose, would it not?"

For a second, I thought the voice that pierced my mind came from Eileen Stirling. It wouldn't have surprised me in the slightest. But it was Anthea. I looked at her. She wore a sorrowful expression, but her violet demon eyes were cold.

"You." Leo took a step toward her. "You betrayed us, didn't you?"

"I am sorry, Ashlyn. But the Darkworld is my master, and I cannot disobey."

She raised her hands to pull the shadows up from around us, lifting the shield.

14

HELL REVEALED

The harpies attacked. I barely re-connected to the Darkworld before the talons pierced my skin. Ice fire flared from my palms and struck the creature, but another took its place. I leapt in front of Claudia before another could take her eyes out. Mrs. Stirling watched us, her face expressionless.

"What's the matter with you?" Leo yelled at her. "What the hell is even going on?"

"Is it not obvious?" she said, barely glancing at him as he threw a handful of fire at another harpy. They left her alone, only attacking us.

"You're the demons' bitch, is that it?" Leo gritted his teeth, drawing on the Darkworld to summon a wall of fire in front of Cyrus to protect his brother from the harpies' claws.

In a brief glance in that direction, I saw that Cyrus's face was greenish and his eyes half-shut.

"You insolent little devil," she said. "It is people like you who are responsible for mankind's sorry state. Demons act according to divine will. They will cleanse us, as written. This is the end of days."

"Bull. Crap." Leo took out another harpy, as I deflected another three from Claudia.

"Leo, look out!" I said.

Another harpy dived at him from the side and he barely dodged in time. The bird-crone flew at me instead, and I punched it in the face so hard the ice on my fist cracked.

"Good one!" Leo shouted.

But I could tell he was tiring, and so was I. The demon in me rose to the surface, but the Darkworld resisted, pushing her back. That had never happened before.

"Come on!" I shouted aloud, hitting three harpies in succession whilst the demon battered at the glass wall around my mind. I glanced up at Eileen Stirling, and one look at her face told me everything I needed to know. She was preventing the demon from taking over me.

"Stay out of my head!"

The Darkworld rose around me, shadows thickening, making it hard to see the harpies. Even Leo, beside me, disappeared. I fought blindly against anything that came near, and still felt the demon battering at the barrier…

I can't win this.

"If you want our help, Ashlyn, you must pay the price."

I heard the half-demon's voice, but still couldn't see her. Rage filled me at her betrayal. Imagine, a demon being dishonest. The irony. *Idiot.*

"Ash, I had no choice. But I can offer you a way out."

I don't make deals with demons! I shouted at her with my mind.

"You promised to help us."

I would, if you weren't trying to get me killed, like everyone else in the universe right now.

"You chose to waste your time, Ashlyn. You could have asked, and you would have found the answers you looked for."

I don't have time for any crap from you!

"Don't you want to know?"

Know what?

"Where Lucifer keeps his demon heart? Demons know everything."

My heart dropped. You're not serious.

"I am. I can take you to someone who knows, deep in the heart of the Darkworld. You will need to come with me."

What—into the Darkworld?

"Yes."

Look, I—even if you're telling the truth, I can't do that now. I have to help my friends.

"If you do not stop Lucifer, your world will fall to the darkness. Only the demons have the answers."

Fine. Fine, I'll come. Just stop the harpies attacking us!

"Do we have an understanding?"

I knew she asked much more than that. She wanted to make a deal. A deal with a demon would end in my death if it went wrong. But I had no choice.

Wait. I want this clear. You're not to harm my friends or me, or allow us to come to any harm, if I uphold my end of the bargain.

A brief hesitation. Then, *"Yes. I agree. Do you agree to uphold your end?"*

Yes.

For a minute, nothing happened. My surroundings remained wrapped in shadows darker than night. Then colour bled back into the world, slowly. First, the grey of the tunnel walls and floor. Then Leo's hand, reaching out, taking mine.

The harpies were gone, and so was Eileen Stirling. Claudia and Cyrus both slumped against the walls. Leo pulled me into a hug.

"Did—did you see what happened?" I asked.

"Couldn't see a thing. Where did she go?"

"I don't know. The half-demon…"

"The bitch. I'll kill her."

I swallowed. How was I going to tell him?

I can't.

You have to.

"Leo…"

"Come on," said Leo. "Let's get out. Better not push our luck further."

I knelt down beside Claudia. My heart sank when I saw a long line of claw-marks on her left arm.

"Shit. One of the harpies got her."

"Cy, too," said Leo, looking up at me. His face was ghostly pale. "Shit. Shit. Come on. We've gotta run. Now."

I nodded, pulling Claudia to her feet, her arm around my shoulders. I staggered the instant she stumbled into my back, but forced myself to stay upright. Leo looked just as off-balance, but it couldn't be helped.

The ten minutes it took us to get out were little more than a blur of pain and tension. Every muscle in my body ached, and I felt mentally bruised, too, from the beating my Darkworld connection had taken. It left no room for fear, not even that Eileen Stirling or the harpies would reappear, or that whatever had stirred up the Darkworld so much would rise up and attack us. All that existed for me was the struggle, and the presence of the others beside me.

Painfully slow, we inched up the stairs. An explosion of noise hit my ears as I leaned on the door to push it open, letting in a stream of natural light.

And firelight. Burning. The street outside was on fire, or so it seemed at first. But then I looked up and saw that the sky was an angry red, full of whirling shapes, which cast shadows red as blood on the ground below. The sky was burning.

"What the hell kind of magic is this?" said Leo.

"The End of Days."

Eileen Stirling stood a few feet away, near the Thames, gazing rapturously at the blazing sky.

"No shit," said Leo. "Okay, this is freaky."

"We have to get back to…" I cast a wary glance at Mrs. Stirling, but she was still preoccupied with the burning, demon-infested sky. Those had to be harpies up there, but some were larger. Other shadow-beasts, perhaps. *Holy hell.*

"Come on," I said.

We hadn't taken more than a few steps before chaos erupted all around us. *Venators* sprang up, as if from nowhere, surrounding us in a neat circle. *Shit. They used Influence to hide themselves.*

The men and women closed in, all wearing the same rapturous expression. It chilled me more than the burning red sky and the wheeling, screeching demons above.

"You are ours, Ashlyn Temple. The Righteous will prevail."

"Oh, gods above," said Leo. "I should have known it was you psychotic religious nuts behind this."

"You will be the first to die, Mr. Blake," said one of the *venators*. "The demons will cleanse the Earth of all sin, and mankind shall be reborn."

"Things will be as they once were, and demons and humans alike will perish."

"Yeah, that's very nice, but way outdated," said Leo. "Yeah, the world's a messed-up place, but wiping out humanity won't solve anything. Do you think the demons really care about sin and salvation or anything like that? These particular demons get a kick out of killing people, and I'm not gonna sit around and throw the blame onto the victims."

If ever I loved him, it was in that moment. Leo faced them without fear, speaking his mind even in the face of death. And I loved him for it. No matter what, these people couldn't take away that. Even if they killed us.

He stepped forward, conjuring a globe of fire. The *venators* closed in.

"You dare use magic against us? Magic is the work of the devil, put here to tempt humans."

Leo gave a short laugh. "What's that you're using on us, then? Skulking in shadows and conjuring pretty lights? Looks like magic to me."

"We have dedicated our lives to the will of the Almighty. He gave us our particular gifts to restore order and cast our judgment on sinners like you."

"See, this is what I hate about you people," said Leo. "You think you were chosen, that magic is some kind of gift? You've no more right than I do to harm people using magic."

"Don't talk about what you don't understand." Eileen Stirling approached. "May I have the honour of purifying Mr. Blake's soul myself?"

"Of course." The *venators* moved aside to let her into the circle.

At that moment, I set the shadows free. I'd felt them gathering around me as we made our way out of the tunnels, but hadn't been able to communicate with them in my exhausted state. But they'd been there, again, the half-people, rallying around Anthea. Ready to help us.

Now, the Darkworld responded, and the shadows darkened on the ground, moving up to meet the red sky in a clash of red and black. Blurred figures started to appear between the *venators* circling us.

"Die. Die. Die."

The Righteous panicked, looking for a way out. Now they were the ones trapped, encircled by walking shadows.

"What devilry have you unleashed?" Eileen Stirling screamed.

The demon stepped in, turning my vision to purple. *"Only what you've earned yourself, human."*

The shadows attacked. Red and black flashed across my violet-tinted sight, and the *venators* fell one at a time, without so much as a scream.

It was so fast. The shadows were silent killers, taking down each Righteous. I watched the rapture fade from their faces, replaced by the stillness of death.

Finally, Mrs. Stirling was the only one remaining. She looked directly at me, and the demon stared back.

"You know nothing, human," she said, using mind-connection to speak to Mrs Stirling directly.

Then the shadow-people closed in, hiding her from view. There was a deafening *snap*. Then, silence. The shadows receded again, and my vision went back to normal. The sky still burned red, but the Darkworld was gone.

I didn't know they could kill people.

"Only at the cost of our own lives," said Anthea. *"My kin gave up their lives for you. Think on that, Ashlyn."*

I staggered back, reeling in shock. Leo caught me. Cyrus had slid to the ground at some point during the chaos.

"I got you." Leo knelt down beside his brother. "We've gotta move!"

Cyrus was still breathing, but the harpy's claw-wound now burned black. I swore as I saw that Claudia's was the same.

"Ash! Leo!"

I looked up. Layla ran toward us, several people I didn't recognise behind her.

"Shit," she said. "Come on, guys, we have to get these two back to headquarters."

The others—presumably other sorcerers in hiding, although none looked familiar—lifted Cyrus and Claudia amongst them as Leo moved forward to check on his brother.

"What's going on up there?" I said to Layla. "How did you know to come here?"

"I got worried when you didn't come back, and I needed to go and buy supplies anyway. I saw the sky and thought the Venantium were under attack. The others are fighting—well, everywhere, really. It's so confusing. One second everything looks normal, and the next—"

She gestured at the sky, which burned as though the Rapture really was upon us.

"The *venators* took us captive," I said. "There was another group of the Righteous in charge, but they're all dead now. I don't know what happened to the rest of the Venantium…"

"There was an evacuation," said Layla. "I walked out into the middle of it, before the demons started attacking again. Then I came here. I got a bad feeling when I didn't see you with the others."

"Thank you," I said, earnestly. "I don't think we could have brought those two back alone."

"Yeah," said Leo, glancing over his shoulder from where he walked alongside the guy carrying his brother. "Do you have anything for harpy wounds?"

"Luckily, we do."

I breathed out. *Please. Don't let them die.*

"It'll be okay, Ash," said Leo, moving back to take my

hand, and sorrow took hold of my heart as I prepared to reveal the final, terrible truth.

"Leo," I said.

"Don't, Ash," he whispered. "Not now. Tell me when we get back. Please. Now's not the time."

I nodded, and squeezed his hand back, as we walked on under the blazing sky.

15

BURNING SKIES

Unease prickled down my spine as we walked alongside the Thames. Reflecting the sky, the water's surface burned and boiled like hellfire, and this was further reflected in the glass-walled apartments we passed. It was like walking through Milton's Hell —a nice little bit of irony for the Venantium, I imagined.

As we crossed the bridge, a sudden tremor went through the Darkworld. I felt it go through the demon, too —shuddering through my entire body. My head throbbed, my ears ringing, as an inhuman scream of pain and rage ripped through the Darkworld. The creatures in the sky spun in flight, black shapes being absorbed in a whirl of shadows that appeared in the middle of the sky. The blackness spread like ink over the red clouds, absorbing the harpies, shadow-beasts, and other monstrosities. The scream echoed, on and on, like a siren. I winced, covering my ears, but it didn't help because it was inside my head. I recognised the voice, even distorted by rage. Mephistopheles.

What happened? The shadows were clearing from the sky,

as though blown by a strong breeze. In a final gust, they were gone, and midnight blue replaced them. Night time. *How long were we down there?* It couldn't have been a full day–could it?

Leo's gaze met mine, his mouth set in a line.

Layla gasped, "What in seven hells was that?"

"The demon's angry," said Leo. "Really angry."

"Mephistopheles," I said. "Something made him really mad. The last time he screamed like that…" *Was when the fortune-teller killed him, sent him back to the Darkworld.*

I remembered the demon grinning through Howard's eyes, and my heart sank. *No.* If he was gone, then Howard was…

We crossed the road. I saw several people gathered ahead, looking in our direction. The *venators* stood throughout the main street, hidden in plain view from passersby, as though waiting for us. Hayley stood at the head of the group. *Shit.* Her face was flushed and she wouldn't meet my eyes. Anger surged within me at her betrayal.

"Well?" said Leo, once she was in earshot.

Layla and the others carrying Cyrus and Claudia slipped past the group and on toward Satan's Pit. The *venators* didn't try to stop them. All their eyes were on me.

"I'm sorry–" Hayley began.

"'Sorry' doesn't cover it," said Leo. "I'd hoped the demons killed you."

"There was only one demon," said another of the *venators*. "And we killed it."

"Look," said Hayley, "Jonathan Stirling came to power at a time when he was sorely needed. I couldn't demean him, not with the Venantium depending on him."

"I don't give a crap about your motives," said Leo. "You're going to leave us alone now, okay? Don't try and make excuses. Just get the hell away from us. And please tell me that Stirling creep met the same fate as his wife."

"His—"

"I take it the bastard's still alive?"

"He… er," someone said hesitantly. I recognised the *venator* as Freya. "He went after the remaining shadow-beasts. Said he'd take down Mephistopheles himself."

"I hope he fell in the Thames," said Leo. "You going to leave us alone now? Our friends are hurt."

Some of the *venators* tried to apologise as we walked past, but Leo brushed them off, and I wasn't feeling particularly generous, either.

We'd almost made it to Satan's Pit when someone grabbed my shoulder. I spun around, thinking it was a *venator* at first, then I took in her appearance. A dishevelled woman in her mid-forties, dirty-blonde hair, and prison-style getup.

Holy shit. It was Howard's mother. Two *venators* had her gripped by the shoulders, restraining her.

I stared at her, and she stared back. Did she know what had happened to her son?

"Ashlyn," she said.

I didn't say anything. This couldn't be happening. At our last encounter, after she'd escaped from prison, she'd told me to give Howard directions on how to find her, presumably meaning the underground shelter. But she'd not been there when we'd arrived. Howard had never seen her again. And now… he was gone. I glanced back at the *venators*, thinking of the scream.

"You said you weren't working with these scum," she said. "They killed him. They killed my son."

My insides lurched, and I looked around, trying to find someone to make eye contact with. My gaze landed on

Hayley, who hovered back. The others had already gone inside the club.

"Is Howard dead?" I asked her.

"Ashlyn... Howard was dead the instant Mephistopheles took him as a host."

"I want to know what happened here."

"You know. We fought. We beat the shadow-beasts back. And when we killed their leader, Mephistopheles, the attack stopped."

"Killed him," I repeated. "Where is he? Where is... Howard?"

"Gone." Howard's mother let out a whoop of laughter that sounded more like a cry of despair. "Gone! Burned him up good, didn't you?"

"When did she get here?"

"She was lurking around the Underground. Came right into the fight, but the demons left her alone. Mephistopheles... he tormented her. It's best that she come with us."

"Dead!" she cried. "Poor Howie. Dead."

Something wasn't right. I felt it in the prickling against my skin, not just because this woman made me wary, but because I was positive that somewhere nearby, the Darkworld had shifted.

I looked back into Howard's mother's eyes, and saw something flicker there. I tensed, taking a step back.

"Hayley," I said, without looking away. "What happened to Mephistopheles's demon heart?"

"His demon heart?" Hayley sounded taken aback. "I don't know. I would have expected... ordinarily we would have a member retrieve it for our collection, but under the circumstances... the body was almost entirely destroyed..."

"Idiot." I shelved away the horror at the mental image her words conjured for later. "Mephistopheles travels from one host to another in a minute. Haven't you learned your lesson from last time?"

"He burned up," she repeated. "There was nothing left."

"Meaning you didn't look." I surreptitiously called on my Darkworld connection, telling the demon to be at the ready. "Meaning you failed to notice, once again, what was directly in front of you."

I stabbed Howard's mother right between the eyes with a dagger of ice-fire.

The demon screeched, eyes suddenly shining vividly violet, demon heart smoking.

"How dare you, Ashyln!" Mephistopheles screamed.

Through our brief connection, a series of images hit me, one after another. Fire everywhere. Shadow-beasts, leaping out of the shadows. Chaos. In the centre stood a single figure, laughing, eyes aglow. Howard.

Then fire flared up from the ground. Hayley came into view, wielding a sword made entirely of writhing flames. She jumped at Howard, slashing from behind, and he was suddenly aflame. Mephistopheles's screech echoed through my ears. I would have swayed, fallen, but I wasn't looking through my own eyes. I was on the sideline, but at the moment Howard fell, I heard a scream from nearby —from me.

I realised with a thrill of horror that I was witnessing Howard's mother's last moments as a human.

She ran forward, and I moved with her. She stroked Howard's ruined forehead, and I saw the demon heart move, latch onto her hand...

The world came back into focus. Hayley gawped at me, as Howard's mother's body crumpled to the ground.

I swayed, disoriented. I could taste bile at the back of my throat.

"Ash!" And Leo was there, and he caught me before I fell.

"What—?" he began, as I went limp in his arms, my entire body trembling.

"She's dead," I choked out. "And so's…"

But I couldn't say it. Leo looked at the woman's body and back at me, mind working.

"Who is she?"

"Howard's mother," I said, swallowing. "She was possessed."

"Shit. Where's the demon heart?"

Fighting revulsion, I knelt down beside her and turned over the body. Her blank eyes stared up at me, and between them, the demon heart still smoked.

Icy hatred for Mephistopheles washed through me.

"What should we do with it?" said Leo, hovering over me.

"I'm going to have to take it," I said. "I'm the only one he can't get at. But if I let it go…"

I had to leave. Now. Where, I didn't know, but I couldn't risk Mephistopheles getting out. Besides, to get to the Darkworld, I had to summon a demon, and I couldn't do that here. I'd find some obscure field in the middle of nowhere, maybe…

"Ash, you aren't leaving."

I paused. Leo held my arm in a firm grip. How did he guess my thoughts?

"It's obvious what you want to do, Ash. But you can't go off alone. If he finds a host and attacks you…"

"Then it's better than him attacking any of you. He'll find a way out no matter what. It's what he does."

I picked up the demon heart, wincing as it burned my skin. I wished I could destroy it utterly… but as long as Mephistopheles remained in the Darkworld, he'd always be able to come back. All he needed was a demon heart and a willing host. *Shit. This really is impossible.*

I felt the demon stir at the back of my mind. *"It's not impossible, Ashlyn. If you hold the heart yourself, bind it with your own, he will be unable to use it to return to this world."*

Really? I asked, disarmed by the demon's response. I knew it was her, this time. Not the half-demon.

"Really."

I reached under my jacket for the pendant. It burned slightly, but not as much as Mephistopheles's. I held one heart in each hand, and, encouraged by the demon, pressed them together.

Both demon hearts glowed, one violet, the other pure white. Smoke curled off the surfaces, and before my eyes, they melded, colours flowing into each other, until they became one double-sided stone. I turned it over, wincing as the cold burned my skin. *Wow.*

"Ash? How did you do that?"

I'd forgotten Hayley and the other *venators* were watching. Unsurprisingly, they gaped at me like I'd just conjured a demon right in front of them.

"I fixed it so he can't come back," I said. To Hayley's blank stare, I said, "If any of you had the demon heart, he'd possess you in an instant. I'm trying to *help* you, not kill you. Even though you left me for dead in a dungeon."

I still shook all over. Perhaps it was irrational, but part of me thought that if we hadn't been stuck in the cells for so long, maybe we could have saved Howard…

"Ashlyn…" Hayley began.

I said, "Did any of you see Berenice? A girl with long black hair and a tattoo on her shoulder? She was with Howard…"

Hayley shook her head. "Sorry, no."

"Shit," I said. I looked back at Leo. "Do you think she's…?"

"I don't know," he said. "We can't exactly ask Mephistopheles. Maybe Layla knows."

Ignoring Hayley and the other *venators*, I followed him into Satan's Pit.

Leo all but ran for the corner and the stairs leading into headquarters. *He's worried about Cyrus,* I thought. So was I, and about Claudia, too. Harpy wounds needed to be treated as quickly as possible, otherwise they could cause paralysis and even death. I knew from experience how painful they were, too.

The medical bay was now in use, with the door flung wide open to let people in and out. Claudia and Cyrus weren't the only patients, and I saw other people bearing the jagged wounds of harpy talons. I had to shut my eyes before the sight of so much blood overwhelmed me.

I had to know if the others were okay. I moved through the room to where Leo knelt beside his brother. Claudia lay on the next bed over. Both were still breathing, to my intense relief.

Exhaustion hit me, almost knocking me off my feet. I felt completely drained, and it didn't escape my attention that part of the problem was the now twice-as-heavy pendant around my neck. As well as the faint heat radiating from it, I also felt its added weight, and a whisper at the back of my mind. *Shit. Please don't tell me Mephistopheles is in my head now.* That was all I needed.

I concentrated on the others instead. Leo needed me. So I pulled up a chair next to the bed. Leo didn't look up. He looked strangely fragile, and my heart broke for him. *He can't lose his brother. He's lost too much already.*

He didn't say a word until most other people had left the room, and we were the only visitors left. Even Layla had left, saying she needed to talk to Hayley. I hoped she'd kick her ass.

Leo didn't say a word. Silence stretched between us, a gaping hole of grief and shock. Both lost in our own thoughts, we waited for dawn.

16

HEART DIVIDED

L ayla came into the room again after a while. "You two should get some sleep," she said. "I'll watch them for a bit. There's nothing you can do now but wait. They're going to be fine as long as I keep applying the medicine."

I found myself thinking of the fortune-teller's collection of medicines. *I never went back to her tent,* I thought. Come to think of it, what had happened to it? Most likely it was still in Blackstone, hidden in plain sight, if she hadn't removed the Influence from it.

I wondered if the skies burned in Blackstone, if demons walked out in the open, terrorising the public. I wished there was something I could do.

Instead, I mumbled to Leo that I needed a shower. I did; I was filthy from the cell and the fight, my skin smeared with grime. Leo nodded mechanically. Bruise-like shadows gathered under his eyes. It was like the Leo I knew was fading away.

It was only when I was in the bathroom, the water

running and the door firmly shut, that I let myself break down.

My sobbing was lost in the flow of the water. I cried angry tears—both at myself and at Mephistopheles, the Darkworld, the universe in general. I gripped the amethyst around my neck, wincing as it seared my hand, and saw a diamond-shaped scar on my chest from where it had burned me.

My problems were only just beginning. If these were the physical effects after only a few hours, what would be the long-term effects, both physical and mental, of letting Mephistopheles share my demon heart? Of containing the monster? Did Lucifer know what had happened to his right-hand demon? Did he care?

Stupid question. Lucifer didn't care about anyone. He could never understand the worry for my friends that crushed my chest. He could never understand love, or real happiness.

I felt the chill of the Darkworld and a voice brush against my consciousness like a moth's wing.

"You can help them, Ashlyn. Return to Blackstone."

The demon. I'd tensed, expecting Mephistopheles to speak to me.

"Are you crazy?" I told the demon, rubbing my eyes. "I'd get killed. It won't help, anyway."

"You need to summon a demon. Have you actually thought about how you're going to go about finding out how?"

I frowned. "Talk to Gareth, maybe?"

"Even he won't have access to that information. No, you need to speak to a true demon, in the Darkworld. But in order to find Lucifer's demon heart, you must return to Blackstone, where it lies."

"That's completely insane. I'd be walking right into Lucifer's hands. How do I know he doesn't know what I'm planning to do?"

"He hasn't read your mind. I would know; I'm part of it."

"Good to know. Since when did you become so snarky and obstinate?"

"I am a reflection of you, Ashlyn."

"Cheers," I muttered. "Never mind, anyway. Black-stone's a death trap. I'd die before I got within a foot of Lucifer."

"Time is on your side. Lucifer is no longer there, as he's targeting the venators. He's looking for something. What... I don't know. But that is what is whispered in the Darkworld."

"Glad I have someone to keep me up to date on the gossip." I shivered. The demon heart felt cold and heavy against my chest, and another consciousness prickled at the edge of my awareness. I pulled the pendant off and set it on the edge of the sink, watching it warily as I stepped into the shower. Even though I didn't speak aloud, I felt less ridiculous talking to myself when it was half-drowned out by running water.

"Are you sure you can keep him out? I refuse to let Mephistopheles hurt anyone else. Least of all through me."

"Yes, I am sure. But you'll have to move fast."

I ran my hands through my hair to get the dirt out. No matter how hard I scrubbed, I didn't feel clean.

"So I have to walk into Lucifer's lair and somehow get hold of the knowledge of how to summon a demon—I'm assuming it isn't the kind of thing they leave lying around, is it? Is there a demon summoning manual?"

"You won't need any book, or even to contact a sorcerer. The Barrier is weak enough that demons will flock to you as soon as you get near. Lucifer has reversed the Venantium's barriers so that they attract rather than repel demons. A nice irony. You only need to contact a demon you trust, and they will instruct you."

"What? A demon I trust? What planet have you been

on? I know demons don't get human feelings, but I'm not exactly buddies with the Darkworld."

"There is one to whom you have spoken, is there not?"

"Apart from Mephistopheles? Wait…"

I'd had… a sort of conversation with a demon in Redthorne, once, if that counted. I wouldn't even begin to know how to go about finding it again, though—especially if malicious demons were the ones ruling Blackstone now.

"I don't even know its name. Kind of an important detail."

"I asked. Belial is your demon."

"*My* demon?"

"The demon you seek."

"Demons. Honestly. I don't know why I trust you, even if you're half of me."

"That is not quite how our relationship works… but no matter. You need to leave as soon as possible."

"What about the others? I have to leave them here?"

"It's for the best, Ashlyn. If they come with you, they leave themselves vulnerable to demonic influence. Yet… I think you should let Leo come with you, if he asks."

"You do? But I thought you said it would put him in danger."

"It is unavoidable. But you need someone you trust, to watch your earthy body whilst you are in the Darkworld and to ensure that nothing harms you. Otherwise, you will be unable to return, and will be trapped in the Darkworld, half-conscious, unless you are willing to take on another host."

Meaning, possess someone. *Hell. Why am I doing this?*

"You are the last hope for demonkind, Ashlyn."

Not helping. If I didn't return, I failed the whole world. Not only would I be doomed to an eternal existence in the Darkworld, a half-life like the shadows had, forever haunted by the memory of being human—the world as everyone knew it would end. Humans would lose their freedom to Lucifer's demons. No one would be able to stop him.

And Mephistopheles would hunt down and kill anyone who had any connection with me.

"Do the demons want me to break the Barrier? I wouldn't see it as an advantage for anyone other than the shadows. They want to be free, but the demons wouldn't be immortal anymore, right?"

"True. But you would be surprised. This was never a fate demons chose for themselves. The terms of the Barrier were dictated by sorcerers. It was the humans who controlled it."

Always the humans, in the end. Was she trying to make me see them as the bad guys?

"Only the truth, that both are culpable. But one particular human must be stopped, and that's why it is so important that you do exactly as I say, Ashlyn."

"You know, I don't think you've ever been so talkative before."

"I speak on behalf of... Anthea. She assumed, rightly, that you would not want to speak to her again."

"Damn right, the traitorous bitch."

"I don't want to demean humans again, but they made her what she is. She envies you, perhaps not as much as her sister did, but it is there. Unlike we half-shadows, you are the master of your own fate."

"Doesn't feel like it right now."

"It will. I think you have a visitor."

I could hear knocking from outside the bathroom. I quickly finished rinsing my hair, dried off, and opened the door to Leo, wearing only a towel.

His jaw practically hit the floor. It might have been amusing under other circumstances. Like without the imminent death and the demon in my head. But now, all I wanted was him. He gave a gasp of surprise as I pinned him to the wall and kissed him, barely stopping for breath.

"Good shower, then?"

"Sorry," I said.

"Don't apologise. Enjoy life when you can, right?"

The bitter edge to his tone didn't escape me.

"Leo, they're going to be fine. Promise."

"It's not that. It's you. Please, Ash, tell me what you're thinking."

I sighed, pulling him over to sit on the bed. "Okay. It's not good news."

And I told him everything that the demon had told me, including my vow to help the half-demons and what that really implied.

"Wouldn't that just be helping Lucifer?" he said. "He wants to break the Barrier, right?"

"Yeah, but he doesn't realise it means he can die. He has no idea what he's doing, really."

"Do *you*? I mean, the demon? You know going into the Darkworld might kill you. Or you might end up like the fortune-teller…"

"Or the half-demons. I know. I'm not expecting a miracle. But if I can just find out how to break the Barrier, and where Lucifer's demon heart is—the two things are linked together. That's what I need to plan. He can read my mind, except when I'm in the Darkworld, so what I need to do is get there as quickly as possible. Then I need to speak to a demon."

Leo sucked in a breath. "Which demon? Ash, I know you've talked to them, but you don't need me to tell you they get a kick out of tricking people."

"I know, but I have, well, my demon steering me in the right direction. I'm more worried about the breaking the Barrier part—I'll have to be in the real world to do it, so that means I'll *have* to come back—assuming nothing possesses my body in the meantime..." I glanced at him. His eyes were fixed on the floor, mouth a tense line.

"I get it," he said, heavily. "You need someone to watch your back. You need me."

I studied the floor, feeling awful for even saying this. "I'd never ask you to put yourself in danger for me. I promised after last time that there was no way I could even bear to face that situation again. I can't deal with it. But... there are so few people I trust anymore. You're the only person I trust who's in fighting condition right now, and the longer I delay it, the worse it'll get. Believe me, I'll fight the higher demons themselves to keep you safe."

"You might have to," he said darkly. "I'm more than a little suspicious about the fact that they haven't been heard of since we left Blackstone. They had the perfect opening to lay waste to the Venantium here, but they left it all to Mephistopheles. I mean, I know higher demons aren't usually particularly interested in destroying humans, but I thought, given that Lucifer has them under his thumb, that it'd be more obvious they're here, in our world, ready to unleash chaos."

"Not chaotic enough for you already?" I said. "I know what you mean. It's weird. But they've been around for ages and haven't done anything major. We didn't even know they were in the Venantium. Maybe that's Lucifer's intention. Fear, and whatever it was you said the other day."

The memory of that conversation triggered an unexpected lump in my throat. It was the last time we'd seen Berenice, before Howard had...

No. Don't think about it.

"Perhaps. Either way, I want to know you're absolutely sure that this is the right thing to do. I trust you with my life, but that demon inside you? Not so much. I know you say she *is* you, but well, some of the things she's done... she's not human, Ash."

"I know that," I said. "I was just talking to her, and sometimes it is like she's a totally different person. But she'd never deceive me. Not like the half-demon or any of the other demons. That much I'm sure of. We need to go to Blackstone."

A pause.

"Okay. Well, we need a plan. Lucifer can read our minds, and I'm willing to bet either he or one of his minions will notice the instant we set foot there."

"Yeah, that's what she told me," I said. "It's because he's reversed the Barriers. But apparently he's looking for something. She doesn't know what, but she's heard rumours. He's focused on something else, so if we act fast..."

"And do what, exactly?"

"Find a demon. Get it to help me into the Darkworld. Get the information I need about how to break the Barrier and beat Lucifer. Come back and do it. Simple." I sighed. "I know it sounds impossible, but she won't leave me be. Neither will Anthea and the other half-demons. They seem to think I can do it, and they won't stop plaguing me until I do. It's like they know something I don't, but they seem to think it'll be easy."

"Demons have a different definition of 'easy,' I don't doubt," said Leo. "But it's pretty obvious that things are snowballing. Demon attacks are happening on a global scale now. If we die in the attempt, well, I guess it's better than surrendering to the demons."

"It's always better," I said. "But there's only one way to stop demons from using my magic after I'm dead." I looked at him, right into his eyes.

Leo frowned. "You can't be serious."

"There's no other way. The last thing I want is a demon using my body as a puppet after I'm dead. I don't believe in an afterlife, but if my ghost or whatever saw my body turned into Lucifer's plaything, I'd be pissed."

"You realise what you're asking me to do?" Leo shook his head. "No one should ever have to."

"We'd better hope it won't come to that," I said, quietly, placing my hand over his. "You know that if the same thing happened to you…"

"It's not the same."

"I know. I know."

I buried my head in his shoulder. The image of Melivia Blackstone, burning alive, filled my mind. That was what I asked Leo. I couldn't kill myself or destroy my human body, if I was separated from it. The only way to ensure I wouldn't be possessed, that the enemy wouldn't use my magic… would be for Leo to kill me first.

17

SEEKING DARKNESS

I t was 7:00 a.m. when we fell into bed, and we only slept a short time. Even our embraces were brief, shadowed with the burden of what was to come. Around midday, I decided it was time to break the news to the others.

Leo stood up when I did, and watched in silence as I packed my meagre possessions back into my rucksack. Maybe Melivia's diary would have a final use. Who knew? I dressed quickly in my comfiest, most practical clothes, a long-sleeved top and jeans, and my jacket. I might have forgotten to retrieve the pendant from the bathroom, were it not for the persistent chill that dragged me toward it, always lurking on the edge of my consciousness. I hung it around my neck, and felt an uncomfortable headache-like sensation brush over my temples.

"Right," I said, as much to myself as to Leo. "It's go time."

"Wait."

One last kiss, breathless and desperate, and I knew that I would always remember this moment, that if I died today, it would be the moment I recalled in my last seconds. One thing demons couldn't take away. The one thing demons could never have.

"Should we say goodbye to Gareth and Layla?" I asked Leo as we left the room.

He hesitated. "We should, really. They've done a lot for us," he said.

Yeah. They'd sheltered us, at the risk of their lives. The time for letting others take the burden was over. I had to face this, ultimately, alone.

I pushed open the door to the infirmary. Layla sat by Cyrus and Claudia, who both appeared to be sleeping. Her laptop was propped open on her knees. Gareth sat against the wall behind his own laptop screen.

"Hi," said Layla. "I didn't want to disturb you, but, well, there's bad news."

My heart plummeted. "What now?" I said.

In response, she turned her laptop around so I could see it. YouTube played a video of a scene of destruction in what looked like a city centre. High-rise buildings surrounded a circle that blazed with a flickering flame, like a colossal bonfire enveloping several roads.

"In China. Demon attack. Same thing happened in Germany and Los Angeles. He's attacking the big cities all over the world. Anywhere with a high population of sorcerers."

"Shit," I said, my throat dry. He could get anywhere in the world, in a heartbeat. No one cold outrun that.

Layla rubbed her eyes, yawning. "Well, guess all we can do is sit back and wait for him to attack us again. Suppose it's only a matter of time."

"Actually…" I said, swallowing. "We're leaving. Leo and me. We're going back to Blackstone."

"You're what?" said Gareth, peering out from behind his screen.

I gave a quick rundown of our plan, ignoring Gareth's attempted interruptions.

Layla sank back in her seat, like the fight had gone out of her. "Okay. Right now, I'd take any chance at hope. I'll tell the others when they wake up."

"Thank you." Leo nodded at his brother. "Wish I could say a proper goodbye to the tosspot. Tell him he's an idiot from me."

"I will do," said Layla.

"Say goodbye from me, too," I said. "Wait... I hate that word."

"Me too," said Leo. "In fact, forget the goodbyes. Tell them we're coming back."

"Yeah," I nodded. "Tell them that."

"Okay," said Layla, putting her laptop down. "I wish I could help."

"Watching these two is the best thing you can do," I said. "Watch out for the *venators*. Jonathan Stirling is probably still alive out there somewhere."

"I'm saving all my energy for when he comes grovelling to me for shelter," said Layla. "Trust me, I haven't run this place for years without learning a thing or two."

"Cool." I turned to Leo. "Let's go."

"Bye!" Gareth waved at us. He looked a bit teary-eyed. *Probably doesn't expect us to come back.* Not that I did, either, but I was so used to putting on a brave face that maybe it didn't matter. It gave the others hope if they thought we were confident in our abilities.

Leo and I climbed the stairs into Satan's Pit and, once out the front doors, didn't look back. It would only make it harder to leave. I looked around, thinking of all the things we could have done in London. There were a lot of things

I'd wanted to do, places I'd wanted to go. I'd wanted to travel the world. I'd wanted to live life. But desire wasn't enough. *You're half-demon. You could never have had a full human life.*

Almost unconsciously, we both pulled on Influence to walk through the crowds and into the tube station without being noticed. We skipped the queues and climbed onto the tube, and once at Euston, onto a train north. Towards Blackstone.

"ASH, WAKE UP!" Leo shook me. "We're nearly there."

I blinked awake. The fields we'd passed for hours gave way to buildings, and I recognised Preston town centre. We had to change to get the train to Redthorne here.

"Maybe it'd be easier to summon the demon there," I said, stretching. "It's just outside Lucifer's range, and it's where I first met that demon, anyway." To think I'd ever considered they might leave me alone. Right now, our hope rested with an enemy who practically had an evolutionary advantage over us. And I'd dragged Leo right into the middle of it. But I knew better than to ask him to stay behind.

"Good point," said Leo. "Okay. Redthorne it is."

We changed trains without a hitch, but I started to get a creeping feeling once we got near Redthorne. It began like an itch, like the Darkworld brushing my consciousness, cold prickling at my skin, and worsened the more time passed. As the train rattled along the line, my hairs stood on end, and I winced as the demon heart burned cold against my skin. It pulsed like a beating heart, growing in intensity until I was unable to stop myself from grabbing at it with my hand.

I stifled a cry as it burned my skin, and let it drop to hang in front of my coat. A diamond-shaped blister marked my palm.

"Ash!"

"Ouch," I said, blinking back tears, and winced as not only the crystal, but the entire pendant pulsed again, the string burning my neck. I reached to pull it over my head, but there was no need. The string had burned away, and the crystal fell into my palm.

"Shit," said Leo. "Put that somewhere safe."

"I would, if it wasn't burning me," I said, shoving it into my coat pocket.

"Do you want me to—?"

"No!" I said. "That's exactly what Mephistopheles wants me to do. I hand this over, you become his plaything again."

"Sorry," said Leo. "Just trying to help."

"I know." I took his hand. His fingers trailed over the burn mark on my palm, and helped alleviate the paradoxically searing coldness that radiated from it.

"We need to get off here," he said, glancing out the window. Characteristically, rain fell heavily, obscuring the platform in a haze of grey.

"No umbrella," I said. "Fine forward planner I am!"

"No one takes on hell with an umbrella," said Leo.

"Now that's something I'd like to see," I said, stepping onto the platform.

A chill wind swept over me like we'd just stepped into an Arctic wilderness. Leo shivered.

"Is Lucifer paying homage to Dante's ninth circle of hell?" he said.

"Probably. I expected rivers of fire, to be honest." My teeth chattered.

Leo's hand was still warm in mine as we left the station.

Rain pooled in corners and dripped from roofs. Everything looked grey and washed out. Few people were around. Hardly anyone walked in the streets, and most of the shops had an abandoned look. I wondered if the ordinary people knew the reason behind the coldness, had the slightest inkling that they lay in the centre of a plot to wipe out humankind. And I'd thought *I* had it bad. At least Leo and I knew what was happening, even if it seemed like the only solution would be a miracle.

I looked around for dark spaces, a clue as to where I might find the demon. *They must know we're here.* My mind was tuned into the Darkworld, and any demon nearby would be able to sense our presence, read our thoughts. I pushed that particular notion aside and peered down an alley I remembered seeing the demon in before.

Nothing. Not so much as a stray shadow. *Something's wrong.* In my pocket, the demon heart stirred, and I felt my hand move toward it of its own accord. *Stop that.*

My hand didn't listen, my fingers scrabbling at my pocket and clasping the smooth, dead-cold stone.

Let go!

My hand thrummed with the vibration as the crystal shook, but my fingers still gripped it, my hand pulling it from my pocket and raising it up to the centre of my forehead. What the hell was happening? We were close to Lucifer… and Mephistopheles was his right hand demon. And his heart was linked to mine now. I scrabbled at it with my fingers, tried desperately to pry Mephistopheles's heart from my own, but it was no use—my control slipped by the second.

No!

My hand moved the last few inches, pressing the demon heart to the centre of my forehead, directly between my eyes. The demon woke.

Violet demon vision washed across everything, including Leo, as he shouted my name. I could no longer hear his voice. Another sound dominated, and it took me a moment to realise that it spoke in my head.

"Come to me, Ashlyn."

"No!" I tried to say, but Mephistopheles tightened his grip and a sharp pain shot through my head.

The closest I'd felt to this was when I'd tried to fight the block on my memories—it was like an intense migraine, but worse. Shadows crept into my vision. I could no longer feel my body, though I saw my arms dangling, dead weights. The only sensation was the cold pain radiating from the centre of my forehead. Laughter echoed in my ears.

"This is going to be fun, Ashlyn," Mephistopheles spoke in my ear. *"Let's break him, together."*

No!

Ice-fire sprang to my palms. Leo stared at me, mouthing my name. *Get away!* I tried to yell. Crap. Somehow touching the demon heart had let Mephistopheles *possess* me. *Let go!*

As Mephistopheles manipulated my body, I fought with everything I had. The blue flames danced from one palm to the other, swirling around as Mephistopheles held up my hands, seeming to admire the flames.

"I liked being able to use real *fire,"* he said. *"You haven't tapped half your potential, though, Ashlyn."*

Get out of my head. Even without control of my body, fear rocked every part of me. I couldn't be possessed. So why—?

"Would you prefer I took him, instead? You're both going to die, anyway." He paused. *"What would you do to save her, Leo Blake? Would you serve a higher demon, as your father did? I am the next great higher demon, and I can offer you more than the others ever*

could. You wanted immortality before, didn't you? You wanted an eternity with the girlfriend you never truly understood?"

Leo's mouth moved. I made out the words, *No fucking way.*

That was *my* Leo.

"She was a fool to bind her heart to mine. Her humanity is gone. She is mine."

He's lying! I shouted, praying desperately that somehow, he'd hear me, the real me. But he gave no sign that he had. He glared at Mephistopheles, and summoned fire to his own hands.

"Want to fight, do you? You know that fire will be fatal to her human body. I, of course, will live on in the Darkworld."

Stop! I screamed, powerless. We'd brought Mephistopheles right near his master, and he must have grown strong enough to influence me where he hadn't before. *No. Leo.*

"Ashlyn, it would be much less tiresome if you stayed out of this. Master Blake and I have a score to settle."

And he threw the ice-fire at Leo.

Just in time, Leo dodged aside. Shadows swirled around him, forming a shield, as Mephistopheles used my Darkworld connection to summon a swathe of blackness. My demon sight could sense him, but I knew he wouldn't be able to see a thing.

Stop.

"Ashlyn, I grow weary of you. Be quiet."

Pain lanced through my forehead and the world faded. I floated. The Darkworld was all around me, and I could make out every shadow's definition, different shades overlapping in a way I'd never noticed before. Figures surrounded me, blurred apart from their vivid, violet eyes. Demons.

Pain hit again and I flashed back to reality—to the

alleyway and Leo, as he laid screaming on the ground. His wrists and ankles were pinned down by ice, and as I watched in numb horror as Mephistopheles threw ice fire at him, hitting him square in the chest.

As I screamed, pain pierced my own forehead again and I was swept back into the Darkworld. The shadows moved closer this time, voices murmuring my name. These were no half-demons but the real thing. The Darkworld wanted me.

No! Leo!

I wrenched myself away. The real world came back, but blurred, like I couldn't maintain a grip on it. Mephistopheles used my body to kick Leo, my foot coated in ice, over and over. Leo's eyes were closed, clenched fists pinned at his sides, a grimace of pain on his face.

"What the hell is going on here?"

The real, human voice cut through the pain. Even Mephistopheles paused, shock emanating from him. A girl stood at the mouth of the alleyway. With blurred vision, I couldn't make out her face—but that voice sounded familiar.

"Ash, you're pathetic. Kick that bastard demon out of your head or I'll do it for you."

Something clicked into place. *Berenice?*

18

WITH DEMON EYES

"**S**eriously, Ash," she said. "Get a grip on yourself or I'll introduce you to a world of pain."

I felt Mephistopheles stir, but Berenice's presence had distracted him. I moved—and my hand actually moved where I told it, to my forehead. I barely felt the pain as I pulled the demon heart away.

My own vision came back. I drew in a deep, shuddering breath. Tears crowded my eyes, and I dropped to my knees beside Leo. Smoke rose from the ice-fire brands on his skin, but his eyes focused on me and a painful smile crossed his face.

"Beat him, Ash," he croaked.

I clenched my fist around the demon heart and realised that I could still feel a cold pressure on my forehead. I only held Mephistopheles's half. *Burn.* My hand came alive with fire. I directed it into the demon heart, into the minute atoms holding the crystal together. Right now, I wanted to utterly destroy it—crush Mephistopheles into a million pieces.

The piece of stone crumbled, and as I opened my hand, the rain washed the ashes from my palm.

I could feel the rain again. It plastered my hair to my forehead, dripped into my eyes to mingle with the tears. I'd hurt Leo. *Really* hurt him. His skin still smoked.

"He's not gone," I said, sniffling. "I only sent him back to the Darkworld."

"Oh, boo hoo," said Berenice. She wore her characteristic at-odds-with-the-world, disdainful expression, one I'd never thought I'd be glad to see. "Your boyfriend's alive. You've got that much."

I winced. *Howard.* She must know he was dead. But... I'd thought she was terrified of Mephistopheles, resigned to his ruling the world. Her behaviour didn't add up.

"How did you get here?" I said, to distract from the uncomfortable silence.

"Oh, I just decided to pay a visit..." Her face twitched, and I saw the raw pain beneath the surface. "Mephistopheles... he tormented me a bit, but when Lucifer ordered him back to London, he left me behind."

"And you just... escaped?" said Leo, through teeth clenched in pain. He managed to sit up, wincing.

Berenice stepped back "Yeah. Lucifer isn't really keeping track of his prisoners at the moment. He doesn't need to."

"He's not?" I said. "Will he know we're here?"

She shook her head. "Hard to tell. His minions are sometimes listening, but not always. He might not even notice you in Blackstone, but he knows when someone goes into the tunnels."

"I don't get it," I said. "I thought he was, you know, all seeing."

A moment passed. Berenice shook her head again. "He doesn't have full control over the higher demons. To say they're being a bit uncooperative is an understatement."

"Really?" I said.

She looked at me, the trace of a smile on her face. "Demons are a tricky bunch, and higher demons don't cave into people without good reason. Even Lucifer."

Wait, what? "I thought a demon's contract was absolute," I said.

Berenice gave a short laugh. "Oh, the demon always gets their way. The human, not so much."

"Since when do you know so much about demon contracts?" said Leo. He held his arm outstretched, which struck me as odd, until I realised he was letting the rain fall onto the burn, soothing it. Another pang went through me. *I did that.* No, Mephistopheles did it.

"I know because I'm in one," said Berenice, and pain flashed into her eyes. Her hands curled into fists, and she bowed her head. "I know because I've been scared every damn minute of every damn day for the past four years of my life."

Leo eyed her, confusion furrowing his brow. "You made a deal with Lucifer?"

"I made a deal with Mephistopheles, when I was sixteen years old. He killed two of my friends and cornered me. I would have said anything to spare my own life. And I did. He owns me."

"He doesn't," said Leo, face a mask of horror. Of course, he hadn't been here when she'd confessed to Claudia and me just… a couple of weeks ago?

"He does," she said, lifting her head to glare at both of us. The rage burning in her eyes actually made me take a step backward. "He owns me, and the only reason I'm not crawling on my knees begging him to spare me right now is because he fucking murdered my boyfriend." Fire shot from her fist, and Leo and I backed out of the way as she punched the wall, leaving a black burn mark. Panting heavily, hand smoking, she turned on us again. "So yeah, I'm fucking angry."

"He's dead," I said, ineffectually. "Mephistopheles. I burned his demon heart to ashes."

Berenice glared at me. "He's far from dead. As long as the Darkworld is there, as long as the Barrier is there… he can't die. 'Cause part of him's inside me, and when he dies… so do I."

No. That can't be true. "But you're still alive."

"I said if he *dies*. He's not dead, and the Barrier makes sure of that. But I'm going to die as soon as Lucifer breaks the Barrier."

"He still means to do that?" I said, exchanging a glance with Leo.

"Hell, yeah. It'll let him unleash his demons on the world. Supposedly. But it's not his priority. He has control over the Darkworld already, and his next master plan is to figure out how to tame those higher demons. I got to hear it in excruciating detail from Mephistopheles."

A lump rose in my throat. "Berenice…"

"Don't you feel sorry for me, you sap. I've known demons are going to kill me for four years. Now I guess I've finally accepted it. I'm not sorry. I just want to take at least one of those bastards down with me." Defiance flared in her eyes.

"You…"

"Told you. I'm fine. Howard knew about it, too. That's why he gave himself up first." Her eyes flashed, and tears glittered on her lashes. "That. Fucking. Idiot. Like us both being dead will solve a thing."

He loved her that much. I knew then why she'd accepted her death. Not because Howard was gone, but maybe it was possible to die with no regrets. I didn't expect to see tomorrow. But I loved Leo. He loved me—human, demon, or both. Nothing else mattered.

"Anyway," said Berenice, blinking the tears away. "Going to tell me why you're here? I take it you didn't just feel nostalgic and want to go back to uni."

"No," I said, hesitantly. "We're here to summon a demon."

Berenice raised an eyebrow. "Didn't you hear a word I said? Demon contracts are absolute."

"I'm already in one," I said. "I'm neck-deep in shit as it is. This is all I can do now. The demons have the answers. I need to get into the Darkworld."

"Holy fuck, you're serious." She blinked a couple of times. "Well, *that'll* draw Lucifer's attention like a magnet. Don't blame me when it goes horribly wrong."

"Believe me, I know. But I have to do it. Are there no demons here at all? Apart from Mephistopheles," I added.

Berenice paused. "They'll be hanging back. To summon one you need a name, anyway."

"Belial," I said, and felt a sudden chill rush over my skin.

"Now you've done it."

"What—wait!"

But shadows were already gathering in the alley, sweeping toward me. I held up my hands and they stopped, a foot away. Leo gaped at me.

"I didn't mean to do that," I said.

"Tough shit," said Berenice, with a short laugh. "You've got your demon now."

Violet eyes stared out of the darkness, and the demon's cold voice cut through my mind.

"I thought you would never come back, Ashlyn."

"Well, I'm here," I said. My voice came out steady, to my surprise.

"You have a favour to ask?"

"You should know. You can read my mind."

"You must speak the words aloud. Such is the nature of a contract."

"Demons," I muttered. "Okay. I want to go into the Darkworld."

"And your reason?"

"To speak to someone who might know how to beat Lucifer."

"A suicide mission."

"It's the only way."

"If that is the case... I see you are already wearing your demon heart."

My hand brushed my forehead. The crystal was still embedded in my skin. It didn't hurt, but felt strange to feel soft skin one second, hard crystal the next.

"Now you need to contact your guide."

"Guide? I thought you were my guide."

"You need to speak to someone who has done this before."

Anthea. Of course.

"I don't want to speak to that bitch," I said. "How about a different half-demon?"

"I will ask, but it may be that they will overpower your will."

"Wait."

But the eyes faded from the dark space. Ice began to crystallise on my hands as the Darkworld moved in closer, surrounding me on all sides. I could no longer see Leo or Berenice.

"Ash!" Leo shouted from behind the darkness.

"I'm here!" I said. "Quit it!" I told the Darkworld, but it continued to move in, shadows lengthening like grasping fingers. "Wait…"

My hands were numb, and the ice travelled up my arms, numbing them, too. It was like my own magic had turned on me and was slowly freezing me into a block of ice.

The demon spoke in the back of my mind. *"Relax, Ash. You're passing into the Darkworld."*

But I didn't want—

My vision turned violet as the shadows formed a complete sphere around me. It was like looking at the night sky, peppered with stars, but everywhere, like floating in outer space. I was reminded of a certain passage from *Paradise Lost*: *...no light, but only darkness visible...*

This was darkness visible, lit only by itself. It unfolded around me like a map, and now I could see different shades amongst the shadows... I would have closed my eyes, but I had no eyes, no body, because this was all in my head...

But it wasn't. An entire landscape of shadows spread before me, as real as I was. A shadow-path unfolded, although there was no need for one because I couldn't walk, couldn't move. I was everywhere and nowhere, all at the same time. Perhaps this was my mind's way of processing the impossible paradox of the Darkworld.

I focused on the apparently solid shapes, however insubstantial they might be. Outlines of shadow-mountains towered over shadow-fields and valleys; a shadow-forest of trees curled around the path, forming before my eyes, until I stood in a clearing surrounded by night. I was reminded of Dante, wandering off the track and onto a path to hell. Except there was no one here but me.

Then I saw the eyes. Countless violet specks shone in the darkness, and once I noticed them, they noticed me, too. My mind was open, and I felt the consciousness of thousands brush past, like people passing by on the street. But all focused on me.

Strange how I'd always imagined the Darkworld as a lifeless, empty place, when right now, it seemed anything but lifeless. Overwhelmed, I retreated to a corner of my mind and tried to pretend it wasn't exposed like a book left open for anyone to pick up and read.

"Ashlyn."

I flinched as Belial's consciousness brushed mine. Now that it was the only sense I possessed apart from limited sight, it made me doubly sensitive.

"You will adjust in time, Ashlyn."

I couldn't feel my own demon, but amongst so many other awarenesses, I might not even recognise her. The thought made me feel even more vulnerable and alone. I drifted in an endless sea, and as that thought crossed my mind, the landscape shifted, becoming sea-like. Black water rippled with shining eyes, all still focused on me like torch beams.

I flinched away. It was the manifestation of every moment of self-conscious insecurity I'd ever had, multiplied sevenfold. I remembered the crippling anxiety and paranoia I'd suffered in childhood, when I hurried through the school corridors with my head bent, feeling that there were a hundred pairs of curious eyes on me, convinced people were whispering about me, judging me. Now there *were* a thousand eyes upon me, and every one of them had just witnessed that old school scene dragged up from the depths of memory.

Now they watched my panic. Every thought I tried to suppress caused another to bubble to the surface. Bad memories, all of them. Being bullied at school. Enduring teasing from the other kids. Being shouted at in class. Stupid, petty things I thought I'd forgotten. But it was like something had pulled a plug and unleashed a tsunami of memories. One led to another in an endless, swirling haze that pulled me in, just long enough to feel the sting and hurt of that particular memory, then spat me out again.

It was nothing like when I'd visited Leo's memories or Claudia's memories. These weren't like video reels. They were too intense, too vivid—far more real than the blackness around me. My own mind held me captive, and I was powerless to resist.

I revisited a childhood memory that had shaped every other nightmare I'd had since, the time I'd got lost in the woods behind Aunt Eve's house, or the woman I'd believed to be my Aunt Eve. Even here, inside my own mind, my memory of her was hazy, blurred by subliminal magic.

Alone in the forest. Running, feet beating on a narrow path, my own ragged breathing echoing in my ears. With memory came sensation, claustrophobia enclosing me like a vice. Branches arched over my head, footsteps sounded behind me, but whenever I turned, heart pounding, there was no one there.

Wake up! a voice told me. *You're dreaming. It isn't real. Wake up.*

It was my own voice, and that much was enough to pull me away from the forest. I wasn't sure whether I'd rather be there, or surrounded by a thousand glittering eyes.

Ignore them, Ash. I'm here.

Where did you go?

I never left.

Even unable to see her, I felt bolstered. *Thanks.*

You don't need to thank me, Ashlyn. Think about what you're here to do.

I'd lost sight—if the term was applied loosely here—of Belial, and it was beyond me to identify him amongst all the other demons.

"How will I find Anthea or the half-demons in here?" The words rang in my head as though I spoke aloud.

"I have sent out a message." Belial's voice sounded in my head. *"They search for you. They will come."*

I mentally shuddered, hoping my sanity would still be intact when they did.

19

IN THE DARKWORLD

I watched the darkness ripple around me, changing shade and shape according to some unknown whim. The eyes continued to stare at me.

"You're doing it yourself, Ashlyn," said Belial. *"The Darkworld will shape itself according to your thoughts."*

"I thought it was separate to me. What about the other demons?"

"You forget that demons do not experience emotion… the exception, of course, being Mephistopheles. You intrigue them because of your complexity, and the Darkworld itself responds. You've changed it."

But I didn't mean to…

"Change can be a good thing, Ashlyn. I have always thought you had the potential."

"Don't expect too much of me. I've an awful lot to do already."

"What you do for one demon affects us all. We are one."

I felt them before I saw their shadowy forms in front of me. The half-demons gathered on the path that had reformed—human-shaped and a lighter shade of darkness to the surroundings. *This is so weird.*

"You will adjust."

Anthea.

"I'm here. Like you asked."

"Yes, you are. Now you are to complete your contract with Belial."

"I still have to do that?"

I searched around for the other demon's consciousness. Belial's voice spoke again, *"I am here, Ashlyn. I require one favour from you. When you break the Barrier, you are to let me go free."*

"Huh? You want to die?"

"This existence is not our choice, Ashlyn. You know that."

"I won't stop you, then. But first I need to find out how to break the Barrier. Who would know that?"

"A demon who that was around at its creation."

"I thought all demons were immortal?"

"We are, but not all are as ancient as the higher demons. They remain the few of the original demons who have not succumbed to madness as a result of their imprisonment. I rather think that most demons would leave gladly."

"You… you don't mind dying? Every demon?"

"Some would fight it. That is inevitable. Creatures of hate like Mephistopheles, whose only outlet is inflicting pain. But in the main, demons know that immortality erodes sanity and life."

"I need to find a demon who was around at the creation of the Barrier—preferably a sane one."

"I told you, Ashlyn. Only the higher demons retain their sanity."

"But they're serving Lucifer! They aren't even here."

"Two are."

"Belphegor… and my father, Lucifer. I have to speak to him?"

"He is the more likely to listen."

"Yeah, he's been a great parent so far. Okay. Fine. Take me to him."

"He will not take kindly to being disturbed."

"You just told me he's my only chance! Can't you take a message to him?"

"You just projected your thoughts to every demon within distance. He will learn you search for him soon, Ashlyn."

It was strange, feeling afraid without the physical symptoms, but I could swear a mental shiver went through me all the same.

"Do not fear, Ashlyn. Here, you are immortal."

Immortal. Like that meant anything, really. Oh God, I needed Leo. I needed grounding. But there *was* no ground, only shadow piled upon shadow alive with glittering eyes, creatures that existed but didn't really live. Was this the mental equivalent of a panic attack? My whirling thoughts were met with curious stares as every nearby pair of eyes turned to face me. I'd probably stirred the whole Darkworld up.

It was strange being a disembodied pair of eyes. I still felt like I could move, like I could look down and around with eyes that were only half-there. But it was a trick. I didn't have a body, and the only thing that moved was my mind. I could project my consciousness outward, searching amongst the myriad curious demons, and, as the panic eased, I found that I could distinguish one from another. Each new being had a slightly different feel, like an individual's thumbprint, but at the moment, all were focused on the same subject. Me. I saw my own face in their minds, and it felt strange because that wasn't what I looked like now, even if I still thought I did. Now I was shadow, eyes in shadow...

"You have a peculiar way of thinking, Ashlyn. Even for a human."

"Thanks." *Seriously? Even demons think I'm a freak?*

"He will speak with you." Another consciousness brushed mine, an unfamiliar demon. No sooner had I recovered than a ripple went through the Darkworld, through the demons, and I became aware of a presence greater than all of them combined into one.

Lucifer was here.

Images filled my mind as it tried to process the other demons' thoughts and impressions. When higher demons spoke through someone, their eyes turned black as the Darkworld itself, and the usual effects of a demon's appearance—the deep coldness, the prickling terror—were multiplied manifold. With no physical body to be affected, my mind struggled to grasp this presence that sent even the other demons into head-bowed, meek obedience. I felt it pass through the area, if we were even in one, felt demon after demon murmur a greeting, acknowledge their superior.

Then Lucifer was before me. If I'd felt exposed before, now I was in a gigantic X-ray machine that showed every facet of my being, every thought I would ever have, every decision I would make. There was no need to speak. Lucifer knew what I wanted, probably better than I did.

"You want to know the heart of the Darkworld."

Yes, I thought, my own mental voice feeble in comparison. "Yes," I said, louder.

"And you wish to know the terms of the contract the human Lucifer made with the demon Mephistopheles. So you had the audacity to come here, from whence few humans have returned, for answers. And you spoke to me."

"You're my father."

"That is, regrettably, the case."

As it turned out, anger wasn't cut off to me entirely. It

pulsed through me, and I felt it ripple through the other demons, too.

"You regret me, too? Shouldn't have slept with Melivia Blackstone, then, should you? I was her 'greatest regret,' apparently. So it's the same with you?"

"You are not my greatest regret, Ashlyn."

"Well, that's good news. But don't you dare blame Melivia for what you did."

"You dare to threaten a higher demon, too?"

"Yes, I dare. It makes no difference to me. You're still a bastard, demon or not. You just left her alone, consumed with regret, and let her ruin my whole life. But I suppose life doesn't mean anything to you, does it?"

"You are correct. But I do not believe she regretted your existence. She protected you—and your heart—on my orders."

"You might have at least acknowledged my existence, rather than letting me believe I was human. Keeping me in the dark did more harm than good. Besides, that doesn't matter now."

"You have done what no one, human or demon, has ever done before, and asked the help of a higher demon. Such audacity, Ashlyn."

"Lucifer—er, the false Lucifer didn't? I thought he was the first to come to the Darkworld."

"Faust is no fool, blinded though he may be. It was Mephistopheles he sought out the first time he came into contact with the Darkworld. He found out through other, lesser demons, that one demon craved the secret of humanity above all others."

"Mephistopheles wants to be human?"

"Mephistopheles was human. He, Ashlyn, is my greatest regret."

Numbness rang through me. The Darkworld itself seemed to hold its breath.

What?

"Mephistopheles was a human-demon. The first. A thousand years or more of your time has passed since he left the mortal world

behind, killed by a sorcerer, hanging onto life out of hate. He's sustained only by the bonds he's formed with humans—like Faust and your friend."

"Berenice. She told me she's bound to him, that she'll die when he does."

"That is true. But he clings to life only through the Darkworld now that you have obliterated his demon heart. If the Barrier is broken, he too, will die."

"But… I don't understand. How can Mephistopheles be so powerful, if he's only a half-demon? None of the others have that kind of power."

"He gains it from Faust. The two are mutually dependent, which is not entirely what Faust intended. He wanted to dominate Mephistopheles. Faust used the magic at his disposal for his own amusement and to win friends and favours, but that was not enough. He wanted the Darkworld. He wanted us. He knew we could kill him if he tried, so he worked out a way of making the higher demons subservient to his commands. He somewhat succeeded, by making himself, by human standards, immortal."

"So how do I beat him?"

"You do not."

"Wait. According to the half-demons, I'm the only one who can beat Lucifer, and according to Belial, you're the only one who can tell me how to do it. I know I have to break the Barrier. But how would I go about doing that?"

"We cannot break the Barrier from this side."

"I know that! My body's still in the physical world. My friends are watching over it. You ought to know, if you can see everything."

"I find it tiresome to wring the thoughts out of mortals. Yours are especially muddled, Ashlyn. You do not really know what you are doing, do you?"

"That's why I'm asking for help. Because you're my dad, and you owe me. Big."

"I owe you nothing. You're still alive, are you not?"

"No thanks to you. People have tried to kill me just for being half-demon. Too many times to count. And now I've had to come right under the other Lucifer's nose because I'm apparently the only person who can kill him."

"You cannot kill him. You can destroy his physical body—if you're morally capable of that, which I suspect you are not. You would also need to destroy his demon heart. But as long as the Darkworld exists, so will he."

"I thought breaking the Barrier would…"

"You are quite right. But breaking the Barrier would mean the end of humanity."

"Does it have to? Isn't there a way to… I don't know, restrict the demons who can get through?"

"That is how it is at the present moment. Only the weakest of spirits can pass through. In order for Faust and Mephistopheles to be rendered mortal, you assign the same fate to the rest of us."

"It can't be impossible. You're the highest demon, aren't you? I thought you knew everything. Weren't you around when the Barrier was made?"

"I never said it was impossible. Only that you risk the fate of humanity if you allow it to be broken."

"Don't make this more difficult than it is already. I only want to save everyone from Lucifer. As long as he exists…"

"I know your heart, Ashlyn. You would sacrifice anything for those you love. Yet willpower alone will not overcome five higher demons."

"Why do they serve him? And why don't you? I'm just curious to know what he could have promised a higher demon."

"He promised the same to all of us. Free reign in the human world. He most certainly does not have them at his mercy. They are equals, working in mutual agreement. If either gained power over the other, they would destroy each other."

"You mean because they're all immortal? It's a stalemate. I thought the whole reason for the Barrier was to stop demons from breaking through to our world? The higher demons are working for Lucifer—I mean, Faust—for that reason, aren't they? They want to rule humanity. I'll just be giving them the key."

"Not so. They might serve Faust because it gives them an advantage at present, but they are higher demons, and not inclined to rash decisions."

"What, you think it's worth risking them killing all of humanity? Even if L—Faust is dead, all the higher demons will be free, won't they? Is there any way to avoid setting free the demons who would kill people?"

"In theory, yes. The higher demons have the say in which of our kin are permitted to pass through the Barrier."

"Wait a minute. Five of you are on Faust's side, though."

"Perhaps it is merely a gameplay decision. Belphegor and I have no desire to rule humanity."

"That doesn't mean I want to risk setting all the demons loose in our world. How would destroying the Barrier make things any better? Isn't that what Faust wants to do anyway?"

"He intends to police the Barrier himself, using my kin as his own border patrol."

"How does he have power over them? It's supposed to be impossible, isn't it?"

"I believe my kin are more supportive of the notion that our kind should be set free."

"But that means if I destroy the Barrier… and Faust is dead… how do I know they won't attack people anyway?"

"They will act on Faust's orders, it is true. You must kill him first."

"So you're saying that the other higher demons are

making a pact with him for the good of demonkind, or whatever?"

"That is one way of putting it, yes."

"But why did you stay out of it?"

"My last attempt to involve myself in human affairs was hardly a success."

"Why her?" The question came out before I could stop it. "Why'd you pick Melivia? You must have known she'd suffered enough already."

"It was... unintentional. I was searching for something quite different when I happened across her. She stood in the way of what I wanted and... you were the outcome."

"Great job."

We'd veered wildly off-topic. I searched for a way to return to my original questions, but Lucifer beat me to it.

"Of all humans to enter the Darkworld, the false Lucifer, Johann Faust, was the first. If the Barrier is broken, you will be the last, Ashlyn."

"So? What does that have to do with anything?"

"Everything. He was the first to discover the path, and the first to break the Barrier."

"Wait. He already broke it?"

"Many of your years ago, the Barrier was quite different to how it is now. Faust changed that when he meddled with magic that he ought to have left alone. In an ancient day sorcerers used their own life force to create the Barrier. In destroying it, Faust unleashed that energy. If it had not been contained, it would have consumed the world."

"But how did he even do that? Is that why he made the contract with Mephistopheles?"

"It was one of his curiosities. Faust was born into a time of discovery, and saw himself as unveiling the secrets of the hidden universe. Specifically, the Darkworld and how the Barrier was formed. His ill-advised contract with Mephistopheles washed all traces of

what you would call humanity out of him. He let the demon share his body and mind. And he found the source of the Barrier's power, and broke it.

"But unbeknownst to him, a secret alliance had been forming, one that would come to be known as the Venantium. They hunted down any demons that broke through, and destroyed them. Fixing the Barrier as it used to be was beyond question. In order to contain the magical energy unleashed by Faust, they did the only thing they could. They found something capable of storing that energy. Do you know what that was?"

"I don't… a giant demon heart?"

"Several demon hearts. One was not enough to contain it. Over time, energy erodes as demon hearts become defunct, but that did not happen in this case. Instead, the demon hearts were, one by one, destroyed. They were originally given to the country's most important and influential magical families to watch. However, this decision was marked as foolish by some, and not without cause. Demon hearts are easy to procure, and at the time, were valued as a sign of wealth and power. The families made no secret of what they really owned, and naturally, were targeted by rogues and other sorcerers looking to unlock the secrets of the Darkworld. Only one such store of energy remained by the dawn of your nineteenth century—and it was owned by the Blackstone family."

An image broke into my mind. A girl in a photograph, wearing an amethyst crystal pendant. A passage in a diary, marked. A note. *Turn to the ending. It will make sense, Ashlyn.*

I watched my own hands turn the pages, and another note fall out. *"Two demons named Lucifer made me what I am. One has my love, the other, my heart, and we are forever bonded. Ashlyn, I am truly sorry. Of all the wrongs I have done, you are my greatest regret."*

Her greatest regret.

No. It can't be. My demon heart can't…

"I am afraid it is true, Ashlyn. Yours is the only source left.

Melivia Blackstone knew nothing of this; her family never considered her important enough to be privy to the family's last great secret. In truth, they had grown complacent, and her mother left it lying carelessly in her jewellery box. Of course the naïve girl couldn't resist stealing it to complement her ensemble, and no one even realised it was missing. After the Blackstones died, the stone was left in the ruins of the house, forgotten, until Melivia took it back after she returned from the Darkworld.

Even then, she knew nothing of its true value. She needed an anchor, a power source, for the child she never meant to have. It was a natural choice, being a family heirloom. But when she learned the truth… it was too late. The heart is yours, as well as the Barrier's. It must be destroyed to break the Barrier—and you, Ashlyn, must die."

20

DECISION

This was impossible. My mind scrambled, trying to come up with anything—any evasion, any denial, anything that might make the world make sense again—it couldn't be possible.

"Does Lucifer know? Faust, I mean?"

"No. He does not."

"Do the half-demons know? Anthea? Would they sacrifice my life to be free?"

"I have no doubt that any demon would see your life as immaterial, Ashlyn. Certainly, I do. You are angry that I played no role in your life. Would you want to watch your child grow up, knowing that her death is necessary for the future of your species?"

"Impossible. I'm not—"

"Human? Perhaps. Your life is tied to that anchor; that much is certain. At the very least, you will lose your demon half if your heart is destroyed."

That can't be... it can't! I searched for my demon half, but she kept silent. Was the horror coursing through me mine, or hers?

"She is you, Ashlyn. You speak to your own shadow... perhaps

your separation enabled her to develop her own identity, but she is still you. You can't escape this. You must forfeit your life, otherwise the false Lucifer will gain supremacy over all humanity."

"I can't destroy my demon heart."

"Then you must ask a friend to do it for you."

"I can't do that to Leo! It's one thing if I'm possessed. If that was true I'd already be dead. But this... this is different."

"Then I wish you the best with your decision."

I felt the presence begin to withdraw.

"Wait!"

"You try my patience. Your thoughts are noisy and confused. Think of a clear question before you bother me again."

"It's hard to think clearly when you've just told me I've got to be a martyr and make my boyfriend kill me!"

"You wished to know, when all is done, how Faust must die, did you not?"

"Some good that'll do me if I'm dead."

But I knew what I had to do. Leo would have to be the one to kill Faust. I had no doubt that he was more than capable of it—that he wanted to do it. I trusted him, wholly and completely.

Even with my death.

"And.... and Faust's demon heart? I need that. I need to destroy it before he kills my friends."

"You saw the note?"

The image played out again, the paper fluttering to the ground, my hand snatching it out of the air to read the last words of Melivia Blackstone...

"Two demons named Lucifer made me what I am. One has my love, the other, my heart, and we are forever bonded. Ashlyn, I am truly sorry. Of all the wrongs I have done, you are my greatest regret."

"One has my love, the other, my heart. What does that mean?"

"I believe she wanted you to work it out for yourself."

"Great. Not only did she accept my death, she wanted to screw with me even more."

I made my mind work, to block out the numbing horror. *Think.* "Her heart... but humans mean something different to demons when they use the word—she destroyed her own heart already, though, when she sacrificed herself." Lucifer's silence made me suspicious. "But... unless she meant that she took care of Faust's when he went back into the Darkworld?"

"I believe she stole it."

"Sounds like her. Crap. Forever bonded..."

An image appeared, prompted by my own thoughts. My heart and Mephistopheles's, melding into one. But her heart was destroyed already. She was gone. Her words might simply be an over-dramatic way of saying he owned her life.

"No, I believe you are right. I watched her take his heart myself. You forget, she could not access her own power through her demon heart; it was essentially useless to her. So she made another. She amassed the power. And... she used it to bind herself to Faust."

No freaking way. And yet... it made sense. "Crap, I keep forgetting you're omniscient. You already knew all this, didn't you? What's the point in making me figure it out?"

"To test you, Ashlyn. To ensure that you are ready for the next step."

"Which is...?"

"To procure the heart."

"I have no idea where she hid it." I felt Lucifer watching me, assessing, waiting for me to say something. Screw it, I was going to die anyway. "Tell me. I know you know."

"You could have worked it out yourself. She hid it in her home."

"The Windermere Cottage. Of course."

Last time I'd been there, I'd fought the demon Vassago and totally demolished the place. Was there even anything left? Come to think of it… wouldn't Vassago have been able to detect its presence?

"She hid it well. He detected the magical energy, but not its location. It covered the entire area."

"That doesn't help. I can't go back there. I'm supposed to confront Faust. Every second I waste, he'll gain more power."

"Then don't. You have powers here, Ashlyn. Use them."

"I don't understand…"

"Then I have nothing more to say to you. In exchange for the information I have given you, however, I expect a favour."

"What is it with demons and bargains?"

A surge of energy shot through me, leaving me reeling. *"You forget I am more than mere demon. I could make every second of your remaining existence a living hell."*

Hell, I knew it. "What's your price? My life's already forfeit."

"Merely that you free me from the Darkworld when the Barrier is broken, and ensure that the other higher demons do not inflict their revenge."

"You're asking me to be your bodyguard? I don't understand what kind of power you demons think I have, but I haven't a clue."

"You are still blinded. Think on this: you have the power that demons have. Disembodied, you could choose to kill to return to life. You can communicate over distance. And you can possess and control others."

"You think I want to do that? I'm no demon."

"Consider your strengths. Now, I have lingered here long enough. If Faust finds out, he will likely claim me under the same contract he inflicted on my brothers. It is of no consequence. But it

will make your life considerably harder if he learns of our corre-spondence."

"Can't I—can't I shield my thoughts from him?"

"*No. Only demons have that privilege.*"

"You just said I was a demon?"

"*The paradox of Ashlyn Temple. Even demons do not know your capabilities. But your mind is transparent to me, and so it will be to all other demons.*"

Great.

"*You can still read others' thoughts whilst you are here. Think on that.*"

I felt the presence begin to withdraw, like a weight lifted off me.

"*Remember our bargain, Ashlyn.*"

The voice faded from my mind, and I was left alone, shuddering in its wake.

Okay. Time to figure this out.

I could read minds. In theory, I could go anywhere I wanted. The Darkworld had no physical barriers. A fleeting thought, that I could simply seek out some dark corner and hide myself away, pushed itself to the forefront of my mind. But it would do no good. The Darkworld wasn't safe, and besides, my human body—and demon heart—were still in Redthorne with the others.

I have to find a way to get to Windermere.

Lucifer said to use my powers…

He must mean that I could get someone else to do it for me. Communicate with someone over distance. In theory, I could talk to Layla and Gareth in London—but that was too far away.

How do I even do that, anyway?

Belial answered, making me jump. "*You use your connec-tion. It spans all human minds, but it will hone in on those with a connection to the Darkworld, and those with whom you share a certain bond."*

Before I could ask how to do that, I felt my mind shift, and the scene changed before my eyes. Now the presences brushing against me felt... different. It was like I looked through tinted, distorted glass, trying to make out familiar faces.

There was one that was so familiar it made my heart ache. *Leo.*

I moved closer, and felt a shudder run through me to see my own lifeless body in his arms.

No. I withdrew. Speaking to Leo now would do no good. I needed someone who was close to the fortune-teller's old cottage...

No sooner had the face flashed before my eyes than my mind honed in on a familiar face.

Alex. She lived right on the doorstep of the lakes.

As the picture became clearer, I saw her and another—Sarah—walking through a town in the Lake District.

They're okay, I thought, relief flooding me. They'd escaped Blackstone after all...

I can't drag them into this.

But it would do no harm asking them to have a look now that I was in this strange, privileged position. *Crap. I can't think like that.* This was a curse, not a privilege. Besides, there was something I had to do.

I honed in, feeling two minds brush against mine. Sarah's was calm, like the surface of a lake. Alex's was as vivid as her personality. I wondered briefly what mine looked like to others—a mess, according to Lucifer.

Focus. I had to make my move, but neither of them had a connection to the Darkworld. Dark spaces were invisible to their eyes.

Oh God. Sorry, Sarah.

Before I could make excuses, I moved in, and felt the lake ripple under my touch. Trying not to disturb the surface of her thoughts, I looked at Alex through Sarah's eyes.

Alex jumped about a foot in the air. "Holy shit, Sarah! What the hell's up with your eyes?" Then she backed off. "No." She shook her head. "Not you. Not you, too. It isn't fair. Get out of her head, you bastard!"

"Alex," I said, through Sarah's voice. "It's me. Ash. Sorry for scaring you."

If possibly, Alex looked even more freaked. She clutched the nearest tree for balance. "You're shitting me. No, I don't believe you. Ash told me you're all liars. Get the hell out of her or I'll end you, I swear!"

"It's true," I said. "I—I am, honestly. Your full name's Alexandra Marianne Delilah Park. Your boyfriend's Rex Cambridge, and he's exactly a month younger than you. You love watching *Lord of the Rings*, but you cry at *The Notebook* when you think no one's looking. You love pink Smarties, and climbing mountains, and you once got Mandeep to dress up as the Grim Reaper and scare the crap out of me. You remember that, right? Oh crap, I'm making a mess of this."

Alex's jaw was slack. "You're reading my mind, or something freaky. But that last part sounded like Ash, I admit. Why are you in Sarah's head?"

"It was the quickest way to talk to you. I'm—I'm in the Darkworld, in Blackstone, right now. I need your help."

"With what? Just saying, I've no issue with hitting my friend in the face if you're a demon."

"Yeah, I don't doubt that," I said. "But I don't think Sarah would appreciate it much. This is weird for me, too, by the way."

Alex frowned. "You do sound like Ash. But I'm gonna need more proof than that."

I expected nothing less of Alex. Sarah's presence pushed at the edge of my consciousness. I tried not intrude on her thoughts, but I could tell that she'd heard me speaking through her mouth, and was aware of everything that was happening.

Sorry! I said, and withdrew, enough to allow her to speak again.

"Oh… my… God," Sarah spluttered.

Alex jumped backward. "Holy crap. You're back."

"I… Ash, you lunatic! Where are you?"

"Is it definitely Ash?"

Sarah let out a shuddering breath. "Yeah, it's Ash. Or it was."

I'm here, I said, projecting my voice into both their minds.

"Okay. This is grade ten on the freaky scale," said Sarah, staring wildly around as though expecting to see me lurking out of sight.

"Damn right," said Alex, unsteadily. "But it is Ash. What do you need our help with?"

"Believe me, I wouldn't drag you into this if I had a choice, but there's something I need from the fortune-teller's old house… it's in Windermere. Where are you now, anyway?"

Alex paused. "Kendal. I don't think…"

I hesitated. Maybe I should just go myself. But time was short, and I had no idea how long I'd already been in the Darkworld. Time passed differently here.

"How long has it been?" I said. "Since we left uni, I mean."

Alex shrugged. "A few days, maybe? It seems longer, but only because it's so bloody confusing. I've been trying to get hold of you, Ash. I was scared about you—and Sarah, too.'

"I'm sorry. I lost my phone, and I had to leave my laptop behind at uni. There was no time…"

"Don't worry about it. You've been out of touch on new developments, though. Sarah's dating Mandeep."

"What?" I yelped. "When did that happen? Have I really been gone that long?"

"Relax, Ash. All right, it's definitely you. No, it's been coming on for ages, I don't blame you for not noticing."

"He's not our flatmate anymore, so it doesn't count," Sarah added.

"Um, that's great. I mean it. Good on you."

Really, it was a reminder that life went on, even when the world was going to hell. I was glad we had something to celebrate. Even if it was only for a minute.

"Anything else I should know about?"

"Not really," said Alex. "I'm reapplying to other unis, but they want some sort of an explanation, and there isn't one. Well, the officials say it was a fire caused by students or something like that—yeah, blame the crazy shit on us."

"The Venantium," I said. "I suppose it's an easy enough story to spread. People will buy it. Anyway. It was near where we got stranded on that trip last year. There's an old cottage—it'll be in ruins. There's something hidden there, concealed. I can…"

I felt Sarah's mind shift beneath mine, and had a sudden idea. Using my thoughts alone, I made her shuffle forward.

Alex gaped at her. "Please tell me you're not making her move."

"Sorry," I said. "I just wanted to try—I remember where it is, so I could help you get there."

"'Spose it's easier than getting lost," said Alex. "But it's damn creepy, to be honest. No offence."

"None taken."

With my own memories in mind, I prepared to steer my friends in the right direction. I hoped that Leo was keeping a close eye out in Blackstone, because if Faust arrived and found him and Berenice, I would have no body to return to.

21

AUNT EVE'S LEGACY

It was easy, in the end. Once Alex, followed by Sarah, who I tried to make look as un-creepy and puppet-like as I could, got the bus to Windermere, I felt the pull of the magic even through the Darkworld. Alex had to run to keep up as I led her down country lanes bordered by dark forests, finally coming to the turning where our minibus had got stuck that night last winter.

Cursing, Alex tramped up the hill behind me. "I'm not used to Sarah being faster than me," she grumbled. "Slow down a bit!"

I did, feeling the pull of the Darkworld skitter over my skin. We were close.

"Into the forest. Wonderful idea," said Alex, as I made for the first path I saw through the trees.

"I did say it was in the middle of nowhere. And we have to walk back?"

"It won't be long."

The truth was, I had no idea where Aunt Eve had hidden the heart. I hadn't found it the last time I'd been here, after all, even if its presence had been everywhere. At the time, I'd put it down to Vassago lurking around.

But now I had someone to ask. Anthea was still there, at the edge of my consciousness, and her whisper guided me through the woods and to the remains of what had once been my aunt's cottage, the place I'd spent summer holidays as a child. The place my Aunt Eve had unmasked herself. What was it about this place that Melivia Blackstone had found so attractive? Probably its isolation. Her former home was gone, after all. And here, Faust would never think to look for her.

All was silent. Leaves fluttered down like shredded skin. White sunlight shone through the trees like lightning, pale and sharp. A light frost sprinkled the ground. Alex shivered slightly in the breeze, but I felt nothing. I was aware of Sarah on the outskirts of my consciousness, watching me control her body with nervous determination. I'd shown her enough of my thoughts to convince her of the absolute urgency of the situation.

"Why have I never come walking here before?" Alex said. "This is nice. Bit confusing, though. I'm glad I have a guide."

"Yeah, it is a bit of a maze," I said. "It's not far now, though…"

The cottage's ruins struck me like a blow. Last time I'd been here, I'd lost control of my powers when fighting Vassago and demolished the place. It was little more than a huddle of crumbled bricks and wooden beams, all overgrown with ivy and brambles. Power thrummed in the air, so strong I could feel it even through Sarah's perception. Alex looked at me, and I gave a brief nod.

I moved Sarah on toward the ruins, slowly, taking one deliberate step at a time. I knew it was here somewhere.

Vassago's words suddenly echoed in my mind. *"I am*

doing nothing. It is this place. It feeds on the power of others. But it gives strength to those who feed on the shadows."

"He didn't know about it, though," I said. "He can't have known it was Faust's heart. Can he?"

"What?" said Alex.

"Um. I was talking to the demons…"

"Right. As you do. What exactly does this thing look like, anyway?"

"A crystal. I don't know what colour, but it'll look like an ordinary precious stone, like the ones you buy at the market."

"Seriously?" Alex blinked at me—at Sarah. "That makes me see the Blackstone market in a whole new light. No wonder they charged the earth."

"Crap." Could it be true? Blackstone was a magnet for sorcerers after all; it wasn't unreasonable to assume they'd been anchors. "Black market demon hearts? Well, that'd have had a certain irony. The Venantium were right there…"

Perhaps they'd even engineered it. One thing was for sure: I couldn't trust anyone in the damn world. Yet here I was. Once again I'd had to put my faith in the fortune-teller.

My mind brushed against the power source. It felt close. I made Sarah bend down and start digging through the rubble, moving chunks of what had once been the top floor. We stood in the hallway, roughly where the stairs used to be. And underneath was…

"A trapdoor," I said. "Seriously?"

I expected it to be locked, but with Alex's help, I managed to get the wooden lid open. A cloud of dust erupted into the air along with such a surge of power it knocked both Alex and Sarah off their feet.

"Holy crap," said Alex. "You know, I haven't had the

best of experiences with cellars. Like a certain haunted house incident."

"Sorry about that," I said. "Anyway, I'm going in."

A set of stairs led downward to a small, square room with no furniture besides a plain, wooden trunk.

I bet it was covered with Influence. This is too obvious. I lifted the lid of the trunk. There it was. A single crystal, threaded on a string like mine had been. Amethyst.

Sorrow rose inside me. Sarah's hands shook as I picked it up, and turned back to the steps.

"Right. Are you okay to come to Blackstone?"

"Gotcha," said Alex. "But you'll have to get us out of these woods, first."

Urgency pulled at me, but I nodded. "Deal. Thanks for this, by the way. You may have just saved humanity."

"Pleasure to help. Come and visit soon, right?"

"Sure thing," I said, as lightly as I could.

The journey back was quicker; two pairs of feet had left imprints on the frosted grounds. I felt the Darkworld tugging at me, pulling me back. I needed to get back to Leo...

"Soon," Alex said. "I'll use my powers to make that train fly, okay?"

"That would definitely help," I said. "Seriously, though. You're amazing."

"See you soon," she said.

The darkness closed over me, my friends disappeared from view, and once again, I was swept into a disembodied state, simultaneously alone and connected with thousands.

I should check on the others in London, I thought—and then thought of Cara. No sooner had her image appeared in my mind than I felt her mind connect with mine, surprise radiating from her.

Crap. I didn't mean to do that.

In spite of myself, I honed in. Images played before me. I recognised Edinburgh Castle from pictures she'd posted on Facebook. So she was safe, at least…

But who were those people she was with? They wore uniform, blue uniform. The Venantium.

What was she doing with them?

"Anyway," she said, her voice hitching slightly, "if in doubt, use their own powers against them. That's what Ash told me."

She's giving the Venantium advice? I moved closer. The other people in the group who weren't dressed in uniform looked like students. Perhaps the Venantium were recruiting. *Does she have the connection?* I thought. It was unlikely, but now wasn't the time to hang about. She was alive, that would have to do for now.

I backed away, into the shadows, searching for other, familiar minds. Claudia and Cyrus. One touch told me they were alive, and safe in London.

That's good.

It was easier to hide than say goodbye, easier to return to the familiar than to complicate things. I'd already said my goodbyes. That just left…

"Ashlyn. There's a problem. Another demon's seen you in Redthorne."

I moved toward Belial. *Crap. How do I get out?*

"That wasn't part of our bargain, Ashlyn. I do not know, as I have never left the Darkworld."

I searched for the half-demons, for Anthea. Where were they? Now was hardly the time to ditch me…

"They've gone," said a voice. *"You're never going back. Oh, Ashlyn, the fun times we will have together."*

A thrill of horror pierced me. Mephistopheles.

22

HUMAN AND DEMON

I felt the other demons move away from me, one at a time, like doors closing one after another. Isolation pressed on me. The Darkworld was all around, a never-ending black void. No pathway back.

Just Mephistopheles and me.

"You ought to have been more careful. Lucifer will be very interested to know that two of your friends are on their way here…"

I recoiled, horror-stricken. What had I done?

"Two more sacrifices, Ashlyn. Did you really think destroying my demon heart would contain me? There are an infinite number of vessels hidden in Blackstone, you foolish girl. I will walk again. But you will not be so fortunate."

I was unable to stop myself from reaching toward Leo. Panic shot through me as a series of images played before me. My own body, limp in Leo's arms. Berenice, white-faced and screaming in the alleyway. The hatch opening on a tunnel underground. Darkness, lit by blue lamps.

The accompanying emotions told me what had happened. Berenice was acting under Mephistopheles's compulsion and had taken Leo—and my body —underground.

To Faust.

No.

"Yes. Berenice was always mine to command. I'll make her kill your boyfriend. Make you watch her torture him."

I could feel pure, harsh glee radiating from Mephistopheles's mind. It pulsed from anger to dangerous joy like a flashing light changing colour. His was the most unstable mind I'd ever encountered, and that made him more frightening than even the higher demons. Even Lucifer—and he'd been human, once, after all.

I had to get the lunatic away from my friends.

But against my will, we moved in closer, to a tunnel winding its way into the distance, but they were passing through a section with no lamps, dark enough that I couldn't see Leo's face, only the outline of him, holding my body. His voice filtered through to me.

"Please, Ash. Please wake up. Don't be dead. Please…"

I fought to break through the Darkworld, but it was like a solid barrier. I didn't know if it was Mephistopheles doing it or if it was simply that I should have asked Anthea beforehand how to return to my body, rather than assuming that it would be as easy as leaving it had been.

All I knew was that I needed my demon heart, an anchor. And right now, it was in Berenice's hands.

The purple light of her demon eyes was the only other light in the tunnel, but the demon heart burned brighter. Her smile was Mephistopheles's: cruel and twisted, filled with the joy of holding the catalyst for the destruction of the Barrier in his hands.

If Faust destroyed it before I could destroy his heart, all was lost.

"You bastard," said Leo. "You fucking bastard. Put that down."

"It's the crux of my plan, Master Blake. Your friend has unintentionally been carrying the energy of a thousand half-demons with her—not to mention the energy of many generations of sacrifice. She's had blood on her hands for her entire existence. You might call it a noble sacrifice."

Leo's eyes were frightened, but his voice was steady. "If the Barrier breaks…"

"She'll die. It's true. But a billion others will be set free, allowed to take this world for our own. We have been denied it for too long."

"Why not break the heart yourself? Why do you need Lucifer to do it for you? Or is this part of the mysterious contract between you?"

"You know of that?"

"Kind of pieced it together, yeah. A human bound to a demon. Like you and Berenice. Parasitic, really, isn't it? I thought you demons hated being dependent on humans. Isn't that why you want to break the Barrier?"

"You have no understanding of our lives, human. We are not meant to live static existences. We are made to be rule, and humans provide the means of doing so. Whilst remaining under our control. It's perfect and right."

"Same old demon talk. No wonder Ash won't wake up. She doesn't want to hear your whining."

"What makes you think she cannot hear us? Ashlyn is trapped in the Darkworld. There's no escape for her. But she will watch me break you, and be unable to do a thing."

"You lie," said Leo. "You fucking liar."

"You are afraid to face the truth. I do believe we are almost here."

They turned a corner, as I watched, screaming helplessly at Leo to turn back and knowing that it would do no good. I was trapped behind glass, unable even to communicate mentally with him. The demon was gone, leaving only me, a single human soul in a sea of demons.

And none of them acknowledged me. They were scared, I realised. Terrified of Mephistopheles.

I was going to have to rethink the notion that demons couldn't feel emotions. Their terror knocked me backward, rocked the Darkworld like the tremor of an earthquake. It was a silent terror. Each demon, like me, was locked in a glass case. Not that there was anything a demon could do from here anyway.

I recognised the chamber instantly. The same one Faust had attempted to break the Barrier in before, or a near-identical one. I'd thought it had been buried underneath rubble, unless Faust had cleared it somehow. Was that what the higher demons had been doing?

But Faust wasn't there. Instead, the five Inner Circle members waited, standing in a perfect circle, holding the demon hearts. Exactly as they had before. Uncannily similar. But there were no scared *venators* watching from the sidelines this time. No fortune-teller to sacrifice herself. No half-demons to defend Leo or my pale, lifeless body.

Berenice approached the higher demons, holding out my demon heart.

"I have acquired the crux," she said. "We must go to Lucifer now."

"Very well," said Mr. Blake, or Mammon, the demon that controlled him.

Leo glared at the demon that controlled his father as their eyes met, but could say nothing.

"Your girlfriend is hurt? I sense that her spirit is not present…"

"That's none of your business," said Leo.

"You still have no respect for your superiors, son of mine. But you will learn… you will learn."

"Like hell I will."

"Before your death, you will accept our new order, Master Blake. Lucifer will pave the way to our future. The destruction of the Barrier will set us free."

"Yeah, so I keep hearing." Leo's voice shook with anger.

Had Lucifer meant it when he'd said that the other higher demons had no interest in ruling humanity? Would I really trust his word? Mammon's expression was one of pure greed. He exulted being in control of an Inner Circle member.

In the end, maybe I couldn't have done it. I couldn't have destroyed my own demon heart. But now Faust was going to do it for me.

The five higher demons—formerly Ms Constantine, Dr Fenton, Mrs Wilcox, Mr Dyson, and Mr Blake of the Inner Circle—walked in unison out of the room, followed by Berenice and Leo. I moved with them, always fighting to break through the Barrier, but I might have as well have been trying to punch through solid concrete with my bare hands.

I heard Leo's quiet whisper in my ear, telling me to hang in there, that he'd get us out of there. But surrounded by higher demons, there was nothing he could do.

I withdrew back to the Darkworld, reaching out in another futile attempt to connect with the half-demons, even a true demon, but a deadly hush had fallen over the Darkworld. I felt a low current of magic thrumming beneath the silence, like still air before a thunderstorm. But no demons. No hope.

I returned to the real world, watching the Inner Circle's progress through the tunnels in fast forward. They came to a familiar stretch of tunnels that I recognised as those beneath Blackstone. One set of stone stairs led to a place I knew well: Blackstone Cemetery. They climbed the narrow staircase, and I followed.

The memorial stone was the first thing I noticed. It had cracked down the middle, and a row of harpies sat atop it, shrieking loudly. They flew everywhere, thick as locusts, especially around the cathedral with its spires reaching into the red sky.

The sky was a vivid crimson, like bloody hellfire, marked with roiling black clouds. Lightning flashed, pure white and blinding. Thunder mingled with the harpies' cries and the shrieks of shadow-beasts. Blurred shadowy shapes prowled past, ghouls clung to the gravestones, and human-sized figures draped in cloaks turned to greet us, revealing the emaciated forms of Skele-Ghouls.

It was hell on earth. Leo swore under his breath, holding onto me like a lifeline. But I was still a prisoner in the Darkworld.

The five stood in a line before the cathedral, as a Skele-Ghoul knocked on the oak doors. I knew who waited inside.

Faust. The first to enter the Darkworld, and now the commander of higher demons and humans alike, wearing a familiar form: Howard. Mephistopheles had handed him over to his boss, as planned.

For an instant, the world faded away, and a sequence of images entered my mind, though from which demon they came, I couldn't tell. I watched two figures in a dark-ened room, a room filled with strange apparatus, symbols carved on the walls and floor. I felt rather than heard the screams of joy from the couple as they looked at something where I hovered, a spectator.

A demon.

Yes, they were a couple, and as they pressed their lips to

one another's in front of the dark form of the demon, I recognised the woman.

Howard's mother. Younger, long curls bouncing from her shoulders—and just as insane as the broken woman I'd seen so recently. Smiling, she turned to face the demonic apparition, the shifting darkness spreading through the room.

A door opened.

Both of them spun around, alarm flickering across their faces. The door opened a crack and then swung on its hinges. A young boy stood on the threshold, no older than about thirteen, face twisted with horror, mouth gaping open in a silent scream.

But the scream I heard reverberating through me came from the woman. *"Howard!"*

Black spilled across my vision again, and I reeled. Through the veil of the Darkworld, I watched adult Howard stride to the open cathedral doors, confident, dressed in a crisp suit not unlike the Venantium's uniform. His height and short-cropped hair had always made him look older than twenty, but the eyes that looked through him had seen centuries. There was no trace left of the troubled young man who'd believed, even after what he'd seen, that his parents were victims. Maybe they were—I knew nothing about the context, nothing even about Howard. Maybe he'd told Berenice the truth. Maybe he'd been too ashamed to.

She was gone, too, now. Two personalities extinguished. Desperate anger coursed through me—*it's not right. None of this is.*

I shrank back as a presence brushed against mine, drawing my full attention back to Blackstone, to the cathedral where Faust stood in Howard's body, in the doorway to the cathedral.

Even the hint of Mephistopheles's touch left me mentally shaken, feeling like he'd pulled out all my thoughts and fears and laid them out for the world to gloat at, like he'd reached into the deepest part of my mind and whispered to my subconscious that I was nothing, only a small human, nothing compared to a centuries-old being with enough hate to destroy the world.

Faust, too, exuded power, like a deadly spider poised to strike. He beckoned Berenice toward him, and she approached, Leo right behind her, holding my body delicately. It was surreal, watching my own limp arm flop over Leo's as he lifted me. I wanted to scream at him to drop my body and run, save himself, but of all the minds I could sense from the Darkworld, his, I couldn't hone in on.

Faust stepped back into the cathedral, beckoning the Inner Circle to follow. I'd pulled back enough that I couldn't hear what was being said—could only watch as everyone moved into the large, abandoned building. Harpies still swooped around the roofs, dark shapes against the burning sky above. I felt other, lesser demons, too—God only knew how many now walked the streets. But that wasn't important now.

As the Inner Circle passed through the doors, Faust beckoned to Leo. He didn't move. Berenice stepped up behind him and shoved him forward, and I watched myself fall. He caught me in time, turning to Berenice with desperate fury etched on his face. But he could sense the power coming from Faust; I could feel it from here, pulsing like a force field that projected an image of fear onto everyone around him.

Muttering curses, Leo carried me into the dark.

Mephistopheles was the last to enter, and he did so in a flourish, moving Berenice's body to embrace Howard's. Faust stiffened, shoved him—her—away. Was it a scene I'd seen before? No, but close. Seeing two people I'd known for over a year acting like this made me ever more aware that appearance wasn't the essence of a person. It should be easy to recognise someone as possessed, but if demons knew you better than you knew yourself, what could you do?

I barely recognised my own body as Leo moved to take my cold, dead hand in his, bowing his head. He'd hung back as close to the door as he dared, but the Inner Circle stood in a line behind him, blocking the way out.

The two demons stood in the centre of the room, underneath a crooked candelabra lit with leaping blue flames, as were the candles lining the walls. Faust took centre stage, and yet the power surging around him was a far cry from the sheer instability of Mephistopheles's spirit. Where the once-human-demon was like a live bomb, Faust was more contained, a predator lying in wait. The two spirits blazed through the veil of the Darkworld, and I saw them set against each other, like fire and ice. But the demon was fire, and the human was ice.

And I knew. I knew there was no bond between them other than the contract. Mephistopheles only obeyed Faust out of necessity, and planned to break free.

It took a minute to process that Mephistopheles was *letting* me read his thoughts. He wanted me to know this. Why? I didn't dare move closer, but all his attention was focused on Lucifer.

I couldn't return to my body. But I still had enough control to shift my disembodied form over to Leo. He didn't notice me either, and I didn't dare get too close for worry I'd get wrapped up in his fear and give the game away.

If I couldn't fight, and we were outnumbered like this, there was only one thing to do. I edged closer to Leo, carefully, and pushed a suggestion into his head. I wouldn't even have called it Influence—but Leo's spine stiffened and his hand dropped to his pocket.

Call for help, I'd said. And from here, I could call anyone, from anywhere in the world. The Darkworld had no boundaries. If I projected the call, Faust or Mephistopheles would notice—but neither seemed to have realised something was up yet.

"We've found it," said Berenice, stepping forward, mouth twisted in a smile at once deferential and gleeful. "Ashlyn's heart is the crux of the Barrier. But there is a slight complication…"

"That will not be a problem." Howard's face was expressionless, but those dark, dark eyes burned within. "I have no fear of extermination. These interfering humans will be intercepted. I've already sent demons to take care of them when they arrive in Redthorne."

Alex and Sarah. Oh God, I'm so sorry.

In spite of myself, I pulled away and focused on Redthorne again. But there were no minds to guide me, only darkness.

"She's trapped in the Darkworld," said Mephistopheles. "I did it myself." As he spoke, the utter confidence in his tone was clear. He didn't feel the need to check up on me.

I reached out to the others, even outside the cathedral, and projected a general message: *come and help.*

"Excellent. I admit I didn't expect any of this—least of all the sleight of hand pulled by Melivia. That woman played me up until the end of her existence." Faust shook his head, as though this was a tragic thing.

Yeah, I thought. *She did.*

"You don't need to worry about her anymore. Can I do it? Can I destroy her heart?"

"That task belongs to me." Howard glanced back toward Leo. "But you may have her body for your own, if you like. The girl is alive?"

"This one?" Mephistopheles grinned and twirled on the spot, tossing Berenice's hair and letting out a maniacal laugh. "Yes. I have not finished my bargain with her. I vowed to make her remaining existence a living hell."

Fury rose within me. He still hadn't let Berenice go. Even now. I watched Leo, who'd withdrawn into a dark corner. I couldn't tell if he was sending out the message like I'd suggested, but I trusted him to.

"I thought that was what you promised, Ashlyn? You demons are not ordinarily so fickle."

"No, we are not. But you taught me, Lucifer... Faust..." Her voice softened, and she moved closer to him. A prickle of fear went through me. She sounded more like Mephistopheles than Berenice, and the demon's voice coming from her mouth seriously creeped me out.

"Don't call me that."

"You made me remember how to be human," Berenice whispered, reaching out a finger to stroke his face. Faust moved aside smoothly, frowning.

"I am not human. You assume too much, demon. Have you forgotten our bargain?"

"How could I forget? You shackled me to you, human."

"I gave you a body. I gave you everything you wanted."

"You took my freedom." The voice coming from Berenice no longer sounded remotely soft—it was harsh as the edge of a blade, and I instinctively edged away. "You forced me to act as your servant. You always knew this was coming, Faust. You cannot hope to command the higher demons. And I do not need your help to gain the power to join them."

A chill raced through me—what was Mephistopheles implying?

"You assume I would have let you join them, and serve at my side."

"I am well aware that you never intended to uphold your end of the bargain. And that, Faust, is why I intend to kill you."

23

FAUST AND MEPHISTOPHELES

Faust stared at Mephistopheles. Then he laughed. He roared, his whole body shaking.

"You've signed your own fate. If you break the contract, you die. That's what happens when you make a deal with the devil."

Yeah, I thought. And I'd almost done the same. But I'd done it to help my friends. Not gain power, or whatever Mephistopheles really wanted.

"Not if I become a higher demon. Thanks to Ashlyn and her persistent questioning of the real Lucifer, I know how to do it. It's simple, really, and remarkably similar to your own plan. To amass the energy of every sorcerer in the world, living or dead—that was your goal. For you, however, I am afraid it was never possible. Energy thrives in the Darkworld. You cannot make it your own. It doesn't *belong* to you. It belongs to the Darkworld. That is why demons can use it and humans cannot. Like the knowledge you always chased, it is immaterial, existing only in possibility. I commend you on your imagination, but it was not to be."

Lucifer was no longer laughing. *So that was his goal.* To possess the power of every sorcerer in the world, living or dead. In a way, it was kind of... disappointing. In the end, he was just another power-crazy sorcerer. But Mephistopheles? Had I really put the idea into his head? *Oh, God. I have to get out of here. I have to.* It wasn't enough to call the others to fight. I needed to—

A cold, dark presence brushed against my mind. If I'd been in my human body, I'd have frozen to the spot—as it was, I was surprised neither Faust nor Mephistopheles had reacted to the fear I was sure radiated from me through the entire Darkworld. *The higher demons.* I'd brushed against them by accident, where they stood silently watching from the door. But more than that—I'd felt my own demon heart in Mephistopheles's hands. *This is wrong.* Mephistopheles had my demon heart, but it belonged to *me.* My consciousness was bound up in it. Surely that meant I could—?

"You are nothing, human," Berenice whispered, still focused on Faust. "Your heart is on its way to me, and I'll destroy it. And I'll destroy the Barrier, and you with it."

"You will never destroy me," said Faust. "I am one with the Darkworld. And our time has ended."

Faust stepped forward, and the shadows moved with him, like a cloak. But somehow, the energy crackling around Mephistopheles was more potent, more sharp and terrifying. And... around me. Somehow, I'd shifted to hover above him, metaphorically speaking. Could either of them sense me? Mephistopheles's anger bled into me, mingling with my own, and his intentions slipped into my head, almost by accident.

Leo still held my body, and he'd moved to the side, as close to the door as possible without colliding with the five immobile figures still watching the show. But Mephistopheles seemed to have forgotten about him.

"Oh, I haven't, Ashlyn. Enjoy the show. It won't take long. Then I will have enough time to torment you. More than enough."

Trapped in the Darkworld, I couldn't even respond. Would Mephistopheles actually kill Faust? Why had he chosen now to strike? Had it really been my questioning Lucifer that had triggered it? Mephistopheles must have been listening the whole time... but had he heard my plea to the others, to Leo? Was he waiting to ambush anyone who showed up to help?

"You will regret this, demon," said Faust.

"You're the one who shouldn't have made a bargain with the devil," said Mephistopheles, and the shadows around Berenice grew thicker. "The devil always gets his due. I will claim you, body and spirit both."

Berenice's hands twisted into claws, her arms elongating. She transformed into a grotesque creature, a monster with three rows of bared teeth in a head bowed with shadowy fur. Countless limbs sprouted, and the creatures moved, spider-like, toward Faust, who watched the whole performance with a look of detached amusement.

"Lack of imagination, demon? I see no need to sully my clothes. Not when I have this."

He held out a hand and a spear of ice materialised and shot toward Mephistopheles. Almost instantly it vanished, leaving a blurred impression in my mind—and it hit me with the force of a blow. I somehow watched through Mephistopheles's eyes, like I'd been drawn over to the demon heart.

But how could I get *out?*

The quiet exploded in a blur of noise. Shadows stabbed, ice-daggers dissolved in fire. Mephistopheles reached into the darkness and pulled out a long sword of flickering black flame, which he grasped in a hand that suddenly looked human-like again. Shrugging off the spider-like guise like a costume, he emerged as Berenice and stabbed at Faust. The blow missed, because Faust now hung, bat-like, from the ceiling, Howard's legs were long and clawed like a giant harpy's.

"You have not seen half of my power!" he roared, at Mephistopheles—at me.

I was no more in control of Berenice's body as I was my own, but somehow... I *sensed* Mephistopheles's commands. Recklessness seized me and I pushed against him. I didn't want to possess her body—far from it—and yet I felt closer to her, the demon heart in her hands, than I did my own body, lying cold in the corner.

Faust gestured toward the five Inner Circle members, inert by the back door.

"Defend me, my servants!"

None of them moved. A ringing silence followed his words, and even Mephistopheles turned to look at the five figures, the higher demons. They hadn't moved or said a word, and I'd half-thought Faust had them under some kind of spell. Apparently not. They seemed to have stopped Mephistopheles's thoughts in their tracks, because I inched forward and actually felt Berenice's hands clenched around the fiery weapon he'd summoned. The fire didn't burn me, of course, because this wasn't my own body.

Kill him. Kill Faust.

Mammon, Mr. Blake, looked up at Mephistopheles, at me, with pitch-black eyes. "We serve no one."

"You will serve me!" Faust's eyes bulged. He dropped from the ceiling, in human form once more—

And I rushed forward, Berenice's body moving at my command, swinging the fiery sword with a finesse I'd never have managed on my own. The sword of fire ran through him, and heat seared my palms—I let go, but no blood poured from the wound. Instead, the burning vanished, to be replaced with another sensation entirely. Mephistopheles's thoughts slid into my mind, and the conclusion clicked into place: he was never trying to kill him.

No, he was trying to do something much, much worse. But even if he hadn't noticed those brief seconds where I'd taken control of his actions, it was only a matter of time. Because there was absolutely no way in hell I'd let him get away with his real plan.

"You cannot harm me with that, demon!" cried Faust.

He thinks I'm Mephistopheles. I withdrew, swiftly, as Faust retaliated with a blow that sent Berenice tumbling toward the ground. She transformed again, black wings sprouting. Mephistopheles laughed, and it sounded positively insane coming from her mouth.

"You have lost your touch, Faust."

A frown touched Faust's features—then the flaming sword materialised in his chest again. He grabbed at it with both hands, to no effect. An inhuman scream came from his mouth as the sword dragged him up toward the ceiling. With a final motion it pinned him in place.

"What—what have you done?"

"I have blocked your access to the Darkworld." Berenice stepped forward underneath his flailing arms, looking up at him calmly.

"You've done what?"

"You cannot draw on its power to free you. The Darkworld listens to me, and only me."

"Impossible. No demon can do that." Faust struggled, but his human form looked limp, helpless against whatever force held him in its grip.

A force I felt within myself, too, radiating up from the demon heart. Even disembodied, we were linked.

"One who possesses the central point of the Barrier can," said Mephistopheles, holding up my demon heart. The small crystal glinted purple in the blue light from the chandelier just behind Faust's helpless form. "Never expected that, did you? It turns out that young Ashlyn had the secret of the Darkworld in her hands all along. Of course, once it's destroyed, the power will fade. So there will have to be a slight adjustment to my plan. It is no matter. I never intended Ashlyn to have the mercy of a quick death."

Horror gripped me. He had no intention of destroying my demon heart, after all. He just wanted to make me suffer. And now, even Faust couldn't stop him. That left only one option to me: kill Berenice... but even that wouldn't kill the demon.

Faust had stretched Howard's face into a hate-filled mask. "You will pay. You will suffer."

"On the contrary, no demon need suffer by humans again. I can police the Darkworld myself, now that I have Ashlyn's heart. As if a human could ever hope to understand us."

Faust roared like an enraged tiger, but the sword held him pinned in place, helpless. *In the end, only a demon could overpower him,* I thought, remembering the fortune-teller's sacrifice. If only I hadn't been so stupid. Of course Mephistopheles was the real danger, the real enemy. Human-demon, a living shadow.

He had to die first. But there was only one way to make that happen.

"You've worn out your human lifespan, Faust. But death comes to all, and demons shall deliver it."

Berenice hovered above the ground, energy crackling around her. Fire flickered along her arms.

"The man who claimed to equal the devil deserves an ironic death," said Mephistopheles. "They are something of a specialty with me…"

Certainty gripped me; I couldn't let him do it. I had to hold him back. Because Faust wasn't as dangerous as Mephistopheles, and I had only seconds, minutes at most, before Mephistopheles realised I could slip into his body—

This time came easier, though vertigo shook me as I was suddenly up in the air, wings spread wide, in Mephistopheles's skin.

"What are you doing, Ashlyn?"

Crap. He'd noticed me. He might have my demon heart, but as long as I kept him out of this body, he couldn't —my head pounded, Berenice's body warping around me —but I couldn't keep hovering and holding him back at the same time. I screamed, more in my head than anything, as I forced Mephistopheles back with everything I possessed.

An explosion rocked the cathedral, so hard that the ceiling began to crumble, the walls shook and bowed. The lights went out in one sweep of darkness, and everything disappeared in a rainfall of rubble. The shock jerked me back from Berenice's body and into nothingness again.

"What is this?" Mephistopheles screamed from behind falling rocks.

"The humans' trump card," said Leo, who'd ducked into an alcove, still holding my body. "Also, incidentally, my cue to bid you farewell."

"What have you done, human?"

"Just made a few calls."

"Whoever is out there cannot hope to overpower me!" screamed Mephistopheles.

"The Venantium would beg to differ," said Leo. "Thanks for not paying the harmless human any attention. That's your weakness, isn't it? What's the good in being able to read everyone's mind if you don't notice what's right in front of you? I figured you'd be more focused on Ash." Did he know I'd given him the idea to call the others?

"I will make you both suffer."

"Same old crap," said Leo. He laid my body down, gently. "Nah. I think I might just kill you first."

And he threw himself around from behind the pillar and lobbed a handful of fire at Mephistopheles.

It missed, which wasn't surprising because of all the smoke and dust from the collapsed ceiling. Berenice strode out of the rubble unharmed, but blazing with anger.

"You arrogant human. How dare—"

"There's the tosspot!" said another voice.

Cyrus stood in the space where there'd been a wall a minute ago. "Need a hand, bro?"

"Good timing," said Leo. "Bit dramatic, wasn't it?"

"I've always thought this place was an eyesore."

Another piece of the ceiling fell down, hitting the floor with a crash. The entire centre of the room was obscured.

"I agree," said Leo. "Is Claudia here? And Layla?"

"Everyone's here. We met halfway. The *venators* are helping out civilians, mostly. And Claudia's back there somewhere, with the other sorcerers from London."

Everyone was here. My call had actually got out in time.

But I'd forgotten about the Inner Circle. As the dust cleared, they became visible again. The five watchers stood unmoving by the wreckage of the door, faces expressionless. Cyrus jumped back when he spotted them.

"Shit," he said. "What's up with them?"

"I don't think the higher demons are interested in the fight," said Leo. "Right, man. Help me. That bastard over there has Ash's demon heart."

"Ash?" Cyrus's eyes widened as he spotted my prone body on the ground. "She's—she's not…?"

"Ash is alive. He's trapped her in the Darkworld. But we're going to get her out."

"Never," Mephistopheles spat, stalking toward them. "You humans will never see her again. But she'll watch you suffer."

No. I wouldn't. Not on my life. I shifted, once again as though my disembodied spirit was tethered to the demon heart, until I hovered where Mephistopheles was. None of his attention was on me at all.

"Ever get the feeling he's all talk?" said Leo.

"Yeah, I'm not impressed. And get out of Berenice's head," Cyrus added to Mephistopheles.

"You worry about this one? She's already dead."

Now was my chance. I shoved Mephistopheles with everything I had, the mental equivalent of throwing myself against a door. Shock that wasn't mine pulsed through me as I saw through Berenice's eyes—just as a voice spoke in my head, projected loud and clear.

"Actually," said Berenice, "I'm not dead."

Disbelief momentarily stunned me. That couldn't have been her. It was impossible—she was possessed.

Berenice—I—froze, fixed in position. The voice came from the Darkworld.

"I figured it out. A way around the contract you forced me into." There was no doubt, it sounded exactly like her. I felt her at the edge of my perception, not a spirit exactly, but something close.

"You lie," said Mephistopheles, through her mouth. I'd let my control slip when Berenice spoke, and now the

demon was back, totally aware of what I'd done, but fixated on Berenice.

"Oh, it's quite simple, really. You said I'm yours, but you've never possessed me before. I'm free to interpret your words in whatever way I want. And I take them to mean that you're tied to me, as I am to you. Alive or dead. You can't possess anyone else."

"What? You speak nonsense. Humans cannot change the word of a demon."

"But I remember your exact wording. 'We are one, human,' you said. You don't tend to forget stuff like that. And now it's in my favour. You're trapped. You're dependent on Ash's heart, aren't you? Well, that means if it's destroyed, you die. I know how to kill you."

"You'd risk her life?"

"Yeah, of course, you murdering prick. I'll destroy it myself."

"Are you mental?" said Leo, hoarsely. I hadn't realised Leo could hear her, but she must be projecting her thoughts at everyone. Cyrus's face was a mask of horror, and Leo—

The heart had to be destroyed. I had to die. That was the original plan. But I'd never had the chance to tell him. Now Mephistopheles was the real danger, we had to kill him. I had to trust the others to finish Faust off without me.

Please. I begged the Darkworld. *Let me go back. Just once.*

And, perhaps because Mephistopheles was distracted, I felt it give in slightly, the shadows shifting to allow me a clearer view. As sorrow flowed through me like blood, I *felt.*

Cold. Ice prickled my skin all over, and my vision flickered. I saw both the scene from above, seeing Leo facing down Berenice, but at the same time, with an odd sense of vertigo, I saw the mostly caved-in ceiling *above* me, like I lay on the ground, looking up. Like being in two places at once. But all I felt was numb.

I concentrated on the second vision, which was clearer, willing myself to return to my body. I felt like a thick presence smothered me, weighing me down, like fighting heavy sleep paralysis. *Come on...* I had to do it now, whilst Mephistopheles was distracted. I had to tell Leo. He had to know. *Please.*

A gasp shot out of my mouth. I breathed in dust and coughed uncontrollably, rolling over on the ground. *Holy hell.* The sensation of *having* sensations made my head spin and my body shake all over.

Leo spun around. "Ash!"

He had me in his arms before I could even sit up. "Ash," he whispered, bowing his head so that his forehead pressed to mine.

My heart clenched. "Leo..."

"You're okay. Oh God, Ash..."

"Kill him. Kill... Lucifer." Ice began to spring up along my arms again, and I felt the Darkworld pulling me back. My hands dropped to my sides before I could embrace him.

"Ash? What's...?"

"I can't stay." My voice cracked. "Please. My friends... Sarah and Alex. They're on the way here with Lucifer's heart. You have to destroy it. I can't..."

"Ash, don't talk like that. You're going to be okay. I won't let Berenice..."

"You have to! Please. It's what my mother wanted all along—what's supposed to happen. My demon heart's the crux of the Barrier. If it's destroyed, the demons are free, like they're meant to be, and Mephistopheles will die, too. He's bound himself to the heart. I was never meant to have it."

"Ash. No. You can't."

"I love you," I choked. My hand found his, held on, tight. "This is—this is okay. Please kill Lucifer. And tell Alex and Sarah… and Cara…" Tears ran down my cheeks, and Leo's face was wet, too. "I'm lucky I knew all of you. I was lucky. You deserve to be happy…"

The Darkworld waited, and so did Berenice. I felt Mephistopheles, too, locked in conflict with the human he'd bound himself to. And with me, too.

I looked directly into Berenice's eyes. "Do it," I said, and let go, this time slipping into Mephistopheles's viewpoint as easily as breathing. For the last time. But now, it was Berenice I felt dominating her own body and contacting the Darkworld alongside me.

"Ash, no!"

Leo's yell rang around what was left of the cathedral, but Berenice had already held up the demon heart, the amethyst crystal, the crux of the Barrier—and summoned fire.

Pain ripped through me, and I was torn away from the waking world, back into the Darkworld.

24

SLIPPING AWAY

Blissful numbness claimed me, and I floated. After the rush of searing pain, I couldn't face anything else. Nothing existed but shadows, and they cradled me. A hum rose all around, growing louder. Emanating from me. Though my body was gone, I felt the darkness like a pulsing presence around me, part of me. The sound of an almighty, splintering *crack* shattered the brief numbness, and then I was free. *The Barrier. It's broken.*

The room spun beneath me. I floated on the ceiling, but no longer encased by darkness. Before my eyes, shadows blended into the scene. The Darkworld was open. Shadowy people passed me by, and although I had no body, I felt their gratitude as they brushed past.

Thank you, Ashlyn.

Anthea was the last to go. I felt regret and sorrow as she passed me, but she didn't stop. Her presence faded with her outline into shadows.

I'd done it. I'd set the half-demons free.

Then… I felt *her*. Pride and sorrow mixed together, radiating from the remainder of the fortune-teller's spirit.

There was so little left of her, I could sense she wasn't able to speak, but that was okay. I sensed her feelings as sure as anything. And then… she was gone, too.

In the visible world, the remains of the cathedral fell with a thunderous crash. I tried to shout a warning to Leo, but he'd already dragged my body out of harm's way, holding himself over me like a shield. I knew he was saying my name, although I couldn't hear it.

Berenice stood in the centre of the chaos. A wild smile lit her features, before dust and rock flew everywhere, hiding her from view.

In the end, the only way to escape Mephistopheles was death.

I couldn't see my demon heart, or what was left of it, but the room crackled with residual energy from the collapsed Barrier. I felt it radiate outward as the walls fell away, opening onto the graveyard outside. The Blackstone family tomb filled my vision, and it had cracked down the exact centre. Now, the Earth trembled as though in an earthquake, and the gravestones shifted, disturbed. Blackstone itself moved.

I saw it all. The sky still burned red, blurred by the large shapes of shadow-beasts. The streets were filled with monsters and *venators* doing battle. Fires leapt up along the streets and flickered in shop windows. Glass shattered, bricks crumbled, and bodies lay in the road. I'd thought I couldn't feel anything, but dread clutched at me as I saw Claudia backed into a corner, two gigantic shadow-beasts bearing down on her with claws glinting.

I watched, as though from a high position above the town. Hideous ghouls dragged themselves through the cobbled avenues, latching onto anyone they passed. Shadows gained a life of their own, creeping up on blue-uniformed *venators* and lashing out. Blood and darkness mingled on the ground. And I was powerless to stop any of it.

Why am I not dead?

The shockwave radiating out from the collapsed cathedral was spreading through the streets. The fighting stopped as monsters and humans alike looked around, confused, as the shadows broke apart. In one moment, the ghouls, shadow-beasts and other monstrosities froze. The broken Barrier had stopped the battle dead in its tracks, and *venators* and sorcerers alike stared at their immobile enemies.

Peace descended, flooding through the Darkworld, flooding through me. Maybe I'd float away into the sky...

Ashlyn.

A voice cut through. I looked everywhere for which demon had spoken to me.

It's me.

Myself. The half-demon—the real me.

I thought I'd lost you, I said. *I'm sorry.*

You have nothing to apologise for. This was inevitable. The fate of a human-demon.

That doesn't make it any easier for me, you know. Leo...

My heart tore. But that made no sense. I had no heart, right?

You have an anchor, said the demon.

What?

A demon needs an anchor to stay in this world. But you... are human.

I'm human-demon. You're me. What are you saying?

We were never truly the same, Ashlyn. I have no anchor. You do.

Leo was my anchor. Him, and the other people I cared about. Love, the one thing demons could never have.

I can't come back. Ash... I'm glad I knew you.

No. That's...

I couldn't see her, but I imagined her smile so vividly it was like looking in a mirror. She was happy for me, and there was no regret in her eyes.

Live out your human life. Be happy.

And I was screaming, screaming my own name, but the last threads of darkness slipped away, and the last words I heard were, *Think about them. Think about your anchor.*

I thought, and my mind filled with images, as though they waited for me. The same memories I'd reawakened in Leo. The same memories that kept me going through the darkness, made me who I was. Ashlyn. Human.

A tremendous roar shook the world. Everything blurred, and then intense cold pierced me all over. Once again, dust choked me and I moved—properly moved. Overwhelmed, I felt my body curve into a foetal position, feet tucked into my chest. My head wouldn't stop spinning.

"Holy hell–Ash!"

I cried. I couldn't stop. Leo had me in his arms, and I was here, really here, for real. This was no dream or illusion, not even a memory. I ached everywhere and I thrilled in every pang as I sat up and wrapped my arms around Leo so tightly, so tight that hell itself couldn't tear me from him.

"Ash—I can't breathe!"

Reality kicked in, as did common sense. I became aware of the Darkworld, still a trembling presence, but no longer the cold, reliable source I'd always been tuned into. It was unstable, but still there, energy waiting for me. I felt it touch me, run through my veins, but not cold. It felt… warm. Something had changed.

The demon was gone. And I felt nothing.

I drew a shuddering breath. "She gave up her life, and let me come back. The demon's gone. Turns out I was me all along." I laughed shakily. "If that even makes sense."

"You know, that does make sense." Leo laughed, equally shaky. "How do you feel?"

"Like hell. And heaven." I laughed again. There was something I was forgetting. As much as I wanted to lose myself in him forever, the sky still boiled red and black, and something gathered in the ruins of the cathedral. "Holy crap. Watch out!"

A dark shape unfurled, a mass of black shadows masking the ruins of the cathedral entirely.

"Lucifer," said Leo. "His heart. You said... Alex and Sarah?"

"Crap. Yeah."

"C'mon."

He pulled me to my feet and we ran, away from the ruins. Sorrow for Berenice beat at me beneath the surface, but that—and everything else—could wait.

Venators were everywhere, all over the town square, most staring up at the shape manifesting in the air as the demons they'd been fighting remained locked in position. But we couldn't afford to look back, or to acknowledge the terror pressing at us from that presence. Now Mephistopheles was dead, Faust must be free to access his power. *Shit.*

Only a few people were moving, and Alex and Sarah were amongst them.

"Guys!" I shouted, and my voice all but disappeared in the endless hum reverberating from the Darkworld. "Over here!"

"There's the nutcase!" said Alex. She and Sarah ran down the street, accompanied by two *venators* and Cara. I couldn't even begin to formulate a question as to how they'd all ended up here together.

Alex pressed the demon heart into my outstretched

hand. "I have to say, I miss the old Blackstone. Not a fan of this décor."

I could tell by her wavering tone that she was half-paralysed with terror, but determined to keep calm for Sarah's sake. Sarah looked like she was about to faint.

"Thanks. You're amazing," I said, sincerely, then turned to Leo. The stone was cold against my hands, a contrast to the strange warmth boiling in my veins.

"Let's do this."

Leo's hands blazed, and he took the heart from me, letting the flames engulf it. I glanced up at the roiling black shape spreading over the sky and saw it shudder, but it didn't look as though the flames had any effect.

"Come on… kill the bastard!"

"Let me help." I reached for the connection, praying it was still there.

Fire.

And for the last time, I saw the world through a demon's eyes. Purple flashed across my vision, ice-fire sprang from my palms, and I put my hands over Leo's, over the demon heart, without a thought to getting burned.

But it didn't hurt. The icy flames mixed with the orange-yellow blaze and engulfed Faust's demon heart. And this time, the beast roared.

The Darkworld shook with it, and everything shifted. The dark shape pulsed from violet to black, like a gigantic demon's eye blotting out the sky. Fire and ice mingled, burned as one. I yelled as the connection bit deeper into me, flowing into my hands like ice water in my veins. Leo and I held the darkness in our hands, and felt it crumble. Faust's demon heart, outlined against the flames, split down the centre, cracks fanning out to break the surface, over and over again. Shards became fragments and disintegrated before our eyes.

The massive shadow in the sky writhed, looking more like a giant storm cloud than anything. Slowly, it turned to grey and then white, vanishing as the sky returned to the pale grey of a winter afternoon.

Then something else appeared in the sky. The human-sized shape looked familiar as it descended, and for an instant, the word *angel* flashed through my mind.

But it was no angel. The voice that spoke in my mind confirmed that.

"Admirable, Ashlyn."

The higher demon, the other Lucifer. He wore a human shape, but it was indistinct, cloaked shadow. He walked out of the sky to land directly in front of us. As the shadows moved away, his form became more defined. A human male with handsome features, and oddly familiar-looking. *Dad?*

"Please don't call me that. I have come here only to put things right. Mammon. Asmodeus. Leviathan. Beezlebub. Satan. Show yourselves. You are wanted in the Darkworld."

Come to think of it... I hadn't seen the five higher demons since Mephistopheles had tried to kill Faust. Instinctively, I tried to feel for their presence, but of course I wasn't part of the Darkworld anymore.

Lucifer nodded, as though he'd heard a reply. *"Yes, we have work to do. The Barrier is unstable. We are needed to police it."*

I managed to speak. "Police it? You're letting them go free?"

"The Five made a poor decision, but demons do not judge. We take care of our own."

I knew that much, but it still bothered me. Five of the Inner Circle were dead. The Venantium would be a shambles without leadership, if what had happened in London was anything to go by.

"I believe you require a contract with us, Ashlyn."

"You what?"

"We will not harm humanity. In return, you will stop the Venantium from creating another Barrier. You will leave the pathway open, as it should be."

I thought that over.

Leo muttered, "Don't let him trick you."

"What will happen?" I asked. "Not having the Barrier there, I mean. If it means demons can come and go, then what about demon hearts? What if someone tried to do what Faust wanted to, tried to get infinite magical energy into one heart?"

"That is precisely why it will need to be policed," said Lucifer. *"Humans are unpredictable, after all. And in order to possess a human, a demon will still require an anchor. However... if the demon is killed, they will not return to the Darkworld, but to nothingness. The same goes for other creatures of the Darkworld. I think this will make them less inclined to cause trouble, do you not?"*

I blinked. Demons could actually die, now? And shadow-beasts, harpies... the implications of this were so big, I couldn't wrap my head around it. Then again, I'd be glad to leave this particular conundrum to the Venantium. "I think that sounds fair," I said, slowly. "Don't harm any humans—that goes for human-demons, too, if there are any. And other humans with... issues. The Vampire's Curse..."

"I meant humanity collectively, Ashlyn. I will not try to trick you. You have done something no human sorcerer has ever achieved before, and helped demonkind. It will never be forgotten."

"Then I'll do it. I'll make the contract."

Lucifer nodded. *"Very well. We will deal with our own, and you with yours. I believe there are many people who wish to speak with you."*

I didn't doubt that. "Okay. Well, um, thank you."

Lucifer turned his back and faded away, becoming a shadow, then nothing.

"Dramatic," said Leo. "So, seeing as you nearly died on me several times, I think I've earned the right to the first question."

"Probably," I said. "But we have an audience."

Venators had started to gather around me. Layla stood with a group of other sorcerers, distinguished only by their lack of uniform. Claudia was amongst them, and Gareth, of all people. And there was Cara, of course.

"Wait," I said, turning to Cara, first. "Just one thing. How did you end up getting into all this?"

"You can speak to your friend later." Hayley.

I couldn't believe she had the nerve to speak to me. Two thug-like *venators* flanked her.

"Er, no," said Cara, looking her up and down. "I'm her best friend. You're no one."

I almost laughed at Hayley's expression. *Way to go, Cara.*

"Anyway," said Cara. "Obviously I was out of my mind with worrying about you, but I couldn't get what you told me about fighting demons—you know, when we were in Australia—out of my head. So when there was a demon attack, I told a few people what you taught me, and we managed to escape. Then I ran into these cool guys—"

She gestured at the unfamiliar *venators.*

"Turns out I'm sort of receptive to the Darkworld, given a bit of practice. They taught me a couple of tricks. Cool, right?"

"Very," I agreed.

Everyone was looking at me. I sighed, feeling tiredness drag at my limbs.

"Want to go sit somewhere?" said Leo, resting a hand on my shoulder.

We ended up in what was left of Blackstone square. The surrounding buildings were mostly demolished, and the cathedral was nothing but rubble. Still, there were stone benches amongst the ruins, and I sank onto one gratefully. Everyone else either stood or sat in the rubble, not caring about all the dust.

I began to speak. No one interrupted, for a wonder. I left nothing out. Not my near-death. Not the truth about my demon heart, and Faust. Or Berenice. Mephistopheles. The half-demons. And Lucifer, my father. It wasn't until I'd finished that talking broke out, questions flying everywhere. I leaned against Leo, eyes closing. Sleep would be a wonderful thing right now.

The key debate concerned who would lead the Venantium now. Hayley was shouted down, but there were other candidates who'd been responsible for keeping the civilians from Blackstone safe and got the students away from campus. That was the kind of leader they needed. As for Jonathan Stirling, he'd apparently been arrested and imprisoned before he could even leave London.

It baffled me to see the *venators* actually agreeing on something, but I knew there had to be people with common sense who wanted change.

But I wouldn't be a part of it.

"What *is* your plan?" Alex asked me, after I'd explained, again, why the heart had been important. "I mean, are you reapplying to uni? Sarah and I have been talking about it… of course, Blackstone's kind of out of the question right now."

"Er… I haven't really thought about it." There it was. I had a future, a life, and hell, was I going to live every second of it. "What about you?" I said to Leo, who still sat at my side.

"Reapply? Repeat second year, you mean?"

"Yeah, the *venators* will sort you out," said Claudia. "I'm gonna go somewhere new. London, maybe. I like it there. Influence'll get me in anywhere."

Leo shrugged. "I'll have to think about that one. I guess I could say major family issues are my excuse."

"*Very* major family issues," said Cyrus. "Shit. I don't suppose we'll ever know what happened to our dad in all this?"

"I personally don't give a crap," said Leo.

"Well, as your brother, I feel duty-bound to tell you to go back to uni."

"I guess I could reapply to Oxford," I said. "Nah. I'll think about it. Might go travelling in the interim. We've got nearly a year."

"A whole glorious year." Claudia laughed. "We're freaking *alive*, people. Whoever thought it possible?"

"Tell me about it," I said. "Well, I'm going to travel the world. And get my degree. And…"

Make plans that would never have been possible before. I felt a pang for the demon. *She could never have appreciated it, could she?*

But I'd never forget her. I'd never forget that she'd given up her entire existence for my sake. Demon or not…

Leo, once again, appeared to read my mind. "Does it feel any different without her there?"

"Honestly?" I said. "I've never felt more alive." And I hugged him.

ABOUT THE AUTHOR

Emma is the New York Times and USA Today Bestselling author of the Changeling Chronicles urban fantasy series.

Emma spent her childhood creating imaginary worlds to compensate for a disappointingly average reality, so it was probably inevitable that she ended up writing fantasy novels. When she's not immersed in her own fictional universes, Emma can be found with her head in a book or wandering around the world in search of adventure.

Find out more about Emma's books at
www.emmaladams.com.